NO EXCUSES

With his rifle in his left hand, Sam drew his Colt and leveled it at the men.

"Stand fast!" he shouted. "Drop the guns! Hands in the air!"

Bootlip Thomas and Murray Bratcher wouldn't hear of it. They came to a halt, but their pistols came up firing. One shot whistled past Sam Burrack's head before he let the hammer fall. Bratcher twisted in a half circle, then collapsed with a bullet through his chest. Another shot grazed Sam's forearm as he turned his aim to Bootlip Thomas, recocking the big Colt, and dropped him facedown in the dusty trail.

Sam stepped forward with caution. He reached out with his boot and kicked the still-breathing Bootlip's pistol away from his hand. Bootlip gasped and tried to raise his face and speak. All that came out was a choked cough.

"Save it," said the Ranger. "I've heard it all before."

JURISDICTION

Ralph Cotton

A SIGNET BOOK

SIGNET
Published by New American Library, a division of
Penguin Group (USA) Inc., 375 Hudson Street,
New York, New York 10014, USA
Penguin Group (Canada), 90 Eglinton Avenue East, Suite 700, Toronto,
Ontario M4P 2Y3, Canada (a division of Pearson Penguin Canada Inc.)
Penguin Books Ltd., 80 Strand, London WC2R 0RL, England
Penguin Ireland, 25 St. Stephen's Green, Dublin 2,
Ireland (a division of Penguin Books Ltd.)
Penguin Group (Australia), 250 Camberwell Road, Camberwell, Victoria 3124,
Australia (a division of Pearson Australia Group Pty. Ltd.)
Penguin Books India Pvt. Ltd., 11 Community Centre, Panchsheel Park,
New Delhi - 110 017, India
Penguin Group (NZ), 67 Apollo Drive, Rosedale, North Shore 0632,
New Zealand (a division of Pearson New Zealand Ltd.)
Penguin Books (South Africa) (Pty.) Ltd., 24 Sturdee Avenue,
Rosebank, Johannesburg 2196, South Africa

Penguin Books Ltd., Registered Offices:
80 Strand, London WC2R 0RL, England

First published by Signet, an imprint of New American Library,
a division of Penguin Group (USA) Inc.

First Printing, March 2002
10   9

For Mary Lynn . . . *of course*.

PART 1

Chapter 1

Ranger Sam Burrack lifted his duster collar against a blast of cold wind laced with sleet, then tugged his sombrero down tighter on his head. He knew he was too far north for this time of year, but there was nothing he could do about it. He'd been on the gang's trail too long to stop now. He couldn't just break away from the hunt and slink home like a dog with its tail between its legs. Besides, he was working alone now—the way he liked it. Nothing against the other Rangers working under Captain Deak McCann out of the badlands outpost, but young Sam felt he always did better working by himself. He nudged the big Appaloosa stallion forward at a walk, keeping a wary eye to the distant northern horizon.

There had been two other Rangers with him at the start of this journey. Their names were Jake Early and Lawrence Wright. Now Wright was dead, the first to fall, a rifleshot lifting him from his saddle as the three of them rode down a narrow path out of the foothills. It had happened three weeks back, no sooner than they'd picked up the outlaws' trail and followed them across the badlands. Sam and Jake Early had wrapped Wright in his canvas riding duster and buried him beneath a mound of rocks near the remnants of the old Spanish mission.

"Don't worry, Lawrence," Sam had heard Jake Early say to the rocky grave. "No matter what happens, we won't stop till we bring every last one of them to justice. We both swear to it." He turned from Wright's grave and looked at Sam Burrack with steel in his eyes.

But young Sam had only nodded slightly and looked away, making no firm promises to either the living or the dead. In the past year, Sam Burrack had seen how quickly a man could play out his string in this vast, harsh wasteland. This land placed no particular value on a man's life, and it made no exceptions.

Sam stared straight ahead in spite of the stinging cold wind. This was not a land born of words and promises, and as it turned out, Jake Early should have kept his promise to himself or at least between himself and the rock pile that had once been Lawrence Wright. Jake Early was now fifty miles back, in Stanton, sweating out a rattlesnake bite that, if it didn't end up killing him slowly and painfully, would likely keep him laid up most of the coming winter.

"You'll get them . . . won't you, Sam?" Jake Early asked through chattering teeth, his tongue swollen, sweat running down his fevered blue cheeks. He'd taken a grip on Sam's forearm there in the doctor's office, and Sam had to peel his fingers back one at a time to get loose. "Promise me you'll get them, Sam!" Jake Early began to sob, the fever taking hold and screaming inside him. "For Lawrence Wright's sake?" His fingernails dug into Sam's forearm. Circumstance had turned Jake delirious, reducing his toughness to hopeless rage the way only this rugged country could do.

"I'm on their trail, Jake," was all Sam replied.

"They'll have the lines repaired before dark," the doctor called out as Sam slung his saddlebags over his shoulder on his way to the door. "You can wire for help, get a marshal and a posse sent up here."

"Thanks all the same," Sam said over his shoulder. "I best keep moving."

"But you need rest, young man," the doctor called out as Sam opened the door and stepped out of the office. "It'll do you no good to run yourself into the ground out there. Besides, you're already outside your jurisdiction."

"Don't I know it," Sam had whispered, closing the door behind him.

Thinking about it, waiting in Stanton and wiring for help might have appeared to be the most reasonable move to make. It was certainly the sort of decision Captain McCann would expect him to make. But it wasn't Sam's way to wait around for help. Besides, had he waited and wired the Ranger outpost, there was a good chance Captain McCann might have called off the hunt. And Sam couldn't abide that. He leaned a bit to one side, shouldering against the growing force of the cold wind. Beneath him, the Appaloosa stallion craned its neck sideways to the lashing sleet. "No, sir," Sam murmured under his breath—he couldn't abide that at all.

And he rode on . . .

The Ganston Gang was not the worst bunch of outlaws to ever lift a pistol, but like most of the cutthroats and border trash that haunted the area around the badlands, they were ruthless enough to demand immediate attention. Young Sam hadn't been a Ranger for more than a year, but he'd already learned that the longer these kind of men went unchecked, the more dark and heinous their crimes became. At times it appeared that people like the Ganstons were almost expecting to get caught, and to not do so only fueled their brashness and propelled them to greater heights of violence, crime and depravity. Then so be it, he thought, stepping down from his saddle in the midafternoon and shaking the remaining beads of sleet from his duster.

He'd ridden the Appaloosa higher in the hill line and slightly above the wind-driven sleet. At the crest of a rising cliff, Sam looked out past the gray swirl of sleet beneath them, then far into the distance in the direction of Hubbler Wells. He'd had to break away from the trail of hoofprints and get out of the weather. By tomorrow morning the sleet would have hammered away most of the prints, but that didn't bother Sam. Come morning he wouldn't need the prints any longer, at least not to know where the gang was headed.

The Ganstons and their gang were riding straight to the wells. He'd bet on it. By now, Hopper Ganston and his brother Earl must have figured anyone on their trail had turned back. The closest Sam and the other two Rangers had been to the gang was the day when someone put the bullet through Lawrence Wright's chest. Shooting a Ranger out of his saddle that way had the gang stoked up and feeling full of themselves, Sam figured. Well . . . maybe it was good, them feeling that way. It would cause them to get sloppy, maybe make a mistake or two, he thought. Then he'd have them cold.

He turned his gaze away from the distance and led the Appaloosa back across a stretch of loose gravel toward the narrow trail. With any luck he could rest the stallion this evening, push forward all night and be in Hubbler Wells by morning. There were seven men riding with Hopper and Earl Ganston, but the numbers didn't dissuade Sam Burrack in the least. Once he got the Ganstons all together in firing range, he knew those numbers would change as fast as he could drop a hammer. "Come on, Black Pot," he said, calling the Appaloosa stallion by name, "let's get some rest. We've got a long, cold ride come nightfall."

Atop the roofs along the main street of Hubbler Wells, most of the possemen lay huddled against the backs of the buildings' facades, as much to keep out of the cold wind as to keep themselves from being seen. On the mercantile roof, some men had drawn close to an upthrusting stovepipe that came up through the roof of the saloon and cast waves of heat. The men rubbed their hands in the warmth of the stovepipe then pressed their hands against their reddened cheeks. "Had I known the weather was going to hell this quick," a voice said in a low growl, "I'd never left Virginia City."

"Ha!" a sarcastic voice scoffed from the other side of the stovepipe. "The truth is, boys, the sheriff of Virginia City was on the verge of escorting Talbert here out of town with a can tied to his backside."

"Shut up, Erskine," Talbert French replied, lifting his eyes from beneath the brim of his battered silk top hat. "You don't know me well enough to say such a thing." The top hat was tied down to Talbert

French's head with a long strip of dirty wool rag that encircled the hat's crown and lay tied in a thick knot at his chin.

"I know as much about you as any sane man would ever want to, Talbert," said Erskine Brock. He spread a flat grin through a week's worth of beard stubble. His new whiskers shined with frost from his steaming breath. "Boys, it might interest you to know that our fellow Talbert French here was once arrested in Abilene for public nakedness."

"That's a damn lie!" Talbert French shouted, half rising to his feet before the man beside him grabbed his arm and pulled him down. Muffled laughter resounded around the warm stovepipe.

"Keep quiet over there, you fools!" Colonel Daniel Fuller hissed from his position against the back of the clapboard facade overlooking the street. "Do you want every loudmouth in this mud hole to know we're up here?" His eyes riveted on Erskine Brock, singling him out as the cause. "I'll horsewhip any peckerwood who causes things to go wrong here—so help me God!"

The men around the stovepipe settled, ducked their heads and found it a good time to resume warming their hands near the stovepipe. "He means it, too," whispered Nells Kroft, his fingertips showing through the missing tips of his ragged wool gloves. The men fell silent, a few of them cursing under their breath at the frigid wind.

At the facade, Daniel Fuller seethed and turned to the man beside him. "Look at them, Red. Look at what the bankers' association has hired to help me." As Fuller spoke, his eyes took in the motley group surrounding the stovepipe, then cut along the facade, appraising each of the possemen with a look of open disdain. "Cowards, drunks and drifters—not a real man in the lot." As his eyes moved along from one man to the next, he silently tried placing names with faces. Some were easier to remember than others.

Herbert Mullins was easy to remember because he was always close at hand, ambitious, looking to get ahead. Art Hickson, Shelby Rudd and Delbert Murry were three Kansans who always kept close together. Fuller looked farther along the line of men. Some of them were simply faces without names, he thought, for the time being at least. Thinking aloud he said, "What's the use? Before this is over, half of them could be dead . . ."

Red Booker swung his head around in surprise upon hearing the colonel's dark prophecy. "Never you mind, Colonel Fuller," he said, steam bellowing from his lips. "You and me never needed much help anyway. We'll take care of the Ganstons . . . by ourselves if we have to."

"Yes, Red, thank you," said Fuller, settling himself a bit, "I believe that is how it must be." His eyes seemed to glaze in quiet reflection for a second. Then he said, "I should have died in the war, Red . . . like any true soldier. God should never have sent me out here, to suffer with idiots and madmen. If there is any true justice in this miserable life—"

"Colonel!" Red Booker's voice cut Fuller short. He had peered over the edge of the facade to the street below while Fuller spoke. Now he ducked down, fast. "There comes the Indian! Big as all get out!"

"Wha—?" Fuller raised up onto his haunches, still keeping down and out of sight. But along the facade, three possemen rose up, cocking their rifles until the sound of Red Booker's harsh whisper stopped them.

"Stay down, you stupid bastards!" Red Booker

grabbed the nearest rifleman and yanked him hard, causing his rifle to fall from his hands onto the tin roof. "Damn it, Bernard, get your rifle and get covered!" The other two men dropped out of sight and huddled against the facade with the others. Bernard Gift snatched up his rifle with one hand, his free hand keeping his ragged derby hat on his head. Steam swirled in his panting breath.

"Excuse the hell out'n me," whispered one of the men to anyone near him, "but it was my understanding we get paid for shooting these robbers, not just watching them."

The man nearest him, a sobering drunkard named Texas Bob Mackay, said in a hushed voice, "That's the Injun Willie John down there. All he's doing is scouting for the gang."

"Injun, ha!" said Talbert French. "If he's Injun I'll spit in my sock. My daddy worked for a big spread near Atlanta back before the war . . . they had nearly two hundred of *that* kind of Injun. He kept them jumping and stepping."

A short muffled laugh arose from the men. "Alls I know is what I heard," said Texas Bob. "Folks call him an Injun, I'm inclined to call him the same."

"Then maybe he's half and half," said French. "But he ain't all Injun."

"I don't really give a blue damn if he's a Chinaman," said Texas Bob. "Kill him and he's all we'll get. Let him go back and bring the Ganstons to us— we'll get every one of them."

Texas Bob's hands trembled, gripping his rifle. He needed a drink so bad his stomach cramped. But he knew he had to fight off the craving. He'd been drunk for a solid two years. It was time he straightened himself out and got down to making a living. Working in a bounty posse was not his first choice, but he had to take what he could get until he could manage to get back in touch with his former comrades.

"Thank you for that helpful insight, Texas Bob," Colonel Fuller whispered along the line of riflemen, the others hurrying over from the stovepipe and taking position among the others. Texas Bob gave Fuller a curious glance, not sure whether or not his words were intended to be sarcastic. But the expression on Fuller's face seemed sincere enough. Fuller nodded in confirmation. "I could use a few more like you, Texas Bob."

The compliment helped calm Texas Bob's raw, quivering gut a little. He swallowed, dry and stiff, and touched a gloved hand to his cracked lips. He couldn't help but ask himself what harm one small shot of rye would do right before a gun battle.

On the cold mud-rutted street, the Indian Willie John saw a familiar face on the boardwalk, and he eased his dapple-gray gelding over toward two ragged boys who stood staring at him. Even as he neared the edge of the boardwalk, his eyes continued scanning the town, scouting it out from within the dark shadow of his lowered hat brim. "The hell are you doing here, Billy Odle?" Willie John asked the thinner of the two. The boy stood with his hand resting on the crude wooden pistol handle shoved down in the waist of his outgrown trousers.

"I live here now, Willie John," the young man replied. His slight smile revealed the gap of a missing front tooth. "What are you doing here?"

Willie John didn't answer. Instead he looked up and down the boardwalk, his eyes checking along the rooflines and alleyways, seeing nothing out of the ordinary for a town like Hubbler Wells. "Where's your folks, boy?"

Billy Odle's hand opened and closed on the pistol butt. "Don't call me *boy*, Injun."

The words snapped Willie John's attention to him. "Don't call me *Injun*, boy."

Willie John sat rigid atop the dapple-gray, looking at the way Billy Odle fondled the pistol handle, for comfort or reassurance, Willie John thought. The boy beside Billy Odle took a step to the side as if any second lead would start flying. Willie John spread a trace of a thin smile. "Don't sass me, Billy. Where's your ma and pa?"

"Oh, all right." Odle let his hand fall from the wooden pistol. "Pa's in prison back in Yuma . . . going to be there for the next year or so. Ma was working in a tent out back of the saloon. But it burned three nights ago. Now she's taking up an empty toolshed over behind the barbershop. You going to go see her?"

Willie John looked away in embarrassment. "Billy, don't you say such a thing," he murmured.

Billy Odle shrugged, not seeing the harm in what he'd said. "Why? She says the more men she can meet here in Hubbler Wells, the sooner we'll have enough money to get out of here and go on to Cleveland."

Willie John only stared, not knowing how to respond.

The boy beside Billy cut in: "The men here say Billy's ma knows every way in the world to—"

"Hey, hey!" Willie John cut the smaller boy off gruffly, saying, "Damn it, boy! Don't you realize that's his ma you're talking about?" Willie John's eyes cut from the younger boy to Billy Odle. "What kind of boy says something like that about your ma?"

Billy shrugged, looked at his friend for support, then back up at Willie John, still not seeing the harm in it. "He's only saying what she'd say herself."

"Lord God . . ." Willie John shook his head, then changed the subject. "What's your pa in prison for? I never knew of him being a criminal."

"Well, he sure enough is," said Billy, seeming to take exception at Willie John's words. "He stole a bunch of stuff from a mercantile store in Wakely . . . broke down the back door and everything. Didn't get no money, but he got all kinds of food! The judge sent him off for three years' hard labor. Is that criminal enough for you?"

"I see," said Willie John, resting his leather wrist gauntlets on his saddle horn. He got the picture of what had happened to the boy and his family since the night he'd last been Billy and his father in Wakely. The family had been struggling along hand-to-mouth even then. It didn't take long for a man to fall flat on his face in this country, Willie John thought. He searched for something to say, something that didn't show pity and take what pride a young boy like Billy Odle might have left. "Are you any good with that gun?" He nodded at the pistol in Billy's waist.

"I'm one of the best," Billy bragged.

"Is that right? I've got ten says you can't beat me," said Willie John.

"You're on!" Billy Odle's hand streaked upward, the pistol coming up pointed at Willie John's face. Willie John feigned reaching for his own pistol, then stopped short as if hopelessly outgunned. "You got

me, Billy," he said, "fair and square." His eyes cut
to the boy beside Billy Odle as his fingers fished inside his vest pocket, came up with a large gold coin
and flipped it down to Billy Odle. "Did you ever see
anything that fast?"

The boy just looked dumb for a second. Then he
said, "Yeah, but if that gun was real, the weight of
it would pull his britches down, I bet."

"Hush up, Alvin," Billy said, shoving the wooden
pistol back down into his waist. "You wish you could
do as well." He turned his eyes back to Willie John,
holding the coin in his closed palm, and said, "Hey,
Willie, I thought you meant ten cents . . . this is a
twenty-dollar gold piece!"

"I never gamble small." Willie John shrugged.
"Ten of that's for you, ten is for your ma. Tell her I
said 'no strings attached.' "

"Gosh, Willie, much obliged," said Billy Odle in
awe, squeezing the gold piece. "Gonna need somebody to take your horse to the livery, Willie? I'll do
it."

"No, not today, Billy." Willie John looked the two
of them up and down and stepped the dapple-gray
closer. "I want to tell you something, though," he
said, leaning slightly down in his saddle, lowering
his voice just between the two of them. "I'm going
to ride up the street and back. When I get back I
don't want to see you here."

"Why?" Billy looked confused.

"Just do like I say, Billy. You and your partner
here clear out, stay out the rest of the evening. Will
you do that for me?"

Billy Odle began getting a picture himself now,
sensing something in the works. His own voice

dropped to a quiet tone. "You getting ready to rob something . . . the bank?"

"Will you do like I told you?" Willie John asked.

"Yeah, if you say so," Billy said. "Only, let me know what you're going to do first."

Willie John saw the boy was playing him for information and he hardened his eyes and backed his dapple-gray a step. "I'm not letting you know a damn thing, boy. Just don't be here when I come back. That's my only warning." He jerked the reins, spinning the horse back to the middle of the street and straightening it forward.

"Is he really an Indian?" Alvin Bartels asked, a touch of suspicion in his voice. "He looks more like a—"

"He's my friend, whatever he is," said Billy Odle, cutting him short.

"Oh . . ." Alvin waited for a second, then asked, "Is he really an outlaw?"

"Oh yes," said Billy Odle, enjoying this new status that had just been given to him: a boy who knew real outlaws. "He's one of the worst kind. He's a killer and a robber and a gunman. He's quicker on the draw than anybody and would shoot down the devil himself if the devil even had the nerve to face him."

"Lord, Billy, and you pulled that wooden gun on him! It's a wonder he didn't shoot you before he could stop himself."

"Naw . . . you saw how fast I was. Besides, like I said, he's a friend of mine," said Billy, watching Willie John's dapple-gray cut into a trot up the middle of the deeply rutted street.

"A friend of yours?" Alvin Bartels sounded skeptical. "He might know your ma and pa, but that's a long ways from being a friend, Billy."

"You saw it with your own eyes, didn't you?" Billy Odle insisted. "Do you think I'd have gotten away with drawing on him if I wasn't his *amigo*?"

Before Alvin could answer, Billy took him by his coat sleeve and pulled him along toward an alley. "Come on, we best get off the street the way he said. I got a feeling him and his outlaw buddies are fixing to let 'er rip."

Alvin followed along. "We're leaving town?"

"What, and miss all the fireworks? Heck no, Alvin," Billy laughed. "We're gonna duck down someplace and watch the fur fly."

"Why on earth would he tell you something like that was about to happen?" Alvin asked, shaking his arm free but following Billy Odle all the same. "How does he know you or me won't blab it to somebody?"

Billy stopped abruptly and turned facing him in the narrow alleyway. "I'll tell you how he knows." He hugged his threadbare outgrown coat tight across his chest, feeling the cold starting to numb his torso. "He knows that men like me and him are two of the kind . . . and that he can trust me no matter what." Billy looked back and forth as if making sure no one was nearby listening. "Pa and me found him on the trail going into Wakely one night when I was only ten years old. He was shot all to hell. We patched him up and gave him water and sent him on his way. He could have shot us, but he didn't. He told us both to keep our mouths shut. And we did. So he knows I'm to be trusted." Billy thumbed himself on the chest. "As far as trusting you goes . . . he figures any friend of mine is a friend of his. He figures if you was to start to tell on him, I'd stop you cold.

That's the way people like me and Willie John think."

"Holy cats!" Alvin Bartels scratched his head and looked back toward the street in awe. The day was turning into quite an adventure.

Atop the roof of the saloon, Red Booker eased back down beside Colonel Daniel Fuller just long enough to report on what the Indian was doing. "He's finished talking to the kids. Now he's riding along the street bold as brass . . . checking out the bank would be my guess. What do you want to do, Colonel?"

Colonel Fuller sat back, leaning against the facade while drawing on an unlit black cigar. Along the roofline the possemen were restless, like hunting dogs pulling at the leash. "We'll do the only smart thing to do, Red," said Fuller. "We'll let him ride out of here and bring the others back to us." Fuller looked along the possemen to Texas Bob. "Isn't that so, Texas Bob?"

Bob Mackay only nodded. Unlike the other men who stood sneaking a look over the edge of the facade, Mackay lay huddled on the tin roof, his rifle held close to his chest. "Yes, sir, that would be my take on it, Colonel," he offered.

"Red," said Fuller, nodding at Texas Bob's reply, "as soon as the Indian leaves, start letting the men go down two and three at a time, get themselves a meal and some hot coffee and warm up. If the Ganstons don't hit soon, we could be up here all night." He lowered his voice to a private whisper between the two of them and added, "Keep a close eye on Texas Bob. He ain't acting right."

"Huh? I ain't noticed nothing." Red Booker looked surprised.

"All the same, do like I ask," said Fuller.

"All right, Colonel," Booker shrugged. Turning to leave, he said over his shoulder, "Folks are gonna start noticing us up here, Colonel."

"Of course they are, Red." Fuller chewed on his cigar. "But let's keep it a secret as long as we can."

On the street below, Willie John silently chastised himself for having stopped to warn the kid, Billy Odle. He shouldn't have done it, and he wasn't sure why he did. Granted the kid and his pa had once kept him from dying, but that was then and this was now. He owed the kid and his father nothing. After all, he should have killed them both just to keep them quiet . . . but he didn't. That squared things as far as he was concerned.

His eyes scanned the roofline again. A few yards past the wooden bank building, he cut the dapple-gray over to a hitch rail, stepped down and raised each of the horse's front hoofs in turn as if inspecting them. Glancing up and along the boardwalk, he saw the familiar face of Huey Sweeney standing hunched up in a heavy greatcoat, wearing a black slouch hat and holding a businessman's valise in his hand. Sweeney gave no sign of warning. Everything was going as planned. Good, Willie John thought, just the way he liked it. When he'd remounted and rode back along the street, he noted that Billy Odle and his pal were gone. He offered himself a thin smile of satisfaction, then heeled the horse out of town at a trot, steam bellowing from the horse's nostrils, Willie John's long coattails flapping on a gust of cold wind.

Chapter 2

At the edge of the flatland, Willie John reined the dapple-gray down and waited behind the cover of an upturned boulder until the soft clop of hooves winded down the hill path toward him. Earl Ganston was the first to ride up around the boulder. "How'd it look in there?" he asked, lifting a nod in the direction of Hubbler Wells. "Did you see Sweeney?"

"Yeah, I saw him." Willie John nodded. He took a chunk of jerked meat from his saddlebags and sliced off a bite of it, lifting the meat to his lips with the knife blade. Chewing as he spoke, he jabbed the knife blade toward the southwest, in the direction of the border. "Everything seemed fine. But I still say we best lay up in Old Mex for the winter."

"Nobody cares what you think. It ain't what me and Hopper's got in mind," said Earl Ganston, a bit testy. "Now, how's Hubbler Wells looking?" He kept a flat, level stare fixed on Willie John, letting him know his place.

Willie John returned the stare, not backing down an inch. "If nobody cares what I think, maybe next time you'll ride in and look things over, eh, Earl?"

As he spoke, Willie John let his hand relax on his pistol butt.

Earl Ganston looked away and spit as his brother Hopper and the others began to ride in and form up around them. "Damn Injun," Earl murmured to himself.

Hopper Ganston sidled his big roan horse in close to Willie John, seeing that some sort of confrontation had just passed between the two men. "What's going on, Willie? Does that bank look ripe in Hubbler Wells?" His gaze moved back and forth between Willie John and Earl; then his eyes rested on his younger brother as he waited for Willie's reply. Earl spit again and looked away from Hopper.

"Everything looks like it should," said Willie, realizing even as he said it that perhaps he hadn't paid as much attention to things as he should have in Hubbler Wells. Something about seeing Billy Odle there had distracted him. "If we're gonna do it today we best get to it. It's a half-hour ride and the bank closes in less than an hour." He looked up and across the gray-streaked sky and added, "We got weather coming."

"Yeah, we do sure enough," said Hopper. "I expect that's why Morgan and his cousin ain't met up with us yet. If they don't hurry up they're going to miss all the fun."

"Bet they'll hate that," said Willie with a wry snap to his voice.

Hopper Ganston caught the tone of Willie John's voice and the expression on his face. He asked, "Something bothering you, Willie? Something going on we oughta know about?"

Willie John looked around at the faces of the other

men, then settled his eyes back on Hopper. "No . . . nothing's bothering me."

Earl Ganston said in a clipped tone, "I think he's seen one of them signs Indians see . . . you know, an owl standing on its head or a coyote chasing a—"

"I ain't one of those kind of Indians," Willie said, cutting Earl off and giving the others a cold stare to quiet any laughter before it got started. "But I will make it known that I think we should cut off here and now and cross the border. If we get weathered in this far north, we'll be easy pickin' for the law."

"Ain't no law onto us yet, Willie," said Hopper Ganston. "Whoever was on our trail a while back is gone sure enough. The way I figure, we've got a free hand here until somebody sics the army on us. Opportunity like this don't come along every day. We got to take our crack at it."

"He's worried about shooting that lawman out of his saddle," Earl Ganston said, "but I don't know why. If we get caught we're all going to hang for something or other, why not for killing a Ranger? In some circles that's the grandest thing a man can do." He grinned at the others, drawing them into his goading of Willie John.

Willie John ignored Earl and the others and spoke to Hopper Ganston. "The town's slow today . . . everybody staying home, getting ready for the winter, I figure. I didn't go past the sheriff's office, but there was no need to. It's only been a month since Leonard Dupré killed Sheriff Sanders. They haven't replaced him yet."

"You don't know that for a fact, now do you, Willie?" Earl Ganston asked in a haughty tone.

"I'd bet my life on it," said Willie John.

"It ain't your life I'm concerned about," said Earl. "It's mine."

Willie John allowed himself a slight smile. "Even better, then, Earl . . . I'd bet *your* life on it."

"All right stop it, you two!" said Hopper Ganston, cutting in before things got out of hand. "We've got plenty to keep us busy." He called back over his shoulder, "Mitchell, Rasdorph, Kerns, you three go with Willie, come in from the other end of town and be ready to give us some cover if we need it."

"Hell, Hopper," Earl Ganston chuckled, "you heard what the Indian said . . . the town's slow today. This ain't no big deal."

"All the same, we're treating it like it is," said Hopper. He lifted his rifle from his saddle boot, checked it and laid it across his lap as the three men he'd called forward formed up around Willie John. "You boys listen to Willie and do what he tells you. Me and Earl and the rest will give you time to get situated. Then we're coming in, taking the bank like we did all the others . . . then riding straight north." He looked from man to man. "Everybody got that? Straight north."

"North? Damn, it's gonna be a cold one, then," said Nian Rasdorph, barely above a whisper. He tugged his battered bowler hat down on his head and lifted his collar to the wind.

"You've got that right," Willie John said, his voice equally low as he heeled the big dapple-gray forward, taking the lead.

Joe Perkins stood up, raising the long bearskin coat from the wooden storage chest and shaking it out before putting it on over his black wool suit. Dust and hair swirled from the coat then descended to the floor. Perkins sneezed and rubbed his palm back and forth across his long handlebar mustache. He took out a wadded up bandanna from his suit pocket, blew his nose with a honking sound like that of a goose, then blotted his nose and said to the telegraph clerk, "How many do you make it to be, Kirby?"

Kirby Bell shrugged nervously. "Like I said, Mr. Perkins, I just got a glance at them. It was Selectman Collins who saw all of them. He said it looked like a dozen or more: rough-looking bunch, he said. Said I better come get you, you being the only man around here with any experience in this kind of thing."

"Yeah?" Joe Perkins lifted his chin a little, liking the feel of somebody sending for his help. Just like the old days, he reminded himself. "Well, if it's robbing they come here for, they'll be sadly disappointed. If it's killing they want . . . they'll find that I am up to the task." He adjusted the brace of heavy Walker Colts on his narrow hips, then reached over and took down his wide-brimmed Stetson and sat it down squarely atop his head, his thin white hair hanging loosely beneath it to his shoulders. As he took out a pair of wire-rimmed spectacles and hooked them on behind his ears, he asked, "Did nobody dare to holler up there and ask them their business?"

Kirby looked down at the cabin floor and shook his head. "Well, no, I don't reckon. See, there's hardly anybody in town today. With the sheriff dead and all, we just naturally figured it best we get you . . . Selectman Collins said so, anyway." He raised his worried eyes to Joe Perkins. "They'll have to be dealt with, that's for sure."

"And you say the telegraph lines are down?" Perkins asked.

"Yep, went dead an hour ago," said Kirby. "I thought that was more than just a little coincidental, too."

"I see. You brought your rifle of course, didn't you, Kirby?" Perkins asked, reaching out and taking his walking cane down from a wall hook.

"My what?" Kirby looked stunned at the very thought of it.

"Your rifle, Kirby," Perkins grinned. "You know, that long shiny thing sitting in your closet? Steel on one end, wood on the other?"

Kirby's face reddened. "I reckon maybe we could wait, Mr. Perkins, see if they really are up to something or just passing through. There could be some good reason—"

"No, Kirby . . ." Joe Perkins looked down, studying his weathered hands as if having to consider the situation. "I fear when an armed body of men has descended upon a town and perched atop its roofs, there can be no good come of it."

"What I mean is, Mr. Perkins, maybe they're lawmen on the trail of outlaws, do you think?"

"No lawmen I've ever known would do something so foolish," said Joe Perkins. "But on the chance that you might be right, we'll inquire of them before we make any bold moves. Now hurry around back and bring the hound. He'll be of use. I've been feeding him lean lately, just in case of trouble like this."

"Should I also bring the wagon?" Kirby asked. "It's a half-mile walk to town."

"Are you suggesting I'm not up to my game?" Joe Perkins gave him a cold stare, leaning on the cane, forming a tripod with his thin legs, the whole of him looking frail and shaky—a skin and calcium remnant

wrapped in the fur of a monster whose mortal reck-
oning had long since passed.

"Uh—no!" Kirby thought quickly, then said, "I
was only concerned about the dog."

Joe Perkins nodded. "Well, perhaps you're right. I
mustn't wear out the hound on the way in—he might
be needed later on the trail. Yes, bring the wagon,
then. I'll wait here and give this thing some more
thought. If we're not careful someone could get hurt
in this fracas."

In moments Kirby Bell had hurried to the shed out
back, dropped the saddle from his horse, hitched the
animal to the small buckboard wagon and raised the
hound. When he returned to the front of the cabin,
Joe Perkins stood leaning on the hickory cane, a large
pocket watch in his hand as if timing the telegraph
clerk's efforts. Rather than attempt climbing onto the
seat beside Kirby, Perkins scuffled to the rear of the
buckboard and fell backward onto its wooden bed.
Then he struggled up to his knees as the hound
lopped back and forth in place barking coarsely, the
big chain slapping the buckboard planks. "What are
we waiting for, telegraph clerk?" Perkins shouted in
a raspy breathless voice. "I doubt they'll come to us."

By the time the buckboard rolled into Hubbler
Wells, Willie John and his three-man party had
drifted in unnoticed and taken position; two across
the street, two at the hitch rail out front of the bank.
Huey Sweeney had stepped out of a saddle shop
where he had spent the last few minutes. Willie John
turned toward the sound of the hound baying from
the seat of the buckboard. Behind the driver he saw
the big bearskin coat and the battered Stetson wob-

bling to the sway of the wagon bed as Joe Perkins struggled to keep himself standing erect, leaning on his hickory cane.

"I don't like this at all," Willie whispered to Nian Rasdorph beside him. As he spoke he gave a slight hand signal to Mitchell and Kerns across the street, telling them to be ready for anything. Sweeney shouted something at Willie John before backing quickly into an alley where he disappeared like a puff of smoke. Then Willie's hand closed around his pistol handle, drew the weapon and held it cocked down the side of his leg, watching the buckboard swing a wide turn in the empty street and stop out front of the saloon.

"What the hell's going on up there?" Earl Ganston whispered to his brother. Earl, Hopper and the six remaining men had already begun riding in slowly from the other end of town. At the sight of the old man standing in the back of the buckboard raising a cane toward the roof, Hopper reined his horse down almost to a halt. The men behind him did the same.

On the roof, Colonel Daniel Fuller cursed in a harsh constrained voice, then said to Red Booker, "What the blazes is that old fool doing down there?"

"Hello the roof," Joe Perkins called out, waving his cane back and forth. Joe held the dog's long chain in his other hand while the animal barked and bounded back and forth, its attention directed upward at the saloon's roofline. Along the rutted street, Willie John and the other gunmen's eyes followed.

"Lord God!" said Daniel Fuller to Red Booker and the men alongside him on the roof. "Here comes the Ganstons . . . and this old fool has given us up."

There was a tense second when every man on the street and atop the roof seemed to freeze in place, watching Perkins and his baying hound. Kirby Bell half rose from the buckboard seat, caught off guard by Joe Perkins's calling out to the armed men above them. He thought surely Perkins would have waited until the few armed townsmen inside the saloon had joined them. But not so. Even as four townsmen bunched up in the bat-wing doors, rifles and shotguns in hand, Joe Perkins raised one of the big Walker Colts and cocked it upward, shakily, at the roofline. "I'll have an answer," Perkins shouted.

"Damn you to living hell, sir!" Daniel Fuller bellowed. "There is a robbery about to take place!"

"A what?" Joe Perkins called out above the baying of the hound.

But still, the street and saloon roof stood tense, motionless, until Willie John made the first move. His eyes shot from the Ganstons, to the townsmen, to the roofline where Fuller and his men had raised up with their rifles now that their cover was blown. Thinking quick, Willie John jumped forward into the street and shouted as he waved his pistol at Perkins and the saloon doors, "They're bank robbers! Shoot them down!"

"Damn that Indian!" Seeing what Willie John was doing, Daniel Fuller shouted to his men, "Somebody shut him up! Fire, men!"

The rifles along the saloon roof opened fire, but hearing Fuller's command had left some of the men confused. Thinking Fuller meant for them to shut up the old man in the buckboard, three rifles swung in Perkins's direction, the shots raising puffs of dust from the bearskin coat as Perkins spun like a top from the impact of whining lead.

Kirby Bell dove from the buckboard seat to the cold, hard ground, the big hound pulling free from

Perkins and leaping right behind him with a loud
yelp as bullets from the roof kicked up a spray of
splinters from the wagon bed. "Don't shoot!" Kirby
screamed, unsure of who he was even pleading to.
The townsmen, seeing Joe Perkins shot and seeing
the Indian and the two men with him fire at the
roofline, misread the situation entirely. They sprang
from the door of the saloon and fired up at Fuller
and his men. But Fuller's men knew who their targets
were. Under fire from the armed townsmen, Red
Booker and the others still managed to throw down a
barrage of deadly fire on Willie John, Nian Rasdorph,
Mitchell and Kerns.

"Get us out of here!" Willie John shouted at Hopper Ganston and the men on horseback who had
fallen back as the firing started. Nian Rasdorph took
a bullet through his chest that drove him backward
against the two horses hitched at the rail. The horses
struggled against their tied reins and whinnied loud
and long in their fright. Willie returned fire as he
snatched at the reins of both horses. Getting their
reins free from the rail and tight in his gloved hand,
he reached down with his gunhand and tried yanking Nian Rasdorph to his feet. "Nian! Let's go!"

A bullet ripped through Willie John's shoulder,
forcing him to stagger back a step. He caught a
glimpse of Earl, Hopper and the others turning in
the street and heading out of town, bullets from the
roofline spitting up dirt at their horses' hoofs. "Damn
it, Hopper!" Willie shouted, falling back quickly into
an alleyway. He pulled the horses along, Nian Rasdorph stumbling along against him. They were both
wounded and bloody now. Willie flattened himself
against the side of a clapboard building and fired up
at the rifles on the saloon roof.

Mitchell and Kerns lay in the street, Mitchell face-down in a dark pool of blood. Kerns was crying out, a hand clasped to his spilling innards, the big hound three feet from him diving in and out at him, bark-ing, snapping. "Help me, Willie!" Kerns screamed above the raging gunfire.

But aside from taking a shot at the hound, there was nothing Willie could do. The dog let out a long yelp as dirt from the shot kicked up against its low-ered muzzle and caused it to turn and run away, not stopping until it disappeared into the horizon. In the street, Joe Perkins had fallen from the wagon, three wounds spitting blood through holes in his bearskin coat. But he was still alive, and still had fight in him. He thrashed and wallowed back and forth under the weight of the coat until he rolled back up onto his knees and raised both Walker Colts and fired.

Joe Perkins's shots ripped chunks of wood from the cornice and facade of the saloon. Rifle smoke drifted in thick clouds, spent brass cartridges littered the dusty street. "Nian, you alive?" asked Willie John, firing at the roof without looking down at Rasdorph, who lay at his feet.

"Yeah, Willie . . . I'm alive," Nian Rasdorph re-plied in a strained voice. "Looks like Mitchell and Kerns are done for, though."

"We've got to make a run for it," said Willie. "Hopper and the boys are gone." On the street, Per-kins fell backward as two more rifle shots hit him, the men on the roof firing mindlessly now, showing no mercy.

"I'm . . . with you, Willie," Nian gasped, raising a weak hand to take his horse's reins from Willie John. "You might . . . have to give me some help up."

On the street, Joe Perkins rolled onto his belly.

Lying prone with more blood seeping through new holes in his coat, he raised the big Walker Colts again. Two shots exploded; two riflemen fell screaming from the roof. "That old man's a shooter," Willie John said absently to himself. Then he looked back down at Nian Rasdorph. "All right, I'll help you up on your horse. But that's all I can do for you. There's no use in lying about it, Nian . . . you're not gonna make it. I can't waste time on you."

"I . . . understand," said the wounded outlaw, looking up with a hand clasped to his bleeding chest. "Ready when you are."

Chapter 3

Seeing that the Ganstons had turned and fled out of town, Daniel Fuller waved his arms and shouted down to the firing townsmen bunched up in the doorway of the saloon. "Hold your fire, for God sakes! We're lawmen up here!"

"Then you best show us some tin *real* quick," called a voice from the saloon. "You've killed old Joe!"

"The old fool in the bearskin coat?" Fuller asked.

"He might have been an old fool, but he was one of us. Somebody's gonna pay for killing him."

"We're sorry we shot him, but that was a terrible mistake on his part. He fired on us first," Fuller replied. "What the hell did you expect us to do?" His eyes went to the crumpled pile of bearskin in the middle of the street as the firing waned below. Alongside Daniel Fuller, Red Booker and the rest of the possemen had stopped shooting on Fuller's command. They stared toward the alleyway and saloon as they quickly reloaded their rifles.

"Let's blame the outlaws that caused all this in the first place," called Fuller. "We've got two of them

wounded, pinned in the alley. Before we do anything, let's flush them out of there. Are you with us?"

A silence passed as the men in the saloon murmured back and forth among themselves. Then, just
as Selectman Collins started to call out to the roofline,
two pistolshots exploded above the sound of hoof-
beats, and Nian Rasdorph came rounding the corner
of the alley, heading up the middle of the dirt street.

"Get that sonofabitch, boys!" Daniel Fuller shouted.

In his wounded condition, Nian Rasdorph rode
low on his horse, wobbling from side to side. Even
so, he managed to keep his pistol firing shot after
shot, alternating his aim between the riflemen along
the roof and the townsmen bunched up in the doorway. "Stay with me, Willie!" Rasdorph shouted back
over his shoulder through a hail of return gunfire.
But Willie John was nowhere near him. Willie John
had never left the alley when Nian made his desperate break for freedom.

"Somebody shoot him, damn it to hell!" Daniel
Fuller raged, hurrying, reloading his rifle and violently yanking the lever back and forth. The roofline
exploded in one long volley of fire, the doorway of
the saloon joining in the fusillade as holes exploded
in Nian Rasdorph's coat from all directions at once.
Blood spewed. The terrified horse spun in a circle
and reared high, sending the wounded outlaw
screaming to the ground. Rasdorph struggled to his
feet, but the hail of bullets pounded him to his knees.
He slung his gun hand toward the roofline, let out a
long scream, then collapsed beneath the hammering
gunfire.

"Hold your fire, men!" said Fuller, waving a gloved
hand in the air. "Jesus," he added, spreading a cruel

smile at Red Booker standing beside him, "I thought that sucker was never going to die."

Along the roof, a voice called out from amid the excited possemen, "What say, Colonel Fuller? Can we go down and look him over?"

"Not so fast, you idiots!" Fuller shouted. "We've still got that Injun cornered down there." Fuller shot a glance down at the saloon, and seeing the townsmen venture forward into the street, he bellowed at them, "Stay put, you fools! That Injun will shoot your eyes out."

"What are we going to do?" shouted Selectman Collins. "We can't sit here all day waiting on one wounded gunman."

"Hear that?" Fuller said to Red Booker. "Now that the fighting's about over, they'll start talking tough. For two cents I'd let them go on in and let the Injun have them."

"What *are* we going to do, Colonel?" asked Booker. "We need to get on the Ganstons' trail while it's still hot."

"In good time, Red," said Fuller. "Right now, bring the men and come with me." He moved back from the edge of the roof. "We'll surround the Injun from all sides and move in real slow. He's been the eyes and ears for the Ganstons. I want to keep him alive if we can. There's a lot he can tell us."

· Hurrying along behind Fuller and waving for the men to follow him, Red Booker said, "That's all well and good, Colonel, but I ain't seen an Injun yet that will tell you anything he don't want you to know."

Fuller offered a dark chuckle. "You haven't seen the way I ask them."

When they had descended the ladder at the rear

of the building, Fuller, Booker and the rest of the posse walked quickly across the street to the saloon. Keeping a close eye on the alley where they knew the Indian lay in wait, Colonel Fuller said to Selectman Collins, "I hope you're good at following orders, sir. If not, we'll likely get some men killed here."

Collins looked at the faces of the other townsmen, then back at Fuller. "We'll do whatever we need to. Who are you, anyway?"

"I'm Colonel Daniel J. Fuller, representing the Midwest Bankers' Association." He gestured a hand toward Red Booker and the rest of the posse. "This is my private militia."

"Oh . . ." Collins looked the men over quickly. "You're bounty hunters, huh?"

Colonel Fuller ignored him, turning toward the alley. "Have you seen any sign of him?"

"No, but he's still in there, waiting to make a break," said Collins. "We caught a glimpse of his horse a minute ago."

"Good," said Fuller. "I want your men to spread out along the boardwalk on this side of the street. My men will take this side. We'll close in slow and easy when I give a signal. I want this man alive."

"We'll do the best we can," said Collins. "But if he starts shooting I can't promise anything."

Fuller gave him a hard stare. "I checked that alley when we came to town. I know it's a dead end. He's in there and there's no place for him to go. You keep your men's fingers off their triggers whilst I talk sense to that Injun. He'll give himself up to me, so long as you boys don't do something stupid."

"Something stupid?" said a voice from amid the armed townsmen. "You mean like setting up an ambush atop the roofs and not letting the town know about it?"

"Who said that?" Fuller demanded, his eyes searching the gathered townsmen.

"I said it." A red-faced man with a long white mustache stepped forward and pushed his bowler hat up off of his forehead. Beneath his coat he wore a long leather smithing apron. "I'm Carl Yates. Joe Perkins is laying dead in the street because of this hare-brained ambush of yours."

Fuller pointed a finger at the man. "I'll deal with you, sir, as soon as this is over."

"You can deal with me then, or now, or any damn time you feel the urge to," said Carl Yates. "Hadn't been for you damn bunch of buzzards—"

"Easy, Carl," said Selectman Collins, stepping in between the two men. "We're all sorry about old Joe. But let's get this situation settled before someone else gets hurt." He turned back to Fuller, saying, "All right, lead the way. We'll spread along the boardwalk and close in."

As Daniel Fuller stepped away from the saloon doorway and down into the street facing the alley, he called out, "You in there, Injun? I know you're wounded. You saw what happened to your buddy. Now, you don't want to end up like that, do you?" Fuller looked over at Nian Rasdorph's bullet-riddled body lying facedown in the street, then moved his men closer with a slow wave of his hand. "Toss out your pistol and we'll come get you, take you to a doctor and let him patch you up. How's that sound?"

No answer came from the alley, only the low nickering of the dapple-gray. Fuller caught a quick glimpse of the horse's muzzle, then saw it duck itself back out of sight at the sound of his voice. "Hey, listen to me, Injun. I don't usually make this kind of offer. If you're smart you'll give yourself up." He motioned the men closer, bringing them in a tighter and tighter circle around the entrance of the alley.

"If he's dead I'm cleaving off his ears for a keepsake," Talbert French whispered to Erskine Brock, the two of them in a crouch, easing forward.

"You ignorant peckerwood, you heard Fuller say he wanted the man alive."

"I know," said French, "but alls I'm saying is *if* he's dead. So far you haven't heard a peep out of him, have you?"

"No, but that might just be his way of drawing us in," whispered Brock. "I figure he's right around the corner of the building just waiting to spring out and make a run for it."

"You two shut up and pay attention," Red Booker hissed at them.

Ten yards from the alley entrance, the circle of men stopped on Fuller's hand signal and stood crouched and ready. "All right, Injun, this is your last chance," said Fuller. "I know what you're thinking . . . but it won't work. You'll make a few feet, maybe even kill one or two of us. But at the end you'll be dead like a dog in the street. Now what's it going to be?"

The only response from the alley was the low sound of the dapple-gray blowing air through its nostrils and scraping a hoof on the cold dirt. The big horse stood close to the clapboard wall, tense and expectant, as if awaiting a command of reins and boot heels. But no command came, and the horse grew more and more nervous.

"You heard me, Injun," said Fuller, getting put out at being ignored. "Come out this very minute or we're coming in!"

Inside the alley the dapple-gray pricked its ears toward Fuller's voice, let out a long low nicker and took a short step forward, its head coming into view past the corner of the building. "Steady, boys, here he comes," Fuller said, raising his cocked pistol, taking aim. "Okay, Injun, that's the way, nice and slow."

The dapple-gray took another short step, then another, until it came into full view, its empty saddle causing Fuller to curse as he let go of a tense breath. A wide smear of blood shone down the right saddle stirrup. "Damn it, boys, easy. He's in there somewhere wounded bad. We might have to drag him out. Everybody move forward real careful-like."

"I've got an idea," Red Booker said almost to himself. He hurried forward in a crouch and grabbed the dangling reins to the big dapple-gray. "Hey in there, Injun," he yelled, keeping the horse between himself and the alley, "I'm coming in. If you ever cared anything at all for this horse, you better hold your fire. He's my shield, do you hear me?"

When no reply came from the alley, Red Booker looked at Daniel Fuller. "Go ahead," said Fuller. "I'm getting tired of fooling with this thug."

Red Booker pushed the dapple-gray forward into the alley. A few tense moments passed while everyone on the street waited in silence for the sound of gunfire. But none came. Finally, Red Booker called out, "There's nobody in here, Colonel. The Injun's got away from us."

"Like hell," Fuller cursed in disbelief, stepping forward into the narrow alley. "I saw him come in here. There's no way out 'less he can fly."

Colonel Fuller looked all around the blind alley. Then his eyes went up to a single window high up the side of the mercantile building. "There's how he got away."

Booker's eyes went up to the window, then he shook his head. "No way, Colonel. The window's closed. He would have had to break it to get through." Booker gauged the distance between the ground and the window. "Besides he never could have reached it, not even standing atop his saddle."

"Then, by God, *you* tell me where he is!" Fuller shouted. He flagged the other men into the narrow littered alley. "Get in here, men. Somebody check that back fence, see if he might've gotten over it."

From amid the men, the mercantile store owner shouldered his way up front. "I'm Murray Fadden. This is my store. I never leave that window open or unlocked except in the hottest part of the summer." He nodded upward. "That's just a large storage room up there. Send somebody with me and we'll go check it."

"Damn right we will," said Fuller. "Come on, men, let's all go see what's up there. Only way that Injun could have gotten away is if he had some help."

Over the rise and fall of debris, discarded household items and garbage of all shape and size, Willie John hurried with Billy Odle right beside him. Weakened by the loss of blood from his shoulder wound, Willie staggered, nearly falling when his boot picked up a tangle of thin wire. He shook his boot free, but Billy noticed the difficulty he had in doing it. "Come on, Willie, hurry!" he coaxed, his voice trembling in urgency.

Willie John's breath sounded heavy and labored. His words came haltingly. "Go on, kid . . . I'm right behind . . . you." He had to grab Billy Odle's shoulder for support. Billy looked up at him with a worried expression.

"The shack is just ahead, Willie. Please! We've got to make it there!"

"Don't worry . . . kid. I'm not . . . done for yet. Let's go," Willie rasped. Willie John looked back along the path, seeing the blood trail he'd left but knowing he was powerless to do anything about it. He didn't mention the trail to Billy Odle. So long as this kid was helping him, Willie didn't want to say anything that might spook him. As they pushed forward again, partly sliding down a mound of refuse and tin cans, Willie said, "Kid . . . this is the second time . . . you've stuck . . . your neck out . . . for me."

"Hush up, Willie," said Billy Odle. "My pa would've done the same had he been here." They hurried across cold flat ground now, toward a tar-paper shack thirty yards ahead.

Willie offered a weak smile. "Thanks, kid."

"Don't tell me thanks," replied Billy. "We'll only stay there long enough for you to catch your breath and get that bleeding stopped. I know a better place not far from here. Don't worry, we've beat them, Willie."

"Where's . . . your pal?" Willie asked, feeling stronger at just the thought of getting away.

"I ran him off when we saw you get shot. We were watching under the boardwalk out front on the railroad hotel. I saw you wounded and knew you might need help. So I told Alvin to get himself home before we got hurt out here. He listens to anything I tell him."

"That's . . . good, kid. But what's your . . . ma gonna say, us busting in like this?"

"This time of day she doesn't know a thing," said Billy. "She's with her customers all night, then all day she stays knocked-out asleep until it's time to go back to the streets and the saloon. Says it's too much on her mind." They hurried on. "It's a hard life being a whore, I reckon."

"I bet," said Willie John, struggling forward, wanting to chastise the boy for calling his mother a whore, but not really having the strength to do it right then.

"Anyway, she won't give us any problems," said Billy Odle.

By the time they'd reached the door of the tar-paper shack, Willie John's loss of blood caught up with him. He felt himself sway to the side as the world grew distant and gray to him. "Hang on, Willie," said Billy, looping the Indian's arm across his shoulder, steadying him as he threw open the shack door. The two of them almost fell to the dirt floor.

Willie John caught a foggy glimpse of a woman lying on the battered bed, half covered by a ragged, soiled quilt. As Willie tried shaking his head to clear his vision, Billy Odle hurried to the bed and threw the loose end of the quilt the rest of the way over his mother, covering all of her except a length of her flowing red hair. "See, she doesn't know there's a world out here," said the boy. "You lay still, Willie, I'll get some water and rags."

There was a short period of time when Willie John may or may not have passed out from his loss of blood. He wasn't sure. All he knew was that one minute Billy Odle was kneeling over him, dabbing a wet rag at the wound in his shoulder; the next minute Billy was saying, "There. That's the best we can do for now. We've got to get out of here pretty soon before they start searching all the back alleys for you."

Willie John felt some of his strength return, and he straightened up, leaning his back against a rough wooden shipping crate in the front corner of the room. He looked around the tiny shack, seeing no accommodation except for the battered bed, a rickety wooden crate for a nightstand and a cracked porcelain pitcher sitting in a wash pan atop it.

As if reading the Indian's thoughts, Billy Odle said, "I don't sleep here, or even come here much. It makes her feel bad, me hanging around. It's bad for business, too."

"Where do you sleep?" Willie John asked.

Billy Odle shrugged. "I was sleeping some up in that storeroom above the mercantile store. But I won't be staying there anymore." He grinned. "Other times I stay at this place where I'm taking you. Nobody knows where it's at, not even Alvin. I found it a while back and decided to keep it to myself, you know, in case I might need it for a hideout if I was ever on the run."

Willie John just looked at him for a second, then said, "Good thinking, kid." He nodded toward the bed. "Maybe we best get out of here before she wakes up." Now that his strength and senses were coming back, he couldn't care less about Billy Odle or his mother or anybody else. What he needed now was to get to this kid's hideout. So far the boy had done a good job helping him get away. If this hideout was as safe as Billy said it was, things would work out fine, provided the kid could keep his mouth shut. But what if he couldn't keep his mouth shut? What if the townsmen caught him and pressured him?

Would the kid tell them? Willie didn't like asking himself that question, but he had to consider it all the same.

"Kid, are you sure nobody knows about this place where we're going?" Willie asked.

"Yeah, I'm certain," said Billy. "If anybody's been there it's been too long ago to make any difference. Why, are you worried?"

"No, kid, I'm not worried at all," said Willie. "I figure I must be in good hands." He offered a thin smile. The fact was, if this place was safe enough for him to hold up a long period of time, he might have to kill Billy. It wasn't something he wanted to do, and it bothered him to even have to think about it. But it was a cold hard fact. If it came down to his life or young Billy Odle's, there was no question. This dumb kid would have to die.

Willie John looked Billy up and down. The boy thought of himself as being tough, a real outlaw in the making. And maybe he was. But Willie John couldn't afford to bet his life on it. Billy Odle had helped him, that was good. But this was not a pleasant world where one good turn deserved another. This was a world of dog eat dog—something Willie John had learned early on.

Tough break, kid, Willie John said to himself, looking away from Billy Odle's eyes, across the cramped shack to the battered bed and the meager belongings of a family put upon by hard times. *But if you want to see what being an outlaw is all about* . . . He looked back into Billy Odle's eyes, his gaze growing cold and hollow. . . . *Here it is, kid, staring you right in the face.* "We'll need some horses. Think you can rustle us up a couple?"

"Yep, without any problems," said Billy. "I know

where there's some good strong ones, a half dozen or more. They're right on the trail we'll be taking."

"Ever stole a horse?" Willie John asked.

"Not until now," Billy Odle said, grinning.

Chapter 4

Sam Burrack had heard the faint rumble of gunfire from a long distance away and pushed the big Appaloosa as hard as he dared for the next mile and a half. He had a pretty good idea what the gunfire was all about, but after riding all night at a brisk clip, he didn't want to get this close to the Ganstons and have to drop the chase just because he'd worn out his horse. His first reaction to the distant riflefire had been to cut away from the trail and swing west. It would do no good to ride straight into Hubbler Wells right now. Whatever havoc the gang had wrought upon the small town would have come and gone by the time he arrived. His best chance at catching up to the Ganstons now was to anticipate which direction they would ride and try to intersect them on the trail. The Ganstons were headed northwest, yet Sam had a hunch they would veer west for a ways after a robbery just to throw off any followers. And from the heavy cracks of pistols and rifles up ahead, there would be followers.

Three miles west of Hubbler Wells, Sam Burrack's hunch paid off. Atop a low cliff overlooking the trail, Sam stepped down from the Appaloosa as the sound of pounding hoofs drew nearer. He drew his rifle from his saddle boot, checked it, levered a round into the chamber and ran a thumb along the sights. Then he backed the Appaloosa out of sight behind a scrub juniper, spun its reins and eased back to the edge of the cliff. Dropping to one knee and raising the rifle to his shoulder, Sam waited as the first three men riding abreast came into view around a turn in the trail. Had he been on the trail of only one man, or perhaps even two or three, he might have fired a warning shot, then given them a chance to surrender. But with odds this long against him . . . no way.

At a distance of eighty yards the first shot picked up the middle rider from his saddle and flung him backward like a loose bundle of rags. Before the other two could get out of the way, Sam quickly levered, aimed and fired again, this time seeing the rider on the right slide down the side of his horse, hang on for a moment then fall away. Before Sam could get off a third shot all of the riders fell back hurriedly around the bend in the trail. *So far, so good . . .*

Quickly, Sam stepped over and unhitched the Appaloosa, mounted and fired two more shots from horseback before heeling the animal away into a wide dash around the trail. From the rocks alongside the trail where the outlaws had dropped from their saddles and taken cover, shots exploded in the direction of the empty cliff. "Hold your fire, damn it!" yelled Hopper Ganston. "Whoever he is, he's gone." He looked at his brother who had dropped behind a short stand of rock a few feet away. "You all right, Earl?"

"Yeah, I'm all right, but poor Jeffries is deader than hell, and Terez is shot plum through. I saw Andy Stebbs grab him and drag him back. Terez will be lucky if he makes it. Got a hole the size of my fist in his chest."

"Well," said Hopper, "this cinches it for me. We've still got one of them blasted Rangers on our tails."

"Damn it to hell, that ain't fair," Earl cursed, yanking his hat from his head and slapping it against his knee. "He's out of his jurisdiction and he knows it! He's breaking the damn law." Earl's voice took a tone of disbelief. "What good is it to make laws if men like him ain't going to abide by them?"

Hopper chuckled under his breath at the irony of his brother's words. "Maybe you oughta write a scorching letter to Congress, brother."

Earl ignored the remark. "This really rips it. We've lost the Indian and three good men back in town . . . now Jeffries and Terez. And we still ain't made a dime out of this deal! What're we going to do to get straightened out?" he asked.

Hopper looked back and forth along the trail in both directions, thinking about it. "Ranger or not, whoever that is shooting at us, you can bet we ain't seen the last of him." He considered it another second then said, "We needed that bank money from Hubbler Wells to hold us over. I hate going to Mexico short on cash. I just never feel quite as welcome when my pockets aren't full."

"I know what you mean," said Earl, still scanning the countryside, his rifle in his hands. "If we're going to get shot at, we might as well be making some money for it."

"Yep." Hopper helped him search for any sign of the person who had done the shooting. "I tell you one thing, I sure miss that Indian already. He kept us clear of stuff like this happening."

"Are we going back to Hubbler Wells?" asked Earl. "Make somebody pay for all this trouble?"

"You can count on it, brother," said Hopper, "just as soon as we can see our way clear. Think Terez will be able to ride if Andy pitches him up on a saddle?"

"I'll go see," said Earl.

Hopper Ganston only shook his head watching his brother scoot away across the dirt toward Andy Stebbs and the wounded outlaw. Then he turned his attention back to the vast empty land, spat and ran a hand across his blistered lips. Was that really one of the Rangers out there, still on their trail? If it was, where the hell did he go? The land before him lay vacant, save for the stir of cold wind whispering through the rocks. *Damned Ranger . . .*

When the men had collected themselves up from the dust, shook themselves off and mounted their half-spooked horses, Hopper rode up beside Earl and held him back as the men rode back warily along the trail. "Let Andy Stebbs and Terez ride up front," said Hopper in a lowered voice. "If that Ranger is back there, Terez is about dead, anyway."

"What about Andy, though?" Earl asked as the men filed past them in a short column of twos.

Hopper just looked at him. They rode on.

A mile later, right where the trail leveled back down and emptied out from among the upthrusts of rock, a rifleshot hammered Andy Stebbs in his shoulder, causing both him and Terez to fall from the saddle as the rest of the men fell back, this time better prepared and immediately returning fire. Sam Burrack ducked down behind rock cover as bullets whistled past him. He hurried back to the Appaloosa, unhitched it, mounted and swung back in the opposite direction.

"See?" said Hopper to Earl. "He's got a good thing going for himself. He can run us back and forth along this stretch of trail until we're all shot to pieces."

"Then let's bust up, every man for himself," said Earl, "since nobody here seems able to shoot that son of a bitch!" He glared at the rest of the men who were once again down from their horse and hugging the ground. Andy Stebbs and Terez lay twenty yards ahead on the trail where they'd fallen.

"No," said Hopper, "busting up might be exactly what he wants us to do." He levered a round into his rifle chamber. "Besides, wouldn't you be a little embarrassed to admit that one fool with a rifle sent the whole damn lot of us running?"

Earl didn't answer. He cursed to himself and scooted sidelong to where he could get a look at the two wounded outlaws. "That just cost us one more man. We better do something quick."

"We're going to," said Hopper. He looked around, making a quick head count. "We'll split up, but not for long." He called over to the three remaining men, "Bootlip, you and Bratcher stay where you are for now. Lester, get over here."

"What's the plan, Hopper?" Earl asked barely above a whisper.

Hopper looked up along the ridgeline above them, then said to his brother, "He's expecting us to run back that way, so he'll be waiting for us. What we've got to do is get where he's at and turn the tables on him. You, Lester and I are going back, but we're going to cut up through the rocks, get him caught between us and Bootlip and Bratcher . . . see how he likes that."

"I don't like it," said Earl. "We'll all be shooting into one another if it comes down to a close fight."

"It's the only choice we've got," said Hopper. "Look how quick he's whittled us down already."

"Damn it," said Earl, knowing his brother was right. "I just want to hit that bank, get some money and go on about our business."

"Yeah, but we've got to get rid of him before we can do anything else," Hopper insisted. "He's hell with that rifle."

Atop the trail, Sam Burrack pulled the Appaloosa back and waited, this time only riding half the distance to the other end of the pass. He knew he had used this cat-and-mouse plan for all it was worth. The Ganstons weren't going to keep falling for it. Now he had to be ready to change tactics, see what the Ganstons had in mind and be prepared. He listened to the sound of three horses race back along the trail. When the rumble of hoofs faded, he stepped down from the Appaloosa and led it forward, the two of them stepping down among the rocks on the steep slope toward the trail.

If he'd been keeping score correctly, there were five men left. Three of them had just headed along the trail. Now was his chance to slip up behind the two they'd left watching for him in the other direction. With any luck he would take these two down and lie in wait for the other three to return at the sound of gunfire. He spread a thin smile. "Keeping 'em off balance, eh Black Pot?" he whispered to the Appaloosa, patting a gloved hand on its muzzle. Once down onto the trail, he mounted and heeled the horse forward, his rifle across his lap.

But before he'd gotten close to the end of the pass where he knew the two men would be waiting, the sound of many rifles and pistols exploded less than fifty yards ahead of him, the suddenness of it causing

Burrack to pull the Appaloosa back and duck it into
a slim crevice alongside the trail. That many guns
could only mean one thing: a posse from Hubbler
Wells. Sam wasn't at all surprised that a posse would
be on these men's trail, but not this soon, and certainly not this many. It always took a while to get a
few townsmen together, get them armed and mounted.
He remembered the large amount of gunfire he'd
heard earlier on his way to Hubbler Wells and began
to get an idea of what had happened. Somebody had
been waiting for the Ganstons. He stepped down
from the saddle and waited, back out of sight, listening to the steady pounding of gunfire.

When there was a lull in the firing, the Ranger
eased forward, leaving the Appaloosa in the cover of
rock. No sooner had he stepped out onto the trail
than he saw the two outlaws running toward him on
foot, one of them limping badly and clutching a hand
to his bloody thigh, both of them carrying pistols and
looking back over their shoulders. With his rifle in
his left hand, Sam drew his big Colt and leveled it
on the men. "Stand fast!" he shouted. "Drop the
guns! Get your hands in the air!"

Bootlip Thomas and Murray Bratcher wouldn't
hear of it. They slid to a halt quick enough, but their
pistols came up firing. One shot whistled past Sam
Burrack's head before he let the hammer fall.
Bratcher twisted in a half circle, then collapsed with
a bullet through his chest. Another shot grazed Sam's
forearm as he turned his aim on Bootlip Thomas,
recocking his big Colt, and dropped him facedown
in the trail.

Sam stepped forward with caution, keeping an eye
back along the trail in case the other three returned—
something he doubted was going to happen right

away. When he neared the two bodies in the trail, he reached out with his boot and kicked Bootlip's pistol away from his hand. Bootlip gasped and tried to raise his face and speak. "Save it," said Sam. "I've heard it all before."

He stood replacing his two spent pistol rounds when some possemen edged forward in a crouch, moving from rock to rock. "I'm a Ranger," Sam called out, not wanting to let them too close before identifying himself. Without holstering his big Colt, he let it drop down his side, his thumb across the hammer. He reached up slowly with his left hand and eased his duster open, revealing the badge on his chest. "Who are you?"

"We'll ask the questions, mister," Red Booker barked, easing up from behind a rock with his rifle aimed and ready.

"I told you who I am," Sam replied. "Now I'd appreciate it if you'd point that Spencer in another direction. If you're a posse we're on the same side here."

"I'll let you know whose side we're on," said Red Booker, "soon as I see that pistol hit the ground."

"You can wait all day and not see that," Sam said. "I'm Arizona Ranger Sam Burrack. I've been in pursuit of these men for a long time. Who are you, mister?"

"We're lawmen," said Booker. "Make no mistake about that. We're detectives for the Midwest Bankers' Association." He stepped forward, the rest of his men spreading out as they did the same until they formed half a circle around Sam. "You're a long way outside your jurisdiction, ain't you, Ranger?"

"Jurisdiction is only a state of mind," said Sam, his Colt still at his side. "If we're going to do any

more talking, lower that rifle and tell your men to
do the same . . . else I'll have to shoot you where
you stand."

Red Booker started to say something, perhaps
mention the fact that there were no less than five
rifles aimed at him, yet the iron in Sam Burrack's
eyes told him that this Ranger was not going to re-
peat himself. The next thing from Sam Burrack
would be a pistol shot. "All right, men, lower them
for now," said Booker, not wanting to sound too
obliging. "This man's a Ranger . . . even if he is a
long ways off his graze."

Once the rifles were lowered and uncocked, Sam
raised his Colt enough to drop it into his holster.
"That must've been Earl and Hopper Ganston who
rode past here a while ago. I need to get after them."
He reached down, picked up the pistol he'd kicked
away from Bootlip Thomas, and shoved it down into
his waistband. "This one's still alive," Sam said,
stooping down and rolling Bootlip over onto his
back.

"Not for long, he ain't," said Erskine Brock, leaning down with a skinning knife, trying to lay the
blade across the wounded outlaw's throat.

Sam Burrack grabbed Brock by his bony wrist,
stood up and slung him to the ground. "Who'd you
say you work for?" Sam asked Red Booker, turning
slightly to him as Erskine Brock scrambled up onto
his knees and shook dust from his long stringy hair
and beard.

"I'm Red Booker. We're riding with Colonel Daniel
Fuller and The Midwest Bankers' Associ—"

Red Booker's words cut short as Erskine Brock let
out a scream and lunged at Sam Burrack with the

skinning knife thrust out before him. Sam took a quick sidestep, brought his Colt up from his holster and with a lightning-fast swipe of the barrel, dealt the man a vicious blow across the bridge of his nose. Erskine Brock's head snapped back; his feet slid out from under him. The other men winced at the sight of blood spurting out of Brock's nostrils. "I've heard of Colonel Fuller," said Sam Burrack, already dismissing Brock, now lying limp in the dirt, "but I can't say it's all been good." He stooped back down, helped Bootlip Thomas up and wiped dirt from his face.

"Thanks, Ranger." Bootlip's eyes cut to where Erskine Brock lay knocked cold.

"Hey," said Red Booker to Sam, "get back away from that man. He's our prisoner, not yours. We're the ones who caught this gang in Hubbler Wells. So don't get no ideas about the bounty money on any of them."

"I'm not chasing bounty," said the Ranger. "But I am interested in the Ganstons. One of the gang killed a Ranger some time back."

"I see," said Booker. "That's why you've crossed your line of jurisdiction . . . a Ranger got killed." He stepped forward, looking down at Erskine Brock as Talbert French and another man dragged him away. "Well, I can't blame you for wanting to avenge one of your own, Ranger. But we'll take it from here. We're paid bounty by the head. Anyway, if you're after Earl and Hopper, don't let us keep you from it. We're taking these bodies back to town and get some photographs taken of them. Colonel Fuller is waiting on us."

"Why's he not out here himself?" Sam asked.

"We've got one of them holed up somewhere back in town," said Booker. "It's the Injun who scouts things out for them."

"You mean Indian Willie John?" said Sam.

"Yep, that's him. He's wounded bad. I expect Fuller's got his claws into him by now. There ain't many places to hide in a town the size of Hubbler Wells. But that's our concern, Ranger. You go on and hit the trail. Some of us will be coming behind you pretty soon."

"They're going to kill me, Ranger . . . no sooner than you're out of sight," Bootlip pleaded. "Ride back with us . . . *please*, for God sakes, I'm begging you."

Sam Burrack turned from the wounded outlaw to Red Booker, giving Booker a scrutinizing look. "You will take this man back to Hubbler Wells if he doesn't die on the way, won't you?"

"Yeah, sure," Red Booker grinned, making little effort to hide his true intentions, "*if* he doesn't die on the way."

Sam Burrack looked away along the trail in the direction the Ganstons had taken, as if having to give some thought to what his next move should be. On the ground, Bootlip Thomas did all he could to persuade the Ranger to ride with him to Hubbler Wells, saying quickly, "Listen, Ranger, if you want the man who killed your pal . . . it's the Injun, Willie John."

Sam Burrack gave him a skeptical look.

Bootlip continued, "I swear that's the truth. He put that poor Ranger friend of yours in his rifle sights at close to three hundred yards away . . . blasted him right out of his saddle." He shook his head, seeming to recoil from the dreaded scene in his mind. "I saw it with my own two eyes. So help me God!" He

raised a bloody finger and crossed his heart to prove
his honesty. "It was plumb awful."

"Aw . . . don't listen to this damn lying snake,
Ranger," said Booker. "He'll say anything if he figures it'll get you riding with us to Hubbler Wells. So
what if it was the Injun done it? He's probably dead
by now. How will you ever know for sure it was
him? Even if he is the one, Colonel Fuller ain't going
to turn him over to you."

Sam considered everything for a moment, taking
another glance at Bootlip Thomas, knowing these
men would more than likely kill him no sooner than
Sam rode out of sight. "Call it self-satisfaction,
Booker," he said, "but I'm riding with you back to
Hubbler Wells."

"Damn it, Ranger," said Red Booker, "that just
ain't at all necessary."

Sam Burrack leaned down to Bootlip Thomas and
helped him stand up. "It might not mean a lot to
you or me, Booker," said Sam, using his hat to dust
off the wounded outlaw, "but to Bootlip here it
might be the most important event in his life."

"That's my thoughts exactly, Ranger," Bootlip said,
his strength returning.

"I'm not going to stand for this, Ranger!" Red
Booker growled, taking a bold step forward, his hand
poising above his pistol grip.

"You'll stand for it, Booker," said Sam Burrack,
"or I'll claim bounty on all three of these men. After
all, I am the one who shot them."

"Yeah, come to think of it," said Bootlip, his voice
growing bolder by the minute, "what did you and
these saddle tramps do to deserve any reward?" He
glared at Red Booker. "This Ranger here did all the
work."

"Don't push me, outlaw," Red Booker growled in warning. He turned to the other men with a disgusted expression. "All right, boys, let's get them bodies loaded and get out of here. Looks like this Ranger is going to be riding with us."

As Red Booker and the men set about loading the bodies onto horseback, Bootlip Thomas eyed Sam Burrack up and down, weighing his chances at getting the drop on this young Ranger when the time came. "I don't know you, Ranger," he said in a disarming tone, "but I sure owe you my life. Thank God you came along when you did. I just hope I can somehow—"

"What's your name?" Sam Burrack asked, cutting him off.

"I'm Buriel Thomas, but everybody calls me Bootlip. Like I was saying, I'm beholden to you, Ranger. I just want you to know how much—"

"Do me a favor, Bootlip," said Sam, interrupting him again. "Don't say anything else unless I ask you to." He looped the outlaw's arm across his shoulder and helped him walk toward the loose horse standing a few yards off the trail. "And just to keep yourself from making a bad mistake, remember this: If I feel your hand get close to my pistol holster I'll put a bullet in you without batting an eye. Do we understand each other?"

"Yes, sir, Ranger." Bootlip Thomas jerked his hand up close to his chest even though it was a good distance from the pistol on Sam Burrack's hip. "Can't blame a man for looking at his odds, can you?"

Sam Burrack didn't answer as they walked on toward the horse.

Chapter 5

Billy Odle didn't search the ramshackle barn any longer than he had to. Once he'd fished a dust-covered bridle and a length of lead rope from a wooden storage bin, he slung both items up under his arm and crept through the darkened barn toward the adjoining corral. In the corral he moved quietly among the horses, trying to decide on the best two before making his pick. But of the seven horses there all were ill-shod and gaunt in the flanks. The fittest-looking animal of the bunch was a lank fan-tailed mule standing saddled and hitched at the rear of the house, thirty yards away. Billy stared across the yard at the mule for a second, then decided he couldn't risk going close enough to either steal it or shoo it away.

He turned back to the horses with a look of disgust. On most of their backs, fleas scurried across festering saddle sores. With no further choosing he slipped the bridle onto a dusty chestnut whose back was clean but whose mane and tail were eaten thin by fleas and mites. *You'll have to do . . .* Then he made a loop in the lead rope, slipped it around the neck of a shaggy smoke-colored mare and eased both ani-

mals along behind him on his way back through the
barn toward open land.

From five hundred yards away atop a stretch of
low hills, Willie John watched from the cover of rock
and dried brush. "Way to go, kid," he murmured to
himself, seeing Billy Odle lead the horses from the
barn. Steam swirled in Willie John's breath and dissipated on the cold wind. He watched Billy Odle
mount the chestnut and ride toward him, leading the
smoke-colored mare behind him. Willie John breathed
in relief for a second. But then his eyes narrowed
warily as he looked past Billy Odle to the rear of the
house. A man rushed out of the house, leaped up
into his saddle and swung his mount in Billy's direction. Willie saw a rifle come up out of a saddle boot.
"Hurry up, kid," he whispered aloud. One thing he
couldn't afford right now was the sound of riflefire
echoing back to Hubbler Wells.

Instinctively Willie John drew his pistol and held
it tight, feeling powerless with it at this distance.
"Come on, damn it!" he cursed to himself, seeing the
man stop his mount long enough to raise the rifle to
his shoulder. Willie held his breath, waiting for the
sound to shatter the silence and roll back across the
land. Almost without realizing it, Willie raised the pistol and cocked it. Then he caught himself and shook
his head. What the hell was he doing, he asked himself, giving the kid a warning shot? What good
would it do? Hadn't he just told himself what the
sound of a gunshot would do right now?

In the distance Willie saw the man take the rifle
down from his shoulder as Billy Odle and the horses
topped a short rise and came down out of the man's
sight. *Got lucky, kid* . . . Willie let go of a tense breath,
lowered the pistol and rubbed his face. Jesus, he'd

better get a grip on himself, he thought. For a second there he was getting too concerned about the brat. He looked back out across the land and saw Billy drawing closer. Two hundred yards behind Billy Odle, Willie saw the rider slap the barrel of his rifle to his animal's rump, staying in pursuit. "All right, kid, get on in. I'll take it from here," Willie whispered. He holstered his pistol and drew the long knife from his bootwell.

When Billy Odle rode up into the cover of the hill trail, he saw the grim look on Willie John's face as he drew the horses to a halt. Misreading the Indian's expression, Billy Odle said, "I'm sorry, Willie, but this was the best of the lot."

Willie John's eyes only skimmed over the horses. "You're being followed, kid. Don't you ever bother checking back on your trail?"

Quickly, Billy Odle looked back and saw a short rise of dust drifting sideways on the cold wind. He saw the mule, the rider, and the rifle in the man's hand. "My gosh! I will from now on, Willie, I swear I will—"

"Get the horses out of sight," said Willie John, slapping a hand on the chestnut's rump.

Billy Odle jerked the horses to one side, holding them back. He turned in his saddle facing Willie, noting for the first time the long knife in his hand. "Don't worry, Willie," he said. "That's Old Man Renfro. He can't keep up with us. He's half blind and riding an old army mule."

"I said, get the horses out of sight," Willie John repeated, his voice more demanding.

"But, Willie, you're not going to kill him are you?" The horses stepped back and forth nervously.

"Kid, he's on my trail. I've got no choice but to

kill him." Willie John fanned the horses forward. "Now get them out of sight."

"The old man's harmless," said Billy Odle, his eyes going back to the long knife Willie John held readily down his thigh. "Can't we just go ahead on? He can't follow us."

"Don't make me say it again, kid." Something had just changed in Willie John's voice, so much that it sounded to Billy like the voice of a stranger. There was an iciness to Willie John's words, and while no threat had been made, none had to be. Billy Odle shrank back and pulled the horses away.

"Stupid kid," Willie said to himself, noticing his hand had grown too tight around the knife handle. He watched until Billy Odle and the horses had disappeared among the rocks. Then he stepped back off the trail and climbed up six feet and perched down on a narrow ledge. "I must be out of my mind fooling with you," he added, speaking to Billy Odle as if the boy were there beside him. "If I ain't careful you'll get me killed." He pressed a hand to his bandaged wound and felt where the wet sticky warmth had seeped through his shirt. "I can't let that happen to me, kid," he whispered in a bitter tone. "That's just how things work." He stropped the knife back and forth across his knee.

Billy Odle had no idea how long he waited, he and the horses tucked back out of sight amid upturned boulders the size of small houses. A deathlike silence set in about him beneath the moan of the wind as he listened for any sound from back along the trail. When it came, it was not the sound of old man Renfro struggling for his life. Instead, it was only the braying of the mule he heard; and the sharpness of the animal's frightened voice sent a dark chill through him. Billy squeezed his eyes shut and pressed his palms tight against his ears.

When Billy finally opened his eyes he saw Willie John standing before him, the knife still in his hand, the blade shiny clean as if nothing had happened. The mule stood behind Willie John with its head lowered, having witnessed the cold-blooded side of man's nature. "Now we can go, kid," said Willie John. As he spoke he ran a hand down the chestnut's muzzle, looking at both horses closely now for the first time. "If this is the best of the lot, I'd hate to see the others."

The iciness was gone from Willie John's voice. Billy Odle breathed easier and rubbed his eyes with his palms, clearing the water from them. "Is he . . . ?"

Willie John's only answer was a short nod. As Billy Odle watched, Willie slipped the saddle from the mule's back, blanket and all, and tossed it over onto the shaggy mare.

"I reckon it's my fault," said Billy Odle. "I should have ran the mule off, so he couldn't follow us, shouldn't I?"

"It makes no difference now whose fault it was, kid," said the Indian with impatience in his voice. "Next time you might want to think out what you're doing, though, if you don't like to see any killing."

Billy Odle nodded and hung his head. Willie John saw him shiver in his thin outgrown coat and suddenly felt sorry for him. The wooden handle of the toy pistol stuck up from Billy's pocket. Willie allowed himself a slight smile and said in a softer tone, "Don't worry, kid, you did good." He reached into his hip pocket, took out a small Uhlinger pistol he'd

found on Old Man Renfro's body and pitched it up
onto Billy's lap. "Here, you might as well hang
onto this."

Billy Odle's eyes lit up. "Golly!" He snatched the
pistol from his lap and examined it, turning it back
and forth in his cold hands. "Thanks, Willie!"

"Don't mention it, kid." Willie's smile widened a
bit. "Just be careful you don't shoot one of us with
it."

"It's loaded?" Billy stared at the pistol in awe.

"What kind of friend would hand you an unloaded
pistol?" Willie John chuckled. Willie slipped the bridle from the mule and strung it to the smoke-colored
mare as he spoke. "How much farther to this hideout
of yours, Billy?" He took the lead rope from the mare
and placed it around the mule's neck. The mule
sawed its mallet head up and down in protest, then
settled and scraped a hoof in the dirt.

"Not that much farther," said Billy. "We'll be there
before you know it." He shoved the Uhlinger into
his coat pocket next to his wooden pistol and rested
his hand on the butt, liking the feel of it. He wanted
to ask Willie what he'd done with the old man's
body—had he moved it off the trail?—but he
couldn't bring himself to talk about the deed right
then.

"Good," said Willie, favoring his wound as he
stepped up into the saddle and turned the mare to
the trail. "This wind is getting colder by the minute.
We need to get out of it." He nudged the mare forward, pulling the mule behind him. "Come up ahead
of me, kid . . . take the lead."

"Yeah, sure thing," Billy Odle said, heeling the
dusty chestnut forward past Willie John. "Just follow me."

Man oh man! Billy thought. *If only Alvin Bartels could see me now.* He lifted his chin and looked back in the direction of Hubbler Wells for a second thinking about it. Then his expression darkened as he thought about his mother and wondered what trouble his leaving might cause her. "Everything all right, kid?" Willie John asked.

Billy turned forward and studied the trail ahead. "Sure, everything's fine, Willie," he said. Billy felt the Indian's eyes on him as he heeled the chestnut's pace up a notch. It was time he got away from his mother anyway, Billy told himself. He couldn't stand being at the shack any more than she could stand him being there. After all, he was bad for business. With his hand growing warm on the handle of the Uhlinger pistol in his pocket, Billy ducked slightly against the cold wind and pushed forward upward, deeper into the hills.

Hattie Odle felt the full force of Colonel Fuller's backhand. His gloved hand sent her spinning backward across the saloon floor, into the woodpile beside the glowing potbellied stove. She struggled to rise to her feet and make a run for it, but her brain was still too fogged by the remnants of opium and whiskey. She rose halfway to her feet and staggered sideways, the throbbing in her jaw not helping her keep balance. "You . . . son . . . of a—"

Her words cut short beneath the next loud slap from Colonel Daniel Fuller. This time he reached out and caught her by her shoulder before she could fall away from him. He shook her, then said nose to nose, "Listen to me, whore! I can spend the better part of the day doing this to you—it can even get worse if need be! Tell me where they went!"

"I . . . don't know what you're . . . talking about,"
Hattie gasped. Blood flowed freely down the corner
of her swollen lips. Her right eye had already begun
to close, the effect of the blows she'd taken when the
colonel and his men came storming into her shack.
She'd been awakened from a drugged stupor by an
angry mob. So far she hadn't managed to make any
sense of it. She'd seen the bloody rags on the dirt
floor. That much she knew was real. Everything else
could well have been a nightmare for all she knew.

"Whip the living hell out of her, Colonel!" Murray
Fadden shouted. "It serves her right, letting that little
rat son of hers use my attic like it was his private
living quarters!" As Fadden bellowed, he took a step
forward from the rest of the men, his fists clenched.
"Let me bust her once or twice. I figure I owe it
to her!"

"Why, Murray," Hattie Odle managed to say in a
pained, slurred voice, "you've always . . . gotten your
money's worth."

Murray Fadden's face reddened. "You low-down
gutter hussy!" He snuck a quick look around the
saloon as if his wife might be present. "Let me have
her, Colonel! I'll beat the truth out of her."

But Colonel Fuller only shoved him back, then
turned his face to Hattie Odle again. "You see, young
woman? You don't have a lot of support going for
you here."

"The hell she don't!" yelled a young woman who
stood halfway up the steep stairs leading to the second floor. "Turn her loose, you son of a bitch!" On
the banister above, three more girls had gathered,
each with defiant looks in their eyes.

"Better do something with Tinnie and the girls,"

Murray Fadden said quickly to Asa Dahl, the saloon owner. "They're fixin' to stick their noses in."

Asa Dahl turned toward the stairs with his thick hand on his hips, his right hand near the billy club he kept shoved down in his belt. "Every one of you whores get back to your rooms, this is none of your business!" Asa shouted.

Tinnie Malone had started to take a step down, but she stopped as Asa Dahl's hand closed around the billy club handle. Tinnie was cautious, but she wasn't through yet. She raised a finger and pointed at Daniel Fuller. "Can't you see she's knocked out on her feet! She can't tell you nothing! That dope's got her mind in a cloud! Turn her loose!" Tinnie shouted.

"This will clear her mind!" Fuller shot Tinnie Malone a dark glare, then reached a hand behind Hattie, entwined his fingers into her hair and jerked her head back at an awkward angle. Stepping over to the glowing side of the potbellied stove, he held her face down close enough for her to feel the stinging heat. "If you want enough face left to ever attract another drunken miner, you best get to telling me what I want to know."

"Oh God, please!" Hattie gasped, trying to press back from the searing heat. "I don't know where he is! He does as he pleases!"

"And he brought the Indian to your shack? What made them come there? Have you hidden him out before? Where did they go?"

"I don't know," she whined, the heat growing more and more intense against her face. "Please! For God sakes! I don't know!"

"Oh, I think you do, little missy," Fuller hissed.

He pulled her face back from the stove just for a second, just long enough to make her think it might be over. Then he slammed her head against it hard. Hattie screamed long and loud. The men looked on with sickly grave expressions, some of them stricken by disbelief. Tinnie Malone screamed as well, and came down the stairs in a lunge, only to be caught around the waist by Asa Dahl and held back. "Turn her loose!" Tinnie shrieked.

Engrossed by what was happening, no one even noticed as Sam Burrack stepped through the doors, followed by Red Booker and the rest of the posse. Not an eye in the crowd seemed to see the Ranger hurry across the floor, the Colt coming up from his holster, and cocking. "Pull her back, mister," Sam demanded. "I'll only say it once." The tip of his pistol barrel jammed up hard under Colonel Fuller's chin.

"Who the hell are you?" Colonel Fuller demanded, slowly backing away from the stove. Sam's pistol held his face at a raised height, making Fuller cut his eyes downward for even a slight glimpse of his face. "You're interfering with legal business here."

"It's like no legal business I've ever seen," Sam said, releasing Fuller's grip from the woman's hair and pulling her away from him. Sam kept the Colt pointed at Fuller, the tip of the barrel an inch from his face. He held Hattie Odle against his chest. Sobbing, Hattie pressed her palms to the hot skin on her face and trembled. "Somebody wet a towel and bring it over here!" Sam shouted over his shoulder.

"Who is this man and why has no one shot him?" barked Fuller, glaring at Red Booker and the rest of the possemen. The men milled uncomfortably, staring at one another as if in search of an answer.

Finally Red Booker stepped forward and spoke up. "He's an Arizona Ranger on the trail of the Ganstons, Colonel. His name is Sam Burrack."

"Oh? A Ranger?" Fuller's expression only changed slightly as he looked Sam up and down. "You look awfully young to be a Ranger."

Sam ignored him as he took the wet towel from Tinnie Malone's hand and helped Hattie Odle press it to her face. She moaned in relief. Sam stepped with her to a chair and helped her down into it, Tinnie assisting him. "There now, ma'am, take it easy. Nobody's going to hurt you," said Sam.

"Rotten sons of bitches," Tinnie Malone whispered, cradling an arm across Hattie's shoulder.

With a thin humorless smile, Fuller said, "You must've lost your way, Ranger. Arizona's a long ride south. What about your jurisdiction?"

Before the Ranger could answer, Red Booker cut in, "That's what I asked him, Colonel. He told me jurisdiction is a state of mind."

"Well, that's real funny, Ranger," Fuller said. He watched Sam Burrack kneel beside the woman's chair and lay his free hand on her shoulder. In his other hand Sam still held the cocked Colt, the barrel never wavering from Colonel Daniel Fuller. "I reckon if you're after the Ganstons, we're all on the same side," Fuller added.

"That's right," Red Booker joined in, speaking to the colonel and the Ranger at the same time. "We've got a prisoner outside what says Ganston's Injun scout shot one of this man's *amigos*. I say we're all after the same thing here."

"Is that right, Ranger?" Fuller asked. "Are we all after the same thing?"

Still ignoring him, Sam asked the woman, "Are

you going to be all right, ma'am?'' She nodded without lifting her face from the wet towel. Sam straightened beside her chair and took a step away from her, his pistol lowering only a little, his thumb still lying across the cocked hammer. "Where's the Indian—Willie John?'' he asked Colonel Fuller. As he spoke, Sam uncocked the Colt, letting the hammer down slow and easy.

Fuller let out a breath of relief. "Well, that's a real interesting question, Ranger. The fact is, we don't know where the Injun's at.'' He gestured a hand toward Hattie Odle. "She knows, but she hasn't told us yet. I was sweating it out of her when you came in. We think her son is involved in all of this some way or another. He helped the Injun get away through the attic of the mercantile store. We found bloody rags on the floor at her shack.''

Sam looked down at Hattie Odle. "Is any of this true?''

"I . . . I don't know what's gone on. They pulled me from my bed and started beating me, accusing me . . . asking me about my son. You saw what he was going to do to me if you hadn't shown up.'' She wept quietly into the wet towel.

"You're a disgrace, Fuller.'' Sam fixed the colonel with a scorching glare.

At length Fuller cleared his throat and said, "All right, things did get a little out of hand. But, Ranger, we've had a hell of a shoot-out here. There were men lying dead in the street. A fine old frontiersman, Elkheart Joe Perkins, was gunned down like a dog. So, you might well expect we got a little angered at this woman hiding one of the murderers.''

"He was ninety-three years old, you know,'' said a voice among the gathered men. A thin red-haired man pressed himself forward and stood with his bowler hat in his hand.

Fuller shook his head. "No . . . I did not know that, sir, but thank you for telling us." Fuller grew visibly impatient. "Now if you don't mind, we're discussing things of importance here." He turned to the ranger. "There, you see? That's what we're up against. The Ganstons think nothing of gunning down an elderly gentleman."

"But it was your men who shot him," the man meekly said.

"And that was a terrible, unavoidable mistake, sir!" Fuller raged. "I dare anyone to step forward and hold my men responsible for what happened out there! We track down dangerous criminals. Of course mistakes are going to happen!"

The red-haired man slipped backward into the crowd. Fuller looked back at Sam Burrack. "Pay no attention to him, Ranger. We have the full support of this town, you can ask Selectman Collins." He looked into the gathered men, searching.

"Here I am," said Collins, inching forward. "It's true, Ranger, we're behind the colonel and his men one hundred percent until this situation is resolved. Even though you're a long ways from home, we hope Hubbler Wells can count on your support, too." Sam noted the trace of desperation in the man's voice.

Before Selectman Collins could say anything more, Colonel Fuller took over the conversation again. "You heard him, Ranger. We'll be leaving straight away. Can't afford to wait around here looking for one man while the whole gang gets away from us. What do you say, Ranger? Will you ride with us on this?"

"I don't think so, Colonel Fuller." Sam Burrack shook his head slowly. "You burn women . . . you shoot old men. I doubt that you and I would get along." He gestured with his pistol barrel toward the saloon door. "Now everybody clear back so the lady and I can leave. I don't have any more time to waste here."

"You're making a big mistake trusting her, Ranger," said Daniel Fuller. "She's nothing but a dope-eating whore. Ask anybody here."

"She's sick, you peckerwood!" Tinnie shouted in Hattie's defense.

"Sick, ha!" said Murray Fadden. "She'll cut your throat for a pipeful of tar opium."

"I'll take my chances," said Sam. "Now clear that door or I'll clear it myself."

Chapter 6

Inside Hattie Odle's shack, Sam Burrack poured cold water from a pitcher, rewetting the bar towel for her to hold to her face. Hattie sat on a wooden stool beside her bed and let Sam tilt her chin up and examine her face closer. He touched one corner of the towel to a cut on her lower lip. "I probably should have gone ahead and cracked Fuller's skull with my pistol barrel," Sam muttered. "Calls himself a lawman, then does something like this."

Hattie Odle looked away and lowered her eyes. "It doesn't hurt so bad now," she offered in a lowered tone. "I'm used to men losing their tempers, the business I'm in." She seemed to be waiting for a response from him. When none came, she looked around the shack and asked, "Where's Tinnie?"

"She said she had to get back to the saloon."

"I hope she's not in any trouble for trying to help me," said Hattie Odle. "That's the first time any of the women there have had anything to do with me. Usually, I'm their competition."

"Well, sometimes when the chips are down, you never know who'll be on your side. Besides, she didn't strike me as being too worried about getting into any trouble over it." He paused for a second, then brushed her hair back from her forehead and said, "Now, I'm going to ask you the same thing the colonel asked, only whatever you tell me I'm going to take as the truth. Did you or your son have anything to do with this?" He gestured a hand toward the bloody rags on the dirt floor.

"No, I swear I didn't," she said firmly. "I wish I could say the same for Billy, but I can't. He's been running wilder and wilder ever since his father went to jail."

"His father?" Sam asked.

Hattie looked up at him as she pressed the wet towel to her cheek. "Yes, his father. I'm a married woman, Ranger," she said with a bitter ironic twist to her tone of voice. "Isn't that the funniest thing you ever heard of? A woman like me— married?"

Sam let it pass without comment. "What about this boy of yours? Any chance the Indian made him do all this at gunpoint?"

"I wish I could say it's so, Ranger," Hattie replied. "But I've lost touch with the boy lately. I don't know what's going on in his mind." Her eyes glistened with tears. "I'm afraid I've lost touch with everything and everybody lately."

"That can happen to any of us from time to time, ma'am," Sam offered. He looked around the small cramped shack and saw the battered tin coffeepot lying on the dirt floor. "Don't suppose you'd have any coffee or tea around here, would you? I could boil us up a pot."

She looked up at him again, her right eye nearly swollen shut as she lowered the wet towel from it.

"There's a bottle of rye under the bed, if the posse-men didn't take it."

"Thank you all the same," said Sam, "but I could use a cup of coffee myself. What about you?"

She looked down at the dark space beneath her bed and touched her tongue to her lips as if anticipating the taste of rye whiskey. But then she took a deep breath to calm herself, looked back up at Sam and said, "Yes, me, too. Coffee sounds good for a change."

They talked while Sam broke kindling across his knee and built a fire in the small tin stove standing in the corner of the shack. She told Sam about her husband going to prison, about how she had worked for a while scrubbing floors and washing dishes at a boarding house in Cottonwood until the owner of the house took ill and died. Sam only listened and nodded now and then as she seemed to purge herself of a year's worth of bad memories. When she stopped for a moment, Sam asked her, "What about the boy? What's all this done to him?"

She looked ashamed. "Billy is a good boy, Ranger. But I'm afraid he's been pushed aside. He's only twelve, turning thirteen. This has all been too much for him to handle." She gestured a tired hand about the shack as if referring to the life she lived.

"I see," Sam said quietly. While a pot of water heated, Sam found a small bag of coffee beans in a battered travel trunk. He wadded the top of the bag good and tight, crushed the beans with his pistol butt and then emptied the bag into the pot as the water showed the first signs of boiling. "If that's the case, I doubt if Willie John had to twist his arm for help. When a boy that age feels abandoned, he's apt to turn to bad company if any's available."

"I didn't *abandon* my son, Ranger," she said, her voice lacking any real conviction. "I've done my best to keep body and soul together for us."

"People can be abandoned in lots of ways. I'm not judging you." He switched the conversation by asking, "What about your son's friends? What kind of boys are they?"

"Billy is sort of a loner," said Hattie. "He only has one friend, a boy named Alvin Bartels. Alvin's a good boy, but he's a little slow. He's like a faithful dog, always following Billy around."

"Then I'll need to go talk to him first thing," said Sam, lifting the pot lid and checking on the boiling coffee. "Where will I find him?"

Before answering, Hattie Odle asked, "Didn't you say you were on the trail of the Ganstons? That you didn't have any time to waste here?"

Sam offered a patient smile, picking up two dusty coffee cups from inside the open travel trunk and rounding a finger in them as he spoke. "I wouldn't call looking for your son and helping the two of you get these possemen off your backs a waste of time, ma'am."

Hattie took the cup as he held it out to her. Then she studied his face as he poured the hot coffee into it. "Thanks, Ranger, I'm much obliged." She hesitated for a moment, then asked, "Is there anything I can do for you . . . I mean for free, for helping us?"

"No, but thank you all the same." Sam blushed and studied his cup as he filled it. "Well, now that you mention it, there is one thing you can do. You can promise me you'll stay away from the opium, at least until we get your son back."

She fell silent, her eyes vacant and lost and seeming drawn to the swirl of steam above her cup. "I can't promise I'll leave it alone, Ranger. But I promise I'll try . . . real hard."

"That's all I ask, ma'am," Sam said. "A hard try is all a promise's made of." He smiled again, and this time, so did Hattie Odle.

When Sam Burrack arrived in the front yard of Alvin Bartels's house, a small wood-frame job on the edge of Hubbler Wells, Alvin shinnied down a tree and hurried over to him before Sam could step up onto the front porch. Seeing the badge on the Ranger's chest, Alvin's breath stopped in his throat. "It wasn't me who done it!" he said.

The Ranger stopped and looked down at him. "Are you sure about that, young man?"

"I swear!" said Alvin crossing his heart. "I didn't do nothing."

Sam Burrack managed to hold back a smile. "Want to tell me what it is you didn't do?"

Alvin looked confused for a second, then said in an almost pleading tone, "I don't know . . . but whatever it was I never done it! Billy made me leave, said I'd get in trouble if I stayed around. So I did leave, just like he said, before the fighting was over. So I never done nothing!"

"All right, take it easy, young man," said Sam, stooping down to put a hand on the boy's shoulder. "I'm not here to cause you any trouble. I wanted to ask you where I might find Billy Odle before he gets himself into some bad trouble. Do you understand?"

"You're not telling my ma and pa I was there, are you?" Alvin asked.

Sam looked at the house and around the yard. "Where are your folks?"

"They're gone out to the new house today. Pa's

building a new place for us on a hundred acres he's buying. I didn't go because I was supposed to go to school."

"So . . . you skipped school, then played around town until you and Billy Odle ended up witnessing the shoot-out? Is that what happened? You just got caught in things before you knew it?"

"Not exactly . . ." Alvin thought about it, scratching his head for a second. "See, Billy knew the Indian, and when the Indian rode in he warned Billy and me to get off the street. Billy said it was because he must've been aiming to rob the bank. So we hid and watched. Except they didn't rob the bank because—"

"Because the posse stopped them," Sam said, finishing his words for him. "But then Billy made you leave . . . so what was the last thing you remember seeing?"

"Well, I remember the Indian was shot and him and another man ducked back into the alley beside the mercantile store. That's when Billy made me leave. He said I'd seen enough. You're not going to tell my pa are you, about me not going to school?"

"No, I'm not going to tell your pa," Sam replied. "Where do you think Billy and the Indian went? Do you and Billy have any secret hideout around here?"

"No, I don't . . . but Billy does. He told me he had one out in the hills. But he wouldn't tell me whereabouts. He can be a real smart aleck sometime . . . always wants to be the one who's seen something nobody else has seen. Only this time, I've got news for him. On my way home from the shooting, I ran smack into one of the outlaws!"

"No kidding?" said Sam, studying the boy's face,

trying to determine whether or not he was telling the truth.

"Yep, the one who's been staying at the hotel for the past couple of days. He was running around the corner of the alley beside the saddle shop and *bam!* We hit head on! He almost drew a pistol on me he was so scared. He hollered for me to stop, but I kept on running, figuring he might have shot me if I didn't."

"How do you know he was one of the outlaws, Alvin?" Sam asked.

"Because I saw him and the Indian looking at one another when the Indian first rode in. They were across the street from one another, but I could tell they were in cahoots, just from the way he acted. Then when the shooting started, I saw him shout at the Indian then disappear."

"I see . . ." Sam turned and looked all around the yard. "What did he look like, Alvin?"

"Tall," said Alvin, holding a hand high over his head to illustrate. "Had on a big wool greatcoat and a brown derby hat. He was carrying a black valise like a businessman carries. I'm not going to get in any trouble for any of this, am I?"

"No," said Sam, "but I want you to do something for me. After I leave, I want you to shinny back up that tree where you were and stay hidden until your folks get home, or until I come back and tell you it's okay to come down. Will you do that for me?"

"Sure, so long as you're not going to tell my pa about me skipping school," said Alvin.

"Listen to me, Alvin," said Sam. "This is more important than skipping school. If that man comes around here, don't let him see you. Do you understand?"

"Yes, I do. That's one reason I was up there to begin with. I knew you wasn't him, that's why I came on down."

"Smart thinking then, young man," said the Ranger. "Now get out of sight and stay put."

Alvin started to turn back toward the tree, but then he stopped and asked, "Do you really think he'll come looking for me?"

"No, Alvin," said Sam. "I think he probably got on a horse and lit out of here before now. But let's not take any chances."

Leaving the boy's yard, Sam walked to the barbershop on Front Street where he found a shaken barber sweeping dust from his boardwalk. "I'll be with you in a minute," the barber said as Sam stepped up beside him. The barber took note of the badge on Sam's chest, then asked, "You weren't with that bunch on the roof earlier, were you?"

"No," said Sam, "I just got into town."

"Whoo-iee, what a sight," the barber said. He wiped a hand across his forehead and started to go into details when Sam stopped him politely.

"I'm hoping you can tell me where a person might purchase some opium if he had a mind to," Sam asked.

The barber eyed him curiously. "You don't look like the type who'd be interested in black tar, Ranger."

"I'm not," said Sam. "I just need to talk to the person who sells it."

"That would be Russell Miegs," he said, jerking a thumb toward the far end of the street. "You can find him at his shack just outside town. Look for a buffalo's skull atop a pole. Miegs calls himself a horse trader, but he does more gambling and drinking than anything else. Don't expect a fair shake from him."

"Much obliged," said Sam, stepping down off the boardwalk.

"Don't you want a haircut and shave, Ranger? You sure could stand it."

"Maybe later," said Sam, picking up the reins to the Appaloosa and walking away.

Beside the horse trader's shack, Sam found Russell Miegs standing at the gate of a small corral. Miegs wore a wisp of a red mustache and goatee. His fingertips stroked his chin as he puffed on a thin cigar. "What can I do for you, Ranger?" he asked as Sam came closer. "I'm all out of horses, I'm afraid." Instinctively he eyed Sam's Appaloosa stallion. "But I'm buying, though, if you're looking for quick cash."

"You're Miegs?"

"Yep, I'm Tucker Miegs . . . everybody calls me Russell. Don't ask me why." Miegs grinned, biting down on his cigar.

"I'm not looking for cash, Miegs," Sam said without returning the smile. "I'm told you're the man to see if I wanted to get my hands on some black-tar opium."

Miegs's smile turned wary. "Hey, I'm not breaking any town law, Ranger, and if I was, you're a long way north of Arizona."

"Take it easy, Miegs," said Sam. "I'm not butting into your business. I've got a friend who's been buying from you lately, but now she wants to quit. I'm asking you to cut her off."

Miegs nodded. "I see . . . Hattie Odle, that's who we're talking about, right?"

"Right," said Sam. "How'd you know?"

Miegs shrugged. "I could tell she wasn't going to last long. Some people can handle black tar, others can't. In Hattie's case, I'd lay four-to-one odds she'll be dead from it before the year's over."

"And you'd be selling it to her right up to the end," said Sam.

"I do what I do, Ranger," Miegs said with a shrug. "Hattie's problem is she ain't cut out to be what she is. She's a whore whose heart ain't in it. You can't blame her for that." His smile came back, more confident. "She smokes tar to face whoring . . . and she has to whore to pay for the tar. Kind of like a dog chasing its own tail, ain't it, Ranger?"

"I suppose so," Sam nodded. "But that's going to change. I want you to turn her down next time she comes to buy from you."

Miegs cocked his head slightly. "Can't help you, Ranger. There's not many to sell to around here yet. My enterprise is what you might call still in its early stages. If Hattie wants it, I've got to sell it to her. Besides, did you ever see what kind of shape a person gets into trying to quit black tar? It would turn your stomach, Ranger. You wouldn't want to do something like that to poor Hattie, would you?"

Sam took a breath, looked back along the street toward town, then turned back to Russell Miegs. "Maybe I need to put it another way, Miegs." Sam stepped in closer, almost nose to nose, raising a finger for emphasis. "If I see Hattie using any more black tar, I'll figure she got it from you . . . then I'll come back here and settle with you."

"Settle with me?" Miegs was not going to be talked down to by some young Ranger riding outside his jurisdiction. "I take that as a threat." He took a step sideways, letting his hand fall to his side and pulled his coat back behind the holstered pistol on his hip.

"I was sort of hoping you might feel this way, Miegs," said Sam, taking a step back, his hands relaxed but ready at his sides.

In the saloon, all talking about the day's excitement stopped, and all heads turned toward the sound of the gunshot coming from the far end of town. "Lord God!" said Selectman Collins. "What's going on now?" Hurrying from the bar and spilling out onto the boardwalk, the townsmen stared toward the lone figure of the Ranger riding the big Appaloosa up the middle of the street at a slow walk. Behind Sam sat Miegs, holding his right leg with both hands, trying to stay the flow of blood. Across Miegs's face, the red welt left by Sam's pistol barrel had already started to swell. Sam circled the stallion in close to Selectman Collins and flung Miegs to the ground at his feet. "He needs a doctor," said Sam.

"The doctor's with the prisoner in the jail," said Collins. He threw his arms up, and as if asking heaven, he exclaimed, "My God! What's happening to this town?"

Sam looked back and forth along the dirt street, then asked Collins, "Where's Fuller and his men?"

"They've already left, Ranger," Collins replied. "They headed south on the Ganstons' trail no sooner than you and the woman left the saloon. Where is Hattie anyway?"

"She's resting," said the Ranger. "Leave her alone for a spell."

"Resting?" Collins shrieked. "Her son has taken up with a murdering thief, and she's resting?"

"Don't go accusing the boy until you know what you're talking about," said Sam.

"Now just one damn minute, Ranger," said Collins. Don't forget this is not your territory here. You can't start issuing orders here. I won't stand for it!"

Sam ignored him. He backed the Appaloosa a step and turned it past Collins. Looking down at Miegs in the dirt, he added, "And don't forget what we talked about, mister."

"What does he mean?" Collins asked Miegs as the Ranger rode away slowly. "What did you talk about?"

Miegs only shook his head and moaned.

Collins dusted his hands up and down his arms and said to the rest of the townsmen, "Well, I think I just let that young Ranger know how we stand on things around here." But when Collins turned around, he cursed under his breath, watching Sam rein the Appaloosa up to the hitch rail out in front of the jail.

Kirby Bell sat at the sheriff's desk with his boots propped up on it as the door swung open and Sam Burrack stepped inside. Bell slowly stood up. "What can I do for you, Ranger?"

Sam nodded at the open cell door as he walked over to it. Inside the cell, a heavyset doctor stood over the cot rolling down his shirt sleeves. On the cot, Bootlip Thomas lay as still as stone. Kirby Bell stood up and followed Sam, saying, "Hey, wait a minute! Did Collins say you could do this?"

"He didn't say I couldn't," Sam replied, giving Bell a narrowed stare. Bell shrank back.

"If you need to talk to him, you better make it quick," the doctor said, throwing his black frock coat across his shoulders and stepping out of the cell. "He's about gone, I'm afraid."

At the cot, Sam looked down at Bootlip and saw his weak eyes open a little and try to focus on him. "Is that . . . you, Ranger?" Bootlip whispered in a labored breath.

"Yep, it's me, Bootlip," Sam said. "You made it here without them killing you."

A faint smile came to the dying outlaw's thick lips. "Yeah, I know. It . . . just didn't seem fair . . . them killing me."

Sam hesitated for a second, then said, "Willie John got away, Bootlip."

Again a faint smile stirred on the thick, parched lips. "I figured he might. He's . . . hard to pin down."

Sam nodded, then asked, "How flush are Hopper and Earl Ganston right about now?"

Bootlip shook his head weakly. "They ain't flush . . . they're nearly broke."

"You mean all the robbing they've done on the way up here, they're broke?"

"It costs . . . money, on the road," said Bootlip.

"So, they need to get themselves some cash before heading over into Old Mex," Sam said, thinking out loud.

"Yep . . ." Bootlip's voice trailed.

"I see," Sam nodded, knowing this was the Ganstons' best place to rob a bank of any size before cutting to the border. This time as Sam spoke, he bent down close to Bootlip to keep Kirby Bell and the doctor from hearing. "They're coming back here, ain't they?"

"Oh yes," Bootlip whispered in reply, "They'll be . . . coming back . . . most any time."

When Sam left the jail he saw Collins and the townsmen gathered at the jail's hitch rail. "I left word with Bell that nobody was to visit that prisoner," said Collins.

"Good idea," said Sam, adjusting his hat down on his head as he unspun his reins. He stepped up into his saddle.

"So . . . did you talk to him?" Collins asked, keeping his composure.

"Yep." Sam backed the Appaloosa, causing some of the townsmen to get out of his way.

"Well!" Collins waved his arms, walking quickly alongside the stallion, "What did he say?"

"He said you better be ready," Sam replied without looking down at him. "The Ganstons are coming back."

"Coming back! But why?" Collins stood with his arms raised, a helpless look on his face watching once again as the Ranger rode away. "Whatever will we do?"

"I don't know, Collins. It's not my jurisdiction, remember?" said Sam.

"I know that, but you have to stay here and help us, Ranger!" Collins called out.

"Nope," Sam called back to him. "I'm going after the Indian."

At the long alleyway behind the strip of buildings along Front Street, Sam stepped down from his saddle and led his Appaloosa behind him. At the rear corner of the saddle shop, he looked all around for bootprints on the cold ground but found nothing. But walking along the alley he found the black valise Alvin Bartels had mentioned lying wide open in the dirt. In their haste, Fuller and his men had overlooked it. He picked it up, looked it over, then put it aside. At the rear of the saddle shop, he saw rubbings where the reins of a horse had been wrapped around a tin downspout. Even in the cold stiff dirt he could tell that this horse had left in a hurry. "All right, Black Pot," he said to the stallion, "let's see where these tracks will take us."

Chapter 7

At a rising pass through the rugged hills, Billy Odle stopped his horse suddenly and looked down at the ground. Beside him Willie John reined up and asked, "What's the matter, kid?" Even as Willie spoke, his eyes scanned the ridges above them where thin flakes of snow had begun sticking to the rocks.

Billy Odle's voice was a cautious whisper, his finger pointing at hoofprints on the ground. "All the time I've been coming up, I've never seen tracks before. Somebody's up ahead of us."

"All right. Take it easy, kid," said Willie, his pistol coming up from across his lap as he stepped his horse to the side. Ten feet above them, he saw the edge of a hat brim move upward then duck back down. He cocked the pistol. Metal on metal resounded clearly on the narrow trail. Then, before Willie could even find a target to aim at, he recognized the voice of Huey Sweeney calling out to him.

"Don't shoot, Willie! It's me—Huey! I'm up here waiting for ya!" Huey Sweeney stood up, his empty hands waving back and forth above his head. "I've been watching you two come up the trail. You're not being followed, I hope."

Billy Odle noticed that Willie John lowered his pistol but kept it cocked across his lap. "I expect we would find somebody back there on our trail, if we looked close enough. Come on down, Sweeney. It makes me nervous, talking up to you this way."

"I'm coming," Huey Sweeney chuckled, stepping carefully down through the rocks. "I swear, I figured you and the boys for dead."

"You nearly figured right," said Willie. "Rasdorph and the other two got spent. I took a bullet . . . barely got away myself." He jerked a nod toward Billy Odle. "This young man helped me out, or I'd still be back there squared off with them."

"That's a damn shame about the others." Sweeney stopped and looked up at him, shaking his head slowly, noting the bandage on Willie's shoulder wound. "I want you to know I hated leaving you and Nian and them back there fighting it out."

"You did what anybody would do, Sweeney," said Willie. "I don't hold it against you." He motioned at the pistol in Huey Sweeney's belt. "Uncock that Colt, Sweeney, before it goes off and leaves you one-legged."

"Oh! Sure," said Sweeney, looking down at the pistol in surprise. Careful not to raise it from his belt with Willie's eyes pinned on him, Sweeney reached down and uncocked the pistol. He shrugged. "I reckon I got a little jumpy waiting up here alone. What do you suppose we oughta do now?"

Willie John nudged his horse in a step closer, looking down at Sweeney. "Are you on foot?" he asked.

"No, I put my horse back there out of sight soon as I first spotted you coming," Sweeney replied.

"Then let's go get it," said Willie.

"Are we going to head right out, try to catch up with Hopper and the gang?" Sweeney asked.

"No. We'd be smart to lay low a few days. Let everybody settle down. Then we can head south and catch up with the others. Unless I miss my guess, Hopper and Earl are going to want to come back and take that bank. It's the nearest around."

"Well . . ." Sweeney seemed to consider things for a moment. Then he said, "All right. It makes sense, I reckon. Lay low, catch up to the others later on." He looked around the land. "Any idea where to lay up?"

"Yep," Willie nodded. "The kid here knows a hiding place up there a ways. Says nobody's been there for a long time."

Billy Odle gave Willie John a stunned expression. "We wasn't supposed to tell anybody, Willie!"

"It's okay, kid. Sweeney is one of us. We've got to stick together, right, Sweeney?"

"Ab-so-damn-lutely." Sweeney grinned. He reached a hand up, wanting Willie to take it and pull him up behind his saddle. "Give me a lift to my horse, Willie."

But Willie refused him and shook his head. "Huh-uh, Sweeney. You best walk back to where you hid your horse. Riding double's a bad idea right now."

"What's wrong, Willie, don't you trust me?" Sweeney asked.

"Look at this plug I'm riding," Willie responded. "He's barely able to carry me." He gave Sweeney a flat smile and stepped the horse back, keeping Sweeney in front of him. "After you, *amigo*," he said.

As Sweeney circled upward into the rocks with Willie John watching his every move, Billy Odle said to Willie in a lowered voice, "I wish you hadn't told him anything about the hideout. I wanted it to be our secret."

"What else should we have done?" said Willie. He looked Billy Odle up and down as the boy seemed to pout and stare toward Sweeney. "Don't worry about him. I know how to handle Huey Sweeney if he causes any problems. Right now, we still don't want any noise carrying back in the direction of Hubbler Wells."

Once again Billy Odle looked surprised. "You mean you're going to—?"

"Shhhh, keep it down, kid," Willie whispered harshly. "This is no time to go tipping our hand."

"But you act like you and him are partners . . . good friends. Like you're going to be looking out for one another."

"Easy, kid," Willie chuckled. "Don't let all the friendly talk fool you. He's out to save his own neck, same as me. We don't owe one another a thing." He turned his gaze from Billy back up in the rocks, watching Sweeney step down toward them, leading his horse. "Nobody owes anybody else a thing in this world, kid. That's something you better learn real quick, if you want to stay alive."

Billy stared at Willie for a second, then said in a timid voice, "But you don't feel like that, do you? I mean about me, the way I helped you?"

"No, kid, don't talk stupid," said Willie, dismissing it. "I'm just telling you how it is with men like Sweeney. After what you and your pa did for me that time . . . and now all this. You and I are buddies, Billy. Don't ever forget it."

When Huey Sweeney brought his horse down from the rocks and mounted it, Willie John motioned him forward up the trail, then fell in behind him. "What am I doing up front?" Sweeney asked, "I don't know where we're headed. Get up here, boy," he said to Billy Odle.

Seeing Billy Odle start to nudge his horse forward, Willie John reached out and grabbed Billy's horse by its bridle, holding the animal back. "Huh-uh. You're good right there, Huey," said Willie John. "Just go the way my partner here tells you to."

A few minutes later, the three of them stepped down from their mounts and Billy led them up onto a slim path that led across a flat rock face. Willie John brought up the rear, still keeping Sweeney in front of him. Looking around, Willie said, "I believe you were right, kid. There's been nobody come this way for a long time."

"This way," said Billy Odle, pointing at what appeared to be nothing more than pure open sky where the land dropped away. Willie and Huey Sweeney gave each other a dubious glance.

"Damn, are you sure about this, boy?" Sweeney asked Billy.

Before Billy could answer, Willie John cut in, saying to Sweeney, "He knows what he's doing, Sweeney."

"That's right," said Billy Odle. "Don't worry about me. I know how to keep up my end of things."

Willie John and Sweeney passed one another a knowing look and followed quietly. "You feeling all right, Willie John?" asked Sweeney. "You look feverish."

"Don't worry about me, I'm feeling fine."

The horses and the mule grew tense, stepping out onto a rim path that stood over three hundred feet above the earth on their right. Beneath them, the tops of long pine and cedar trees swayed on the cold air in a light swirl of snowflakes. On their left stood almost seamless rock, reaching straight up fifty feet or more. "My God," said Huey Sweeney, "why would anybody have ever come to a place like this unless they were stone-cold crazy."

After a few more yards, they stopped and looked back into the opening beneath an overhanging shelf of rock. Sweeney and Willie John stood speechless for a moment staring at ancient wooden ladders laid against flat hand-set stones, leading upward to stone doorways filled with the blackness of night. "An Injun ruins," Sweeney finally whispered. "And we're talking about *ancient* Injuns!"

Billy Odle put his hands on his hips in satisfaction, saying to Willie John, "Well, what do you think? Is this a hideout or not?" All three of them turned a slow complete circle, Willie and Sweeney taking in the wide common area where petrified firewood lay in a heap, and where on the surrounding walls ancient hands had left pictures painted with the stain from berries, colored clay and bloodroot.

"Yes, kid," Willie whispered as if in awe, "it's a hideout sure enough." He stood with his free hand pressed to his shoulder wound where fresh blood had seeped through. "You're sure nobody knows about it? Your friend maybe?"

"No, I told you," said Billy Odle. "Nobody knows about it except me."

Willie turned to Sweeney with a faint smile. "He told me he's kept this place a secret in case he needed to hide out someday."

Sweeney laughed under his breath. "You must think you're an outlaw in the making, boy."

"I don't like being called 'boy,' " Billy snapped at him. He shot a glance at Willie John for support but saw none.

"Yeah?" said Sweeney. "Well, sometimes it ain't what you *like* in life, boy . . . but what you have to get used to."

Observing Billy Odle, Willie John saw a dark shine of fire in the young man's eyes. But then Willie saw how quickly the lad was able to check himself down and turn away from Sweeney's taunting. "I'll go up along the rim and rustle up some brush and kindling," Billy said in a tight tone. "We're out of the wind here, but it'll turn colder come dark."

Billy turned to walk away, but Willie John caught his arm. "Good work, Billy," said Willie John, meaning it.

Billy nodded and walked on, feeling his chest fill with pride.

Huey Sweeney stood watching until Billy Odle was out of sight. "Damn, Willie," Sweeney chuckled. "Looks like you found yourself a guardian angel— for a while anyway. Where'd you run into this pup?"

"It's a long story. I met his dad once when I'd been shot and was on the dodge. The kid feels like we've become friends."

"Yeah?" Sweeney grinned. "Well, he's got lots to learn, you can see that in his eyes. Anybody out here in the cold when they could be laid up somewhere near a warm stove ain't got much sense anyway you look at it."

"He's a good kid," said Willie John. "Him and his family's had some bad breaks lately."

"Bad breaks?" Sweeney acted surprised. "Don't tell me you're feeling sorry for somebody, Willie. I don't believe it!"

Willie walked away, leading his horse and the mule deeper underneath the shelf overhang. "Believe what you want to believe, Sweeney," he growled.

Sam Burrack had picked up the Ganston Gang's hoofprints easily enough once he'd gotten around past the town garbage dump and headed north toward the hill line. Judging from the length of the horse's stride, the rider had been pushing hard. But once Sam followed the prints a few miles onto the flatland, he saw where the horse had slowed down, almost to a walk in some places; yet, the direction never wavered. The rider wanted the protection of the rock trails and hill passes. Once at the base of the hills, Sam swung off to the left and found two more sets of prints—the ones left by Billy Odle and Willie John. He nudged the Appaloosa forward, taking his rifle from his saddle scabbard and placing it across his lap.

Atop a rocky perch in the distance, Lester Phelps saw the lone rider coming. He slid back from the edge of the cliff, stood up, dusted himself with his cold hands and turned to Hopper and Earl Ganston. "It's one of the lawmen who were on us before we hit Hubbler Wells. There's not a doubt in my mind."

"Damn it!" said Hopper. "We've got to get him off our rumps if we're ever going to do ourselves any good!"

"I can nail him in another hundred yards, if he keeps coming the way he is," said Lester.

Hopper and Earl Ganston squinted out across the flatlands at the tiny figure beneath them in a light swirl of snow. "Like hell you will," said Earl.

"I've got him," said Lester. "You can count on it."

Earl and Hopper looked at one another. "Lester is

one hell of a shot with that big Spencer, Earl, I got to admit it," said Hopper.

"All right, then," said Earl, turning to Lester. "Give us a ten minute head start toward Hubbler Wells, then let him have it."

"Whoa, wait a minute," said Lester. "I wasn't figuring on you two leaving me out here."

"Why not, Lester?" Hopper asked. "It won't take all three of us to pull that trigger, will it?"

"No, but damn it—" Lester's protest was cut short by Earl Ganston.

"Lester, there's no reason for us not to get a jump toward Hubbler Wells, just in case something goes wrong. We'll see if you got him or not. If you miss, won't it be better if the two of us are in position to swing around behind him, and keep him off your back?"

Lester scratched his head. "Well, since you put it that way."

"It's the only way that makes sense, Lester," Hopper joined in.

"All right, go on, then," Lester said grudgingly. "I'll be along in a few minutes." He slid the Spencer rifle from the saddle boot and ran a hand along the barrel.

On the flatland, Sam brought the Appaloosa to a halt and stepped down for a second for a closer look at the hoofprints, noting how the swirl of snow had begun to increase over the past half hour. By the time he reached the hill trail, the snow might cover the prints altogether. He stooped down and brushed a gloved hand back and forth on the ground.

Lester Phelps leveled his rifle and kept the sights trained on the Ranger, following him as he stood up and stepped back into the saddle atop the Appaloosa stallion. Taking in a deep breath and holding it, Lester squeezed slow and steadily on the trigger, his aim pinned to Sam Burrack's chest.

At a distance of over two hundred yards, Sam saw the shot a split second before he heard it. The bullet fell short and struck the cold ground near the stallion's hoofs, sending a stinging spray of rock and dirt against the animal's foreleg. The stallion reared and twisted in the air. Before he could settle it, Sam felt a second bullet whistle past his head. He brought the stallion down, batting his heels to its side. Black Pot sped forward, but Sam could already feel the difference in the stallion's gait. He reined hard to the left and slid the stallion into the cover of a narrow crevice. Jumping down from the saddle, he yanked his rifle from its boot.

Lester Phelps's eyes searched frantically through the light swirl of snow, knowing he'd missed his shot, and knowing what kind of trouble he was in, losing sight of the Ranger. He looked off in the direction Hopper and Earl Ganston had taken. Now he was worried. There was only two hundred yards between himself and a man he'd just tried to kill. He looked back down in the Ranger's direction for only a second. Then he jumped to his feet and sprang to his horse, his heart starting to pound in his chest. "Wait for me, boys!" he called out in a weak voice, knowing the Ganstons were too far ahead to hear him.

Once on his horse, Lester used his rifle barrel to bat the horse's rump. He raced along the trail, looking back in spite of the fact that the Ranger couldn't possibly be close behind him. If there was any way for the Ranger to see him, it would be as he sped along a short stretch of trail that lay exposed to the flatlands where it dipped down along the side of the hills. But that stretch of trail was no more than fifty yards long. He spurred the horse hard as he reached it, then ducked low in his saddle.

By the time Lester heard the rifle shot below, the white-hot pain had sliced through his left side and blew out a hole through his right side. It took a second for him to realize he'd been shot. As the crack of a rifle resounded across the hills, Lester felt his legs let go of the saddle. His arms flew up involuntarily, letting go of the reins. For a moment he seemed suspended in air. Then the ground came up fast, hitting him full force on his back.

Lester couldn't begin to guess how long he had laid there. He was sure he'd been knocked unconscious, and what had brought him to was the sound of a horse's hoofs moving toward him. At first he thought it was Earl and Hopper coming back for him; but when he felt the warm wet muzzle touch his cheek, he looked closely and realized it was his own horse. The spooked animal had run a short ways down the trail, then circled back. Lester raised his bloody right hand from the gaping wound in his side, then looked down at the wound itself and winced. "We got to get out of here," he murmured to the horse. Reaching up, he took hold of a stirrup and raised himself to his knees. But then he stopped cold at the sound of a pistol cocking a few feet in front of him.

"Turn loose of the horse, mister," said Sam Burrack. "You're not going anywhere."

"Like hell, I ain't," Lester rasped, seeing the Ranger more clearly now. What he saw was a cocked Colt in a gloved hand and a long riding duster standing beneath the lowered brim of a gray sombrero.

"You can go on and finish me off . . . if you've a mind to. But otherwise I'm leaving here."

"You've put me afoot, mister," said Sam. "Now I've got to have your horse." He stepped closer, the Appaloosa stallion limping behind him.

"You taking me back, lawman?" Lester gave him a curious look.

"Do you think you'd make it?" Sam asked.

"Nope . . . I'm done for," Lester wheezed.

"Then there you are," Sam replied. He jerked a nod toward the Appaloosa stallion. "But I'm taking him back to get his leg treated. I'm sort of in a hurry."

"There's bounty on me," said Lester. "I'm worth hauling back dead. You make something, I get a good wooden box. What do you say?"

"I'll tell the bounty hunters where to find you. But I'm not after any reward money," said Sam. "Now turn loose of that horse."

A look of resolve came over the wounded outlaw's face. "You want it, you'll have to take it," said Lester, clutching the stirrup with one hand, his free hand going to the pistol on his hip.

"That's what I figured," said Sam.

The pistol shot rolled across the plain like summer thunder.

PART 2

Chapter 8

Sam Burrack had been sitting atop Lester Phelps's dun, looking back toward the hills through the increasing snowfall, knowing that whatever traces remained of the Odle boy and the wounded Indian would be gone by morning. But there was nothing he could do about it now, Sam reminded himself. He looked back at the Appaloosa stallion on the lead rope behind him. Then he heard the sound of a hoof striking a rock and saw Red Booker leading his horse toward him.

"Don't shoot, Ranger," said Booker, drawing nearer, "it's only me."

"Where's the rest of the posse?" Sam asked.

"They're coming along," said Red Booker. "We've had no luck finding the Ganstons, so we're headed back for Hubbler Wells. How's it going for you? Any sign of that Injun or the kid?"

"No," Sam lied. "I caught up to one of the gang, though."

Booker looked at the horse beneath the Ranger, then at the Appaloosa on the lead rope. "What happened?"

"He clipped my stallion with gravel. I had to take his horse to get back to town."

"Is he dead?" Booker asked, looking around as if to find a body.

"Yep. He's an hour or better back there, just above the flatlands on a hill trail. If you want the bounty, he's all yours."

"Colonel Fuller will be much obliged," said Booker. The Ranger couldn't help but notice a begrudging attitude.

"It was nothing I did," said Sam. "I just happened along. He tried to ambush me. I shot him."

"I didn't say anything, did I?" said Booker.

"You didn't have to," Sam replied.

Before either man could speak again, Colonel Fuller's voice called out from a few yards away. "Red? Who's that with you?" the colonel asked.

"It's the Ranger, Burrack," said Barker.

"Oh? The Ranger, eh?" Fuller came forward at the head of the riders.

Sam and Booker both sat silent, watching Fuller and the others appear gradually from the white swirl. "Well, young man," Fuller said to Sam Burrack, looking around and seeing no outlaws draped across his horse's back, "I see you've had no luck, either."

"He shot another one, Colonel," Booker cut in. "Said the body is back there for the taking along the hill trail."

"I'll be damned," the colonel growled under his steaming breath. A grumble stirred among the men. Then Talbert French nudged his horse forward a step.

"I ain't proud," said French. "If he's offering, I say let's take him up on it."

"Is that it, Ranger?" Fuller asked. "You don't want to claim the bounty?"

"If I did, I'd be toting the body with me, Colonel," said Sam, shaking his head. "I told you, I'm only after the man who killed my fellow Ranger."

"Then what do you say, Colonel?" Talbert French asked, getting eager. "It's honest money."

Colonel Fuller nodded, looking a little embarrassed. "Yeah, all right, go on, French." He waved the man away. "Take Texas Bob with you."

"I haven't seen Texas Bob since last night, Colonel," said French. "I fear he's deserted on us."

"That damned drunkard," Fuller grumbled under his breath, looking all around as if Texas Bob might appear. "Then take Erskine Brock with you. Between the two of you, maybe you won't get lost."

"You might want to wait about sending them back there, Colonel Fuller," Sam offered in a quiet tone. "The way this snow is falling, it's going to be hard traveling by nightfall. Might be wise to wait till morning."

"I think my men are capable of riding a few miles on their own, Ranger," said Fuller. "The rest of us are going to make a wide swing west on our way back to town."

"Suit yourselves," said Sam. "See you in Hubbler Wells." Without another word he nudged the dun forward, leading the injured Appaloosa. He wasn't going to mention the hoofprints he'd been following when Lester Phelps ambushed him. For the boy's sake, Sam wanted to keep the posse away from Willie John's trail. By the time these two made it back to Lester's body, Sam could only hope the snow had covered all tracks into the hills. From the looks of the weather, anybody up in those hills wasn't going anywhere for a while. He'd get back on their trail as soon as the snowfall lifted.

Ten yards along the flatland trail, Sam looked back long enough to see that two of Fuller's men had separated from the others and were headed in the direction of the body he'd left lying in the dirt. "Fools," he murmured under his breath. Seeing the two men turn in their saddles and look toward him through the thickening white swirl, Sam shook his head and rode on.

"He's too damn uppity and cocksure of himself to suit me," said Talbert French, tugging his hat down tighter on his head and tucking a ragged wool muffler up across his face. He turned his horse, Erskine Brock doing the same beside him and they moved forward at a slow walk.

"Maybe he knows what he's talking about," said Erskine Brock. "I can't see no harm in waiting for this weather to lift. It ain't like that body's going anywhere, is it?"

"Coyotes will get to it by then, you idiot," Talbert French sneered behind his muffler. "If you're scared, you can just as well stay here."

"I ain't scared of nothing," Brock snapped back at him, "but I don't see no sense in taking unnecessary chances, either."

"Relax," said French. "Suppose I was to tell you I had three full bottles of unopened rye in my saddlebags? Would that calm you any?"

"Are you joshing me, Talbert?" Brock gave him a dubious look. "Where in the world would you get three bottles of rye whiskey?"

French cut him a glance, his eyes revealing little above the edge of the ragged muffler. "It fell out of the sky to me. Where do you think I got it? I got it from the bar when everybody was watching that Ranger buffalo the colonel." He tapped his gloved fingers to the side of his hat. "Some of us use our heads, Erskine."

Brock grinned now. "Well, pull it out if you've got it. It's a welcome companion in this weather."

"I thought that might change your mood some," said French, bringing his horse to a halt as he reached a hand back into his saddlebags. "I've been waiting for an opportunity to take a snort. I wasn't about to mention it to none of them buzzards, take a chance on them telling Booker or the colonel about it." He pulled up a corked bottle, inspected it closely in the falling snow, then pitched it to Erskine Brock.

"Whoa! Be careful," said Brock, catching the bottle with both hands.

"Don't worry, Brock," said French. "There's plenty more where that came from." He nudged the horse forward.

For the next hour they pushed on through the blowing snow until they had moved upward onto the hill trail where the rock served as a partial wind-break. The first bottle of rye was nearly gone when the two of them stepped down from their saddles and let their reins fall to the ground. They left the horses and walked a few feet across the trail for a closer look at the body lying almost completely covered by a building white drift.

"There now, we found him. That wasn't so hard to do, was it?" French asked in a whiskey-tilted voice. He reached out with his boot toe and scraped snow from the dead man's face. He chuckled, saying down to the corpse, "May you rest in peace, you frozen dead sonuvabitch."

Erskine Brock looked all around through the swirling snow with bleary eyes and said, "I don't want to hang around here if it's all the same with you."

"Suits me," said French. But he stood with his head cocked slightly, staring at the grim dead face. "They never seem so damn tough once you find them all shot-up like this, do they?"

"No, I reckon not," said Brock, still shooting nervous glances along the trail. "Let's get him across your horse and go."

"*My* horse?" French gave him a hard, drunken stare. "What's the matter with your horse?"

"Nothing," said Brock, his voice sounding more and more shaky. "I just want to get him loaded and get out of here. This place is perfect for an ambush."

"Ambush, ha!" French reached out for the bottle dangling in Brock's hand. "This one's done his last ambushing, is my guess. It ain't the dead you need to worry about, it's the—"

Talbert French's words stopped abruptly beneath the roar of a six-gun as the bullet slammed him squarely between his shoulder blades. Warm blood splattered onto Brock's face. Brock turned, the whiskey bottle falling from his hand as he snatched his pistol up from his holster. But he never got a shot at the figure standing obscured in the blowing snow with the reins to Brock's and French's horses in his hand. Brock saw the blossom of fire spring up around the smoking pistol barrel. The shot lifted him onto his toes, then dropped him five feet back, his pistol flying from his hand.

Brock wrestled upright onto his knees and clutched the gaping hole in his chest as the figure stepped forward through the blizzard. "Don't shoot . . . I'm done for," he pleaded, feeling his blood spill out from between his fingers.

Huey Sweeney stepped forward, taking his time, a half-grin on his face beneath his lowered hat brim. The pistol bucked in his hand, then fell silent as its echo careened higher into the hills and out across the flatlands below.

In one of the small rooms above the Paradise Saloon, Hattie Odle was rolled up into a ball on the bed, her arms hugging her stomach. Tinnie Malone spoke to the other four women gathered around her in a hushed voice. "I couldn't leave her there in this shape. There was no fire in the stove. She would have caught her death tonight. I had to bring her here at least long enough to warm her up some."

Clare Annette, a tall, stout woman with a high pile of flaxen hair shook her head and pulled her plume-trimmed gown snugly across her large bosom. "Tinnie, if Asa finds out what you're doing, helping her, he's gonna make it tough on all of us."

"Look at this poor thing, Clare," Tinnie whispered. "I couldn't leave her there all alone. I know the kind of hell you go through getting that black tar out of your system. What would you have done if you'd found her instead of me?"

Clare Annette let out a breath of exasperation. "The thing of it is, I wouldn't have gone looking for her in the first place. You know we're not supposed to have anything to do with her." She leaned slightly and winced, watching Hattie Odle tremble in a cold sweat. "Jesus!" Clare Annette reached down, pulled up a long corner of blanket and lay it over Hattie Odle, tucking it around her. "All right, Tinnie, we can keep her in here until I get a customer. But then she's got to go. I don't want Asa jumping on me over this."

"Asa can go to hell, as far as I care," said Tinnie. "I'll take any blame that comes." She looked to one of the other women, a thin older brunette with a large artificial mole grease-painted on her cheek. "Turkey, will you get some firewood from your room? We'll go warm up her shack for her before we take her back there."

"Confound it, Tinnie," Turkey O'Brien protested. "I barely got enough wood to last the night as it is." She looked at the others standing staring at her, then sighed, "Hell . . . okay. But let's all chip in some."

"Thanks, Turkey, we will," said Tinnie. "Won't we, girls?"

"Sure," said a young woman named Jersey Lori Smitts, speaking for the others. "I'll sit with her some tonight, if that'll help." Jersey Lori glanced at the others. "Maybe we can split it up some, take turns with one another through the night?"

"Count me in, then," Turkey O'Brien nodded, reaching down a hand and wiping Hattie Odle's hair back from her forehead. "This poor little thing is going to need all the help she can get."

"What was the fool Ranger thinking, leaving her alone to sweat out opium?" Jersey Lori asked, her voice still hushed.

"Don't bl-blame hi-him," Hattie managed to say, trembling. "I t-told him t-to . . ." Her voice trailed off.

The women looked at one another, then Turkey said, "You didn't tell him how bad it is, did you?"

Hattie Odle shook her head as her whole body shuddered. "I cou-couldn't," she moaned. "M-my b-boy . . ."

"What did she say?" asked Jersey Lori, reaching down and taking a pillow and tucking it beneath Hattie's head.

"She's worried about her boy, Billy," said Tinnie. "All the townsmen think he left here with that wounded Indian." She lowered her voice to the others, trying to keep it from Hattie Odle, saying, "God help him if he did . . . that Indian is a straight-up killer, if it's the same Willie John I knew in Abilene."

"Oh, it's the same one all right," said Clare Annette. "As far as ever seeing that child of hers again . . ." Shielding her words with the side of her hand as if keeping it a secret, she nodded down at Hattie Odle. ". . . I wouldn't count on it if I was her."

"Shame on you for saying such a thing, Clare," Tinnie whispered.

"I'm just being honest," Clare added.

"Shame on all of us, if you ask me," said Jersey Lori. "We all had a hand in whatever happens to her boy."

"What in tarnation is that supposed to mean?" Turkey O'Brien asked, propping a thin hand on her hip and giving Jersey Lori an offended look.

"It means if we hadn't shunned this woman and treated her so poorly to begin with, maybe all this other stuff would never have happened."

"Bull!" said Turkey. "We shunned her because Asa told us to. And so what if we did? He's the one keeping us in business. He gave her the chance to be a part of our group, and she turned him down. We had every right not to welcome her with open arms, with her taking on customers that should've belonged to us."

"She never took any customers that I wasn't glad to get rid of," said Lori. "And you know why she turned Asa down? She's not like us. She was only doing this for a little while, just to get back on her feet. She didn't want to get tied in with Asa, and I don't blame her. He would never have let her leave."

Turkey O'Brien chuckled. "Lori, honey, you tell me if there's one of us here who didn't tell ourselves we'd only start whoring for just a *little* while." She spread a wry grin and passed it from one woman to the next. "Just long enough to save up some money . . . to pay off a debt . . . to get some good-for-nothing grifter out of jail. Truth is, I came into the business because I like sleeping past sunup."

Turkey stared at Jersey Lori, still waiting for an explanation. "What's any of this got to do with us causing her boy to be riding with Willie John?"

Jersey Lori didn't answer. Instead, she looked to Tinnie for some support.

"So, Turkey," said Tinnie, letting out a breath, "now that we all know your likes and dislikes, can we count on your help with Hattie or not?"

"Oh, of course, I'll do my part helping her," said Turkey. "I just wanted to make sure I said my piece first."

Tinnie shook her head in exasperation, snatched up a wool coat and threw it around her shoulders. "I'm going to take some firewood to her shack and start heating it up. I'll be back as quick as I can."

Tinnie left the room and headed down the stairs, throwing the hood of the coat up over her head. Hoping not to be noticed, she stayed close to the wall and hurried along to the rear of the saloon where a door led out into the alley. But as she slipped out and closed the door behind her, at a table near the glowing stove, Asa Dahl, Tucker Miegs, and Miegs's brother, Pierson sat watching. Tucker Miegs's wounded leg was wrapped with a thick bandage beneath his striped trouser leg. He held a brass-handled cane close to his side. Beads of sweat dotted his forehead. A bottle of rye sat in front of him. "What do you suppose that one's up to?" he asked Asa Dahl.

"I don't know, but I'm damn sure going to find out," Asa replied. He started to rise from his chair, but Miegs's hand clamped his forearm and sat him down.

"Take it easy, Asa," said Miegs, his voice a bit thick from the rye. The pain in his leg throbbed without mercy. "I've never seen a whore yet that won't show you everything . . . if you keep your mouth shut and watch."

"Don't try to tell me about whores," Asa said.

"I won't," said Tucker Miegs, "but maybe my brother will." He nodded at Pierson sitting beside him. Pierson raised his eyes slowly to Asa Dahl as he finished a shot of rye and slid the glass forward.

"Maybe somebody better tell you something, Asa," said Pierson Miegs in a flat hiss of a voice. "I leave town for a few hours, then come back finding my brother shot and put out of the dope business. All of it because he did you a favor—getting that whore hooked on black tar."

"One whore on opium ain't exactly a business," Asa Dahl offered, his voice not sounding up to the task of facing Pierson Miegs.

"It was a start," said Pierson, a thin mirthless smile spreading beneath his pencil-thin mustache. "Who knows what it might have built into, hadn't been for you and that Odle woman."

"It wasn't my fault that damned Ranger took an interest in her," said Miegs in his own defense. "Things got out of hand so quick here. I couldn't do

nothing about it! Nobody could. One minute everything was going on its usual way, the next minute
we had bounty hunters, bank robbers and Rangers
sticking their noses into everything."

"Only one Ranger," Pierson Miegs corrected him.

"All it took was one," said Asa Dahl. "You can
ask Tucker, here. That Ranger hardly spoke a word
to anybody. He rode right in and buffaloed the whole
posse before he was in town five minutes."

"Oh my!" said Pierson in a sarcastic tone. "He
must be really tough." His right hand now rested on
the tied-down pistol on his hip.

"What the hell was I supposed to do?" Asa Dahl
asked, his tone growing bolder. "Was I supposed to
hurl myself between him and your brother here? Get
myself shot up, too?" Asa Dahl pointed a finger. "Let
me tell you one thing, Pierson—"

"Easy, Asa," said Tucker Miegs, cutting him off.
"Let's get things back like they ought to be here."
Sweat trickled down Tucker Miegs's forehead from
the pain in his leg. "Nothing's going to ever be right
unless we pull things back together." He mopped a
damp handkerchief across his brow, then turned his
attention to his brother. "He's telling you the truth,
Pierson. He couldn't do nothing to stop it. He wasn't
there, had no idea what was happening. But I saw it
clear as day. That Ranger didn't come there just to
tell me to stop selling Hattie Odle dope. Nossiree.
That sneaking devil *wanted* to shoot me!"

"Then why didn't you shoot him first?" Pierson
asked in a haughty tone.

Tucker's shoulders slumped with a deep sigh.
"Why didn't I shoot him first . . ." His voice trailed
as if he needed to think about it. "Because he was

so fast, I never had a chance to get a shot at him. How's that for a reason?''

''There's no kind of excuse for letting a man shame you down that way, shooting you in the leg. It'd looked better on you if he'd put a slug in your chest.''

''Well, I'm greatly moved by your concern, *brother*,'' Tucker Miegs fumed. ''And I apologize if my being alive has brought you any embarrassment!''

Pierson Miegs slurred something under his breath. Then he took his time filling his shotglass with rye. ''He gets back here, maybe I better show you how it's done.'' He tossed back the shot of rye and let out a hiss. ''Somebody's going to have to put the iron to him . . . reckon it's got to be me.''

Chapter 9

Evening had turned the sky a dull gray as Sam stepped down from his saddle and led the Appaloosa and the dun to the livery barn off the main street of Hubbler Wells. Both animals were wet from the snow, their tails and manes flecked with ice. Finding no attendant in the barn, Sam put the two into separate stalls. Then he dried them both, first with a handful of straw, then with a wad of clean burlap he found atop a feed bin. By the time he'd finished drying the Appaloosa stallion and began inspecting the injured foreleg, an old man stepped in behind him and rested his elbow on the stall rail. "Did he throw a shoe?" the old man asked.

"No, he caught some sharp gravel kicked up from a bullet," said Sam. "He'll be all right. I just didn't want to take any chances." Sam stood up dusting his hands together and turned to face the old man.

"Say! You're that Ranger who kept the colonel from burning a whore, ain't ya?" The old man looked excited. "You shot that dope peddler, too, didn't you?"

"How much for the two stalls and board?" Sam asked, as he pulled a coin from his vest pocket.

"A dime apiece for any grain you might have fed them," said the old man. "But I make it a practice to never charge for stalls when it's a lawman doing his job."

"Haven't you heard?" Sam offered a thin smile. "I'm out of my jurisdiction."

"Not with me, you're not." The old man touched the drooping brim of his battered slouch hat. "I'm Marvin Giddle—call me Marvin. Long as you're here, you pay for the grain only . . . the rest is on me. Call it my civic duty."

Sam tipped his hat in return. "Much obliged, Marvin. I'm Sam Burrack. I don't suppose anything else has happened here since I left, has it?"

"Nope, except that Tucker Miegs's brother, Pierson, rode in. He's the gunfighter of the family. You might want to keep a close eye on him. He's already made a couple of threats aloud, saying what he'll do to the man who shot his brother."

"Aloud, huh?" said Sam. "Where was this at, the saloon?"

"Yep, where else does a braggart always sing his song?" Marvin Giddle grinned, running his rough fingers through his wiry white beard. "You don't look real worried about it, Ranger."

"I'm too tired to be worried," said Sam. "Is there a good restaurant open?"

"Yep, Mama Carver's, right past the saloon on the other side of the street," said Marvin, pointing. "Tell her I sent you. Her and I help one another out all we can."

"I'll tell her," said Sam. "What does this Pierson Miegs look like?"

"Oh, you can't miss him, Ranger. He's wearing a long black frock, a black hat with a snakeskin band

and a pair of big Remingtons pinned to his belly. Got himself a little slick mustache that he can't keep his fingers off of."

"Thanks," said Sam. "I'll recognize him."

"Any chance you might kill him, Ranger?"

"There's always that possibility," said Sam. "But I'd like to think maybe he won't be there when I step through the door."

"Oh, I see . . ." Marvin Giddle seemed disappointed for just a second. Then he perked up, saying, "But if he is? And if he gives you no choice? You'll shoot him, right?"

Sam just stared at him. "You act like a man itching to see a fight."

"No, but I'd love to see somebody put a few holes in that bastard right where he buttons his shirt. I've seen what a rotten piece of work he is. He's got it coming. I'd advise you to watch your back when you're around him."

"Thanks, Marvin, I'll be sure and do that," said Sam. Raising his big Colt from his hip, the Ranger checked it and lowered it back into his holster. Then he turned his duster collar up and walked out into the blowing snow. He had one stop to make before going to Mama Carver's restaurant. He turned into the alley that led to Hattie Odle's shack behind the barbershop.

At the sound of the door opening behind her, Tinnie stood up from checking the crackling fire in the small stove and turned toward Sam Burrack. Glancing around the tiny shack, Sam asked, "Where's Hattie Odle? Is she all right?"

Tinnie looked him up and down, putting a hand on her hip. "She's all right now. I took her up to one of our rooms above the Paradise for a while, until I get a warm fire going. I found her back here about to freeze."

Sam looked around. "Why is she living back here? What's wrong with that little hotel across the street?"

"Nothing, except it's a flea-trap," said Tinnie. "The problem is Asa Dahl owns an interest in it. He's making things hard on Hattie. Has been ever since she refused to work for him."

"I see."

"Did you find her boy?" Tinnie asked.

"No," said Sam, "I didn't. I had some trouble with my mount. I'm headed back out in the morning if the weather will let me. I want to talk to Hattie before I leave, try to let her know I'm still looking."

"Ranger, I don't know if you noticed or not, but Hattie Odle has been so knocked out on black tar lately, she's lucky she knows her own name."

"I knew she'd been using it," Sam replied, "but I didn't know how bad." He searched her eyes for an answer.

Tinnie shook her head. "She's as bad on it as anybody I've ever seen, the little fool. If I'd known before, I would have tried to stop her."

The Ranger sighed, taking off his sombrero and batting it against his leg to free it of melting snow. "How come you didn't know about it before? Don't you women look out for one another like they do most places?" As he asked, he nodded toward the crackling stove. "I see you're doing it now."

"Yes, *now*," said Tinnie, looking a little ashamed. "Now that it's probably too late to help her or her boy either one."

"His name is Billy," said Sam.

"What?"

"Her boy," said Sam. "His name is Billy."

"I know that," Tinnie replied, giving him a curious glance.

"And as far as it being too late . . . it's never too late to do some good for somebody," said Sam. "Most places that goes without saying."

"Ranger," said Tinnie, "this town ain't like most places. It hasn't been for quite some time. Nobody looks out for one another here anymore—at least not for any of the right reasons. In this town everybody minds their own business if they know what's good for them. The leaders of Hubbler Wells are all scared to death the railroad owners are going to look us over and not like what they see. Now that some of the copper and lead mines are closing down, if the railroad doesn't put in a siding stop here, this town will be dead in another year."

"I see," Sam responded. "So men like Selectman Collins and the others want to put on an image whether it's real or not, just for the sake of survival."

"Yeah," said Tinnie, "I suppose that's as good a way to say it as any." She grinned. "Of course I prefer saying they're just a bunch of phony bastards. If anything kills this town, it will be them."

"They won't kill this town." Sam offered a slight smile in return. "It's been my experience that nothing or nobody can kill a town . . . a town only dies of natural causes."

Tinnie cocked her head in surprise at Sam's words. "Hey, I thought you were one of those silent types."

"Ordinarily I am," Sam replied. "Maybe it's because people hardly ever ask anything that I might have an opinion on."

"Oh?" Tinnie's smile turned playful. "What makes you know so much about why something lives or dies?" No sooner than she'd said it, Tinnie realized the irony of what she'd just asked him.

"See?" said Sam. "When I do have something to say, I don't always know when to shut up." He became aware of the weight of her eyes resting on the big Colt on his hip. His palm dropped to the pistol butt, and, looking into his eyes, Tinnie saw something inside him draw away from her.

"Well . . . I best get going," Sam said. "I still have things that need doing." He put on his wet sombrero and leveled it across his forehead. "I'll come back by and check on Hattie before I turn in. Do you mind packing the rest of her things? Get her ready to move out of here?"

"Ready to move? Where? She's got no place to go." Tinnie gave him a questioning look.

"I thought of a place," said Sam.

"Oh? Where?"

"Dahl's hotel," he said matter-of-factly.

"I should have guessed," Tinnie chuckled. She folded her arms across her bosom and looked down at the dirt floor, shaking her head. "Whores and lawmen, eh, Ranger?"

"Beg your pardon?" Now it was Sam who gave her a curious look.

"Whores and lawmen," she repeated. "I always said the two have things in common that neither of us wants to admit."

Sam stared at her for a second. "None that I know of," he said with finality.

"Well, I know of lots," said Tinnie. "For one thing, on the outside we allow the rest of the world to soil us dirty as pigs. But inside nothing's ever supposed to touch us . . . we're not supposed to let it, are we?" She leveled a knowing gaze on him.

Sam touched his fingertips to the brim of his sombrero, backing to the door. "I don't know, ma'am," he said; he gave one last quick glance around the small shack with its battered bed and the belongings of two people—mother and son—packed into a travel trunk sitting on the cold dirt floor. "Are we?"

At the bar, Selectman Collins and Asa Dahl stood huddled over their whiskey glasses in conversation. Tucker Miegs and his brother Pierson still sat at a table nearest to the big ornate potbellied stove. In a rear corner, Clare Annette plunked on a twangy piano for three grizzled old copper miners who stood with beer mugs in their grimy hands and hung on every note. Moments earlier, Daniel Fuller and his possemen had returned to town and taken over the far corner of the bar. They drank their whiskey and blew on their cold hands and batted snow and ice from their hats and shoulders.

When Selectman Collins had asked how things had gone, Fuller only grunted in passing. Then Red Booker came back to them with a shotglass in his hand and told them the bad news. Two men had gone off in search of the body of one of the outlaws the Ranger had shot. But neither man had returned. As Red Booker told the story, both Collins and Asa Dahl had listened, nodding with interest. No sooner had Red Booker walked back down to stand beside Fuller at the end of the bar, than Selectman Collins let out a breath and spoke to Asa in a bitter, low-ered tone.

"As if either of us should give a damn," Collins said. He threw back a shot of whiskey and blotted his mouth with a folded handkerchief. "All we need is for a railroad representative to show up while this town is in an uproar. It will be the last time we hear anything about a rail spur coming here, I can safely promise you that."

"Relax," said Asa Dahl, "it's only going to be for anther day or two. They'll be off after the Ganstons, and we'll never see them again."

"It's easier for you to relax, Asa," said Collins, nodding along the bar. "At least you're making something from them being here."

"You're damn right I am," replied Asa Dahl, "and that's going to be the case whether this town stands or folds. If all goes well with the railroad, I'll make a fortune . . . if not, I'll squeeze every dollar I can out of this town until the last horse heads over the hill. Can you blame me?"

Collins rubbed his neck and poured himself another drink. "No, I suppose not. I just wish things would settle down . . . that stupid whore's kid running loose with that Injun, the Ganstons hitting town, this posse and all. It's too much trouble happening at once. It looks bad to outsiders."

"Speaking of too much trouble," said Dahl, nudging Collins in the side, "look who's coming here."

"Oh Jesus, no!" said Collins, turning enough to see Sam Burrack walk across the floor to the stove and rub his hands together in front of its open iron door. Collins's eyes went to Tucker and Pierson Miegs sitting at the table, only six feet away from the Ranger. Both of the Miegs brothers' eyes looked like hot glowing coals as they stared at Sam in silence. From her piano stool, Clare Annette took note of the brothers' frame of mind and stopped playing the piano in hopes that it would bring Sam's attention to them. But Sam didn't seem interested in anything but warming his hands and rolling a toothpick back and forth across his lower lip.

After a few leaden minutes of silence, Sam turned to the piano, then looked along the bar at the expectant faces all around, then back to the stove. "What are you doing in town?" Sam asked without looking at Tucker Miegs.

Tucker Miegs boiled. "You never told me to get out of town, Ranger!"

"I shouldn't have to tell you," said Sam, warming his hands, talking as if to the stove. "A bullet in the leg and a cracked head oughta be enough."

"I've as much right here as anybody else," said Tucker. "I quit doing what you accused me of doing—that should be enough."

"Hold it one damned minute, brother!" shouted Pierson Miegs, springing up from his chair and sending it sliding across the floor behind him. "You don't have to answer to this two-bit desert rat! This ain't Arizona Territory, and you've got no more power here than a one-horn goat, far as I'm concerned."

"You've got a point," said Sam. "It's something you can discuss a few miles down the road." He still spoke without looking at Pierson Miegs.

"Like hell! If you want me out of town, Ranger, you best be prepared to put me out!" Miegs stepped sideways away from the table and stopped, facing Sam Burrack with his hand poised near his pistol. "Hey, look at me when I talk to you," he demanded. "You shamed my brother Tucker like he was a dog! Now it's time to pay up. I'm here to collect."

As Pierson spoke, Sam reached down and lifted his pistol from his holster slowly, as if to check it. Pierson Miegs watched him, but for some reason didn't make a move until the big Colt up and leveled and cocked toward his chest. "Wait a minute!" he said taking a step backward. "I didn't know you were drawing!"

"What did you think I was doing?" asked Sam. "Are you new to this part of the country?" The tooth-pick rolled across his lower lip and settled in the corner of the Ranger's mouth.

Pierson looked painfully embarrassed and rattled. "I mean—that is, I knew you were drawing that pistol . . . but I wasn't ready yet. I thought—"

"You weren't ready yet?" Sam asked, cutting him off, taking a step closer, forcing Pierson to take another step back. "You mean you expect me to wait for you?"

"No, that's not what I meant," Pierson Miegs stammered.

At the table, Tucker Miegs sat helpless and shook his head in disgust. "He got you, brother."

"What exactly did you mean, then?" asked Sam, advancing another step, Pierson stepping back against his will beneath the cover of the big Colt.

With much effort Pierson Miegs managed to stop his retreat and hold his ground. "Holster that Colt and I'll show you what I mean," he growled.

"You don't want me to holster it," Sam warned.

"I'll take my chances," Pierson Miegs hissed, feel-ing his courage coming back to him. He watched Sam slowly uncock the big Colt. Then Miegs began working his fingers open and closed as Sam slipped the Colt down in his holster. "Now, let's see who gets run out of—"

Pierson Miegs's words cut short against the toe of Sam's boot slamming upward into his crotch. Letting out a tortured grunt, Pierson rose onto his toes and bowed forward at the waist, his hands clasping tightly between his legs.

"Dumb bastard," Tucker Miegs murmured to himself.

Sam took Pierson by his collar and the tail of his coat and guided him swiftly halfway across the saloon to where a thick supporting timber stood in the middle of the floor. Pitching him the rest of the way forward like a sack of grain, Sam stepped aside as Pierson slammed headlong into the wooden beam. The building trembled. Dust sprinkled down from the rafters. "Lord God!" said a voice from the bar. Sam walked over, stooped down, and lifted Pierson's pistol from his holster. He stood up facing Tucker Miegs.

"I want you both out of town. Stay out until you know I'm gone," said Sam.

"Look at me, Ranger," Tucker Miegs whined. "I'm leg-shot! I can't get out of town. Hell, I'm lucky I can even get around at all." He gestured with his hand toward the street. "And in this weather? You just as well kill me as run me out in this!"

"As soon as this weather lets up," said Sam, "you better both be gone." He shoved Pierson's pistol down into his belt. "I don't want to look over my shoulder and have to see either one of you again."

Tucker stood up supporting himself on his cane and limped over to where his brother laid knocked cold. "What am I supposed to do? I can't lift him."

Sam looked along the bar for volunteers. At the piano, two of the miners looked at one another, set down their beer mugs and came forward. "Much obliged," said Sam, walking past them on his way to the bar. He stopped where Asa Dahl and Selectman Collins stood staring with their drinks in their hands. "I'm taking a room at your hotel tonight, Dahl. I don't suppose it's full up is it?"

"I'm only a silent partner," Dahl replied, "but I'm certain there are plenty of vacancies."

"Good," said Sam, "because Hattie Odle needs a room, too. I'll get her moved in right away."

"Now wait just a damn minute, Ranger!" Dahl slammed his glass down on the bar. "I'm not allowing that doped-up woman in the hotel. You saw the shape she's in . . . she's in a black-tar stupor. The other hotel owners won't have her."

"I bet they will if you ask them real nice-like," said Sam. "I know you'd like to do whatever you can to see that woman get herself straightened out . . ." He leaned closer, looking Dahl in the eyes. "Ain't that right?"

At the end of the bar, Fuller, Booker and the others watched, listening intently. Asa Dahl felt their eyes on him and grew uncomfortable. He managed a shrug. "Well . . . sure, I hate seeing anybody in that kind of shape. But you can't expect me to vouch for her to my business partners."

"Why not?" Sam stared hard at him. "I've cut off her dope supply. She'll have somebody looking after her."

"Oh? Who?" asked Dahl, cocking his brow slightly.

"One of your sporting women," said Sam. "I figure some of them will want to volunteer to help look after her, soon as they hear it's all right with you." Sam's eyes shifted to Clare Annette who sat quietly at the piano. "Will you pass the word along, ma'am?"

Clare Annette only nodded cautiously.

Asa Dahl bristled. "I'm not some horse-trading dope peddler, Ranger. You can't treat me like you did the Miegs brothers. I own established, legal businesses here. Your duty is to protect people like me, not push them into doing—"

"But, you're forgetting, Dahl, I'm out of my jurisdiction," Sam said, cutting him off. He took the toothpick from his lips and put it in his shirt pocket. "I'm going over to the hotel and renting two rooms, one for Hattie Odle and one for me. If you plan on trying to stop me, Dahl, you be waiting on the boardwalk when I bring her there."

Sam turned and walked away, down to the end of the bar where Fuller and his possemen stood watching. Before Sam came to a stop, Fuller turned from the bar with a look of contempt, saying to Red Booker, "I'll be at the restaurant." He left without giving Sam a glance. Red Booker chuckled as the colonel stepped out the door behind the two miners carrying Pierson Miegs between them. Tucker Miegs also followed, limping on his cane. Asa Dahl slammed his shotglass down onto the bar and he and Selectman Collins turned and left the saloon as well. "Let's get out of here," Dahl hissed, shooting the Ranger an angry glance.

"You sure can kill a social gathering real quick," Red Booker said to Sam Burrack. "Hell, that man just left his own saloon because of you!"

Sam offered a thin smile. "I didn't ask him to leave."

"That's true," said Red Booker, raising a hand to flag the bartender. "Can I buy you a drink?"

"Much obliged," said Sam.

"Tell me something," Booker asked Sam as the bartender poured a shotglass of whiskey. "Do you always have this much trouble getting along with townfolk?"

"I'll admit I do better out there," said Sam, nodding

toward the endless land beyond the saloon door. "It's easier getting along with wolves and rattlesnakes than it is with some people." He raised his whiskey. "Did your men find the body I left up along the trail?"

"They never came back," Booker said in a flat tone. "We heard some shots from a long way off. If those two don't show up before long, I'll figure they're either dead or holed up in the hills against this weather. It looks like the Ganstons have some luck on their side. This snow will wipe out any trace of them. They'll be wintering in Mexico."

"Maybe not," said Sam. "That outlaw who tried to ambush me said the Ganstons would be headed back here to rob the bank."

Booker seemed to consider it for a second. "Naw, I doubt that, Ranger. They're headed south."

Sam touched his fingertips to his hat brim. "Suit yourself. I just thought I oughta mention it." He finished his drink and sat his empty glass on the bar.

Chapter 10

Snow stood a foot deep on the hill trail leading up into the cliff ruins. Beside the waning fire, Willie John tried to push himself up from the ground, but his trembling hands felt too weak and unsteady. He sank back onto his back and looked across the low flickering flames at Huey Sweeney. He wasn't about to ask Sweeney for help. He couldn't risk showing the extent of his wound or his weakness. "Where's the kid?" he asked, trying to keep his voice level and strong.

"Gone for some firewood," said Sweeney, jerking his head toward the entrance of the overhang without taking his eyes off of Willie John. "He'll be right back." Sweeney rose into a crouch and moved closer around the fire, slowly, like a lesser wolf seeking permission from the pack leader. "Say, Willie, that wound still looks pretty fierce . . . still bleeding and all. I'm real concerned whether or not you're going to make it."

"I'll make it, Sweeney." Willie spoke in a labored voice. He let his weak right hand lay on his pistol butt, although he doubted very much if he could have raised the big Colt right then if called upon. "You don't have to concern yourself about me. Fact is, if you want to take those two new horses you brought in last evening and go . . . I'll understand."

"Sure enough?" Sweeney seemed pleased. "You mean there'd be no hard feelings over it? We'd still be friends if ever we met up again? My, my, I appreciate that."

Willie John saw Sweeney's mocking demeanor and only stared at him, waiting for his next move. Sweeney had grown bolder and bolder since he'd returned last evening with the two fresh horses and the bottles of rye.

"You know . . ." said Sweeney, squinting as if in contemplation of something. "I've been wanting to ask you ever since you and the kid showed up. Is it true what everybody was saying? About how you had near ten thousand dollars squirreled away for your trip to Mexico?"

"Do I look like a fool to you?" Willie John said, keeping up the pretense of being in control. He knew that if Sweeney made a move on him right now, it was all over. He was powerless to defend himself. "I know what all the men were saying . . . but it wasn't true. How the hell would I have managed to keep ten thousand dollars, the way I spend money?" he offered a weak half smile.

"That's what I told myself at first," said Huey Sweeney, not wanting to let the matter go. He tapped a finger to his forehead. "But then I got ta thinking about it. I never really *saw* you spend any money anywhere we went. I only heard you talk it afterwards. Never knew you to gamble much, never saw you squander anything on women. So I figured an

Injun buck like you with no vices to speak of . . . hell, maybe you did save up that much over a period of time."

An Injun buck. There it was, Willie John thought. Yesterday he'd been Willie . . . now that he'd grown weaker and the rye had Sweeney feeling braver, whatever respect there might have been there was gone. Sweeney was testing him now. Seeing how far he could push, the lesser wolf readying its position, ready to take over whatever dark realm there was to command. "Call me that again, Sweeney," Willie said in a level tone, forcing his hand to close around his pistol butt, "you won't have to go around wondering whether or not I'll blow your head off. You'll know it for a fact."

There was a silence in which Willie John held Sweeney's stare without a waver of an eye or a twitch of doubt. Huey Sweeney looked deep into Willie John's cold, cagey eyes and could not read what was there. This could all be a bluff. But with a man like Willie John, you didn't take that kind of chance . . . not yet. He needed to pull back now and check again later. He smiled apologetically. "Easy, Willie. I meant no harm. It just sort of slipped out, you know? The two of us never had a cross word in our lives, did we?"

"No," said Willie, "but this is a brand new day."

Sweeney chuckled. "That it is." He eased his hand down to his side as he spoke, letting it get closer to his pistol butt, seeing what Willie would make of it. When he made a quick jerky move with his hand, he saw the look on Willie's face harden even more, the Indian's hand growing tighter on his holstered pistol until Huey Sweeney backed down and put his hand around the bottle at his side. "Dang it, Willie!"

said Sweeney, "I just wanted to toss you this bottle of ole scat."

"Then toss it," said Willie, his eyes, hand and expression still frozen. He felt his energy draining quickly, yet he managed to raise his free hand, knowing there was little chance of him catching the bottle, not even from four feet away.

Huey Sweeney watched Willie's eyes, still judging, still wondering, still unable to decide his odds. But before he raised the bottle to toss it over, a sound near the mouth of the overhang caused him to spin around with his pistol coming up, cocked and ready. Then he uncoiled and let out a breath, seeing Billy Odle standing with an armload of snow-streaked brush and downed tree limbs.

"Damn it, boy!" said Huey Sweeney. "Let somebody know you're coming . . . you'll get your fool self killed that way."

Billy's face turned stark white behind the red blotches of cold in his cheeks. "I'm—I'm sorry," he said in a shaky voice, steam wafting from his mouth. He hurried forward and dropped the bundle beside the fire. Then he looked at Willie John. "Are you all right, Willie?"

"Yeah, kid, I'm fine," said Willie, his hand still on his pistol butt, his eyes still locked on Sweeney. "Never been better." He nodded at the bottle in Sweeney's hand, asking Billy Odle, "How about handing me that bottle of rye, kid . . . keep Huey from spilling it."

"Sure," said Billy, yet he hesitated stepping closer, seeing the cocked pistol in Sweeney's hand.

"Don't mind the pistol, kid," said Willie John. "He's fixin' to put it away, right, Huey?" Willie John's eyes were dark polished steel.

Sweeney didn't answer. Instead he uncocked the pistol and dropped it back into his holster. Ignoring Billy Odle's outreached hand for the whiskey bottle, Sweeney placed the bottle on the ground, stood up and looked down at Willie John. "Think I'll go take a look at the weather," he said.

"The snow's halfway up to my knees and still falling," Billy Odle said, trying to be helpful. "I had a hard time walking in it."

"Is that a fact," said Sweeney, walking away. "Then I'll be real careful." At the opening of the cliff overhang, Sweeney said without looking back at Willie, "I need that money, Injun . . . think it over."

No sooner had Huey Sweeney walked outside into the morning gray, than Billy Odle turned to Willie John with a puzzled expression on his face. "Pay him no mind, Billy. The whiskey has him walking in circles."

Now that Sweeney was out of sight, Billy saw the effort it took for Willie John to sit up on his own. "And you're *not* doing all right like you said, are you?"

"No, Billy," said Willie John, lying back down on the blanket, a sheen of sweat on his forehead. "I'm not all right. But I can't let him see it. He's ready to shoot me down and take off with the horses."

"How could he do something like that?" said Billy.

"It's easy for him," said Willie John with a weak attempt at a smile. "He figures I'm not going to be around long anyway. Why's he wasting time hanging around here?" He swallowed back a dry knot in his throat.

"But you've been riding together, watching out for one another. I thought you two were friends. He should be doing everything he can to—"

Willie John cut him off. "Listen to me. You've got a lot to learn about this world we live in . . . too bad I don't have time to teach you."

"But I won't let him hurt you, Willie. You just tell me, I'll do whatever needs doing." Billy drew back the corner of his ill-fitting coat and rested his palm on the pistol in his waist. Willie John saw the serious intent in the boy's eyes and knew he would try something that foolish if only Willie said the word.

"Thanks, Billy, but that's not what I need you to do right now." He clasped Billy's forearm, looking up into his eyes. He knew there was no use trying to shoo the boy away. Billy was like a stray pup. He would only run in short circles and come right back. "What I need, Billy, is some medicine from town. I'm not going to pull through if I don't beat this infection." He gestured toward the bloody wound. "It's not going to heal without medicine."

"You—you want me to ride to town? Get some medicine from the doctor?" Billy looked stunned. "I thought you couldn't trust me enough to let me out of your sight?"

"Forget me saying that, Billy. I trust you. Believe me, I trust you more than anybody in the world right now. Will you do this for me? It'll take you the rest of the day and all night to get there. It's going to be . . . a rough ride in the snow."

Billy's chest swelled with pride at Willie's words. "If that's what you want, Willie, you bet I'll do it. I'll do it right now, no matter about the snow." He started to rise up, but Willie caught his forearm.

"Not so fast, kid," said Willie. His hand curled around the butt of the pistol in Billy's waist. "Don't take this with you. It could get you in trouble if you run into any lawmen."

"But, Willie, I—"

"Use your head, Billy. If you get yourself killed, how will I ever get that medicine? You won't be needing this, anyway." He drew the pistol from Billy's waist, then glanced toward the front of the cliff overhang. "Now close your coat and flip this blanket over me. I can't stay warm. One minute I'm burning up, the next I'm freezing. I really need that medicine, Billy."

"What do I ask for?" said Billy.

"Do you speak Mexican, kid?"

"No," said Billy. "Not a lick."

Willie John seemed to consider it for a second, then he said, "Listen carefully, Billy. You'll have to make up a story. Tell that doctor a neighbor sent you for something to treat an injured horse. Tell him the neighbor said the medicine you came for is *haga creer* . . . that nothing else will do. Can you say that?"

"Haga creer," said Billy, testing himself.

"That's right," said Willie. "And be sure and say what I just told you to say."

"My neighbor said the medicine I want is *haga creer,"* Billy rehearsed aloud.

"That's fine, kid." Willie John slumped on the blanket, allowing Billy to cover him with the loose corners. "Now get you a horse and get going. I'm counting on you."

"What is *haga creer*?" asked Billy. "Some kind of strong Mexican herb?"

"Yep," said Willie. "I never liked using it. But times like this, it might be the only thing that'll help."

Huey Sweeney stepped back under the overhang just as Billy Odle stood up buttoning his coat, making ready for the ride. "Hey, where you going now,

boy?" Sweeney said. "I don't like you out there
traipsing around, making footprints all over hell."
Sweeney took a sidestep as if blocking Billy from the
horses and the front entrance of the cave overhang.

Before Billy Odle could answer, Willie John cut in
saying, "Get out of his way, Sweeney, I'm sending
him on an errand."

"What? And have him bring the law down on us?
I don't think so, Injun. That fever's affected your
mind."

"You told me to think about it, Sweeney. That's
what I've done. Now step aside . . . let him get a
horse and get out of here. I need medicine."

Huey Sweeney ran it back and forth in his
whiskey-blurred mind for a second until he realized
what Willie John was doing. The Indian was buying
the boy's life with the money he had stashed. All
right, Sweeney thought, he could go along with that.
Evidently Willie John was in worse shape than he'd
suspected. A while ago was nothing but a bluff. But
now the Indian was ready to make a deal for the kid.
"All right, boy," said Sweeney, a thin nasty smile on
his lips, "get mounted and get out of here." He took
a step closer to Willie John, noting how the Indian's
hands were quivering slightly in their weakness. "I'll
attend to our *amigo* here."

Billy could see something dark at work between
the two of them, but he couldn't put his finger on it,
let alone begin to understand it. These were outlaws
in the outlaw world—the world he wanted to be a
part of. The only way that was going to happen was
if he learned to do what he was told without questioning it. He hurried, throwing a saddle up atop one
of the horses they'd taken from the Renfro corral.
When the horse was readied, Billy led it to the front

of the overhang and looked back at the two men. Sweeney stood facing Willie John with his feet spread shoulder-width apart. Billy Odle started to say something, but Willie John didn't give him the chance. "Get going, Billy. Me and Sweeney need to talk."

Huey Sweeney took a step forward as Billy Odle led the horse out and down the narrow, snow-covered path toward the trail. "Not so fast, Sweeney," said Willie John, causing the half-drunken outlaw to stop mid-step, "I need an hour . . . let the kid get out of here a safe distance."

"I never known of you giving a damn about anybody but yourself, Injun." Huey Sweeney gave him a sly grin.

"You want the money, don't you?" said Willie John.

"What do you think?" said Sweeney, grinning, his hand poised near his pistol.

"And you know there's no amount of torture going to make me tell you unless I'm ready?" Sweat ran down Willie John's forehead. Sweeney took note of his condition and let his hand relax.

"Yeah," said Sweeney, "I reckon I can wait a little while. It ain't like I've got plans to be somewhere." He stepped close with caution, reached down and picked up the bottle of whiskey. He raised it, took a drink and offered it out to Willie John. "Might as well finish this off with me. We've had many a drink together, eh, pal?"

"That's a fact." Willie took the bottle with trembling hands, holding it carefully. He sipped from it and tried handing it back up to Sweeney. But his strength gave out and he let the bottle slump until Sweeney stooped down and caught it before it fell.

"Look at me," said Willie John, "I've never been in such a sorry shape in my life."

"And to think I let you bluff me a while ago," Sweeney grinned, sitting down near the fire and tipping the bottle toward Willie John in salute. "I got to hand it to you, Injun . . . you've never been short on guts." He sipped the whiskey, then lowered the bottle and said, "Hell, you should just as well go on and tell me now where that money is, don't you think? That kid won't hear nothing, not this far back in the hillside."

"A few more minutes," said Willie John.

Sweeney shrugged. "At least tell me how much we're talking about. I heard ten thousand . . . is that close?"

"It's close enough," said Willie John. "It's enough to throw one wild winter in Old Mex. A man can't ask for more than that can he?"

"He might ask," Sweeney grinned, "but he wouldn't get it." They sat in silence for a few moments longer, then Sweeney said, "I ain't carrying a watch; reckon it's long enough?"

"Why don't you take it easy, Sweeney," said Willie. "You're holding the only winning cards in this deck. You know I would never have sent him out of here if I thought I was coming out of this alive. The shape I'm in, I couldn't outrun a posse even if you didn't kill me. You've got my word."

"Yeah, I already thought about all that," said Sweeney, seeming satisfied with himself. "I have to admit, Injun, your hide's pretty much nailed to the wall this time. What I don't get, though, is all this concern you have over that snot-nosed kid. It just ain't like you."

"I don't know," said Willie. "Call it a case of conscience here at the end, I suppose." His words trembled a bit as a fevered shiver ran the length of him. He drew the blanket up tight under his chin with both hands and gritted his teeth before going on.

"A conscience?" Sweeney chuckled and sipped the whiskey, shaking his head. "Injun, who'll ever believe that?"

"Laugh if you want to, Sweeney," said Willie John in a weakening voice, "but I've become a changed man . . . seeing that boy, and the faith he had in me. Nobody ever looked up to me that way." There was a tearful sound to his voice. "It makes me wish I could go back now and live my whole sorry life over—maybe do something decent, instead of being the rotten bastard I've always been."

"Stop it, Willie John," said Sweeney, looking away as he held the bottle over to him. "Here, take a drink. We need to get this thing done with."

"See, Sweeney, you know it's true. We've both been a foul piece of work our whole miserable lives. What kind of men ride together, then turn on one another this way? You . . . getting all set to kill me for money. Look at me, Sweeney. Tell me what low devils we are."

"Shut up, Injun, I mean it," said Sweeney. He refused to face Willie John. "Don't give me no deathbed sermon. Maybe you're stricken by some kind of conscience here when you're dying, but not me. I'm still well and kicking. I'll take that money, cross that border and before you know it I'll be—"

The muffled sound of the pistol shot through the thick folds of the blanket clapped like low thunder in the confined area. A long streak of fire flared then fell, causing the horses to tense up for a second and flatten their ears back. The mule began a long steady bray as Huey Sweeney fell backward on the dirt and rolled away from the fire, his pistol spilling from his holster where he had placed it loose and ready. Blood spewed high from the middle of his chest until he managed to clasp both hands to it and cursed in a hoarse whisper, "You dirty, sneakin', lousy . . ." His words trailed away behind clenched teeth. Then he sobbed in rage, "I believed . . . you. An Injun's word . . . is supposed to mean something!"

"I've told you people time and again." Willie John flipped the blanket off himself and struggled up to his feet, Billy Odle's gun hanging limp in his hand. He clasped his free hand to his shoulder wound and rocked back and forth on his feet. "I ain't that kind of Indian." He struggled forward. Taking both thumbs to cock the pistol again, he aimed it down at Sweeney.

"The boy?" Sweeney rasped. "The . . . money? What you said . . . about conscience? All lies?"

"You tell me," said Willie John, slinging the smoking blanket around the barrel of the pistol. "You know so much." The pistol bucked in his hand, a lick of flame exploding through the blanket.

Willie John limped over to the frightened animals and settled the braying mule. The horses turned quiet but remained tense and restless, stepping back and forth in place as Willie clung to one by its mane, holding on for a moment to regain his strength. He shook the blanket until the smoke dissipated from it, then he threw it up over the horse's back. Too weak to even try to toss a saddle, he pulled the horse and the mule to one side, slipped the reins to the other animals free and shooed them from the cave. The mule honked and bucked in place, the motion of it causing pain in Willie John's shoulder. "Easy, mule," he said, "or I'll dress you out right here."

Limping, he led the two animals toward the entrance, stopping long enough to pick up Sweeney's big great coat from the ground and toss it over the horse's blanketed back. "Conscience?" he murmured, looking down. "Conscience?" he repeated, louder this time even though the effort sent pain throughout his chest and shoulders. For reasons he did not understand, hot rage boiled inside him. Gathering all of his strength, he drew back a boot and kicked Sweeney's dead face. "There's *conscience* for you . . . you stupid sonuvabitch!"

Chapter 11

Tinnie Malone crossed the street early, before any of the townsmen had gathered to clear the snow away. The snow was still falling straight down, slow and steady. Sam Burrack stood at the window of the hotel and watched her approach. He smiled to himself, seeing Tinnie curse under her breath. In her agitation at the weather, she slung her striped wool muffler up around her throat and hunched her shoulders inside the heavy man's overcoat she wore. Her hands stayed inside the coat's folds, keeping her hem hiked high and dry, almost to her knees.

Sam met her as she stepped inside the hotel door and stomped her feet on the braided entrance rug. Behind the desk, the clerk lowered his spectacles on his nose and shot her a look of disdain. She returned his look, saying in a gruff tone of voice, "What do you expect me to do, stand outside?"

"Indeed," the clerk murmured, picking up a mop from behind the counter and heading over to the door with it.

Tinnie shook snow from the heavy coat and stepped off the rug, joining Sam. "How is she?" Tinnie asked.

"Sleeping, finally," said Sam. At a round oak serving table, he picked up an empty white china cup, handed it to Tinnie and saw her smile gratefully as he lifted a silver pot and poured coffee for her. "She was up off and on until almost dawn, cussing one minute and praying the next . . . shivering, getting sick all over the place, then trying to get past me to leave." He shook his head and set the pot back down on the table. "I swear it was worse than trying to contain a she-panther."

Tinnie sipped her coffee, studying the Ranger's face closely, taking note of the fierce jagged scar that ran the length of his right jawline. "Tell me something, Ranger," she said. "Are you this kind to everybody you meet?" As she spoke, she gestured a nod up toward the rooms at the top of the stairs where Hattie Odle lay sleeping.

"No," said Sam, his fingertips idly brushing past the scar on his face, aware of it now that he'd seen her notice it. "Ordinarily I pistol-whip a person as soon as I meet them; it gets us off on the right foot."

She smiled at his dark joke. "You know what I mean, Ranger. There's not many people who'd waste their time on somebody like Hattie Odle."

Sam sipped his coffee, then lowered the cup. "I hope I never think that helping somebody is a waste of my time." He looked her up and down, then added, "I notice you seem to have time yourself."

Without responding, Tinnie sipped her coffee again and then put the cup down on the serving tray. "Come on, let's take this upstairs. She'll be better today than she was yesterday. She's getting it out of her system."

"I hope so," said Sam. "I need to get on the trail, see if I can find her boy—and Willie John."

"In this weather?" said Tinnie. "From the looks of the sky we've got lots of snow to come, maybe a squall before it's over."

"All the more reason I need to get out there and back," said Sam, his voice laced with urgency.

They had started up the stairs, but Tinnie stopped with the serving tray in her hands and looked him up and down. "Excuse me for getting personal, but do you have a woman somewhere, Ranger? A wife, a fiancée?"

Sam blushed. "No, ma'am, I'm unattached. This work hasn't allowed me much time for myself since I started." He stepped forward up the stairs, Tinnie beside him, smiling to himself at the way he'd described himself as unattached.

"I see," said Tinnie. "How long have you been doing this work?"

Sam seemed to consider it for a second, then he said, "A little over a year, ma'am."

They stopped at the top of the stairs. "Do me a favor, Ranger, call me 'Tinnie' . . . I don't feel like a 'ma'am.' "

Sam nodded. "All right, Tinnie, and you call me Sam, if you please."

"Fine," said Tinnie. "How did you come to be a Ranger, Sam?"

"It's not worth talking about, Tinnie," said Sam. "I started doing this work because it needs to be done. That's as well as I can explain it." He quickly changed the subject. "Do you think Dahl will give Hattie Odle any trouble once I'm out of town?"

"Who knows? Asa Dahl is a snake. He'll do whatever suits him, so long as it lines his pockets some way."

"Then why do you work for him?" Sam asked.

She stopped outside the door to Hattie Odle's room and considered it. "That's a good question, Ranger. I wish I knew the answer. Remember what I said about whores and lawmen? About us being a lot alike?"

"Yeah, I remember you saying it," Sam replied, "but I never said I agreed with it."

She smiled. "Well, whether you agree with that or not, it's a fact that women in my line of work do some peculiar things. Working for men like Asa Dahl is one of them."

Sam opened the door for her and stepped aside as she walked in carrying the coffee tray.

Looking around the corner of the bank building down on the snow-covered street, Hopper Ganston looked back and forth in each direction for a second. Then he ducked back out of sight and turned to his brother Earl, his breath swirling like steam out of his mouth. "They're gathering with shovels at the far end of town. We won't get a better chance at this than we've got right now."

"There's no horse at any hitch rails?" asked Earl, checking the pistol in his gloved hand.

"Not a one," said Hopper. "It's like what we just saw at the livery barn. Everybody stabled their mounts before the snow got heavy."

The first thing they had done upon entering the town was to slip into the livery barn and look all around in the looming darkness. "That felt strange," said Earl, "seeing all them horses just standing around bare-backed, the whole town unprepared."

Hopper said, "It felt even stranger seeing Willie John's big dapple-gray there among them, Willie's saddle and tack laying over that rail—like ole Willie had just left and was coming right back for it."

"Seeing that horse there told me one thing," said Earl. "Willie's gone on to his happy hunting ground." He spread a wicked grin. "Too bad we never found out where he kept his money stashed."

"Yeah, too bad," said Hopper, leaning forward and checking along the street once again. "One thing's for certain, this whole town is unsaddled and unbridled. It's like an answer to a robber's prayer."

"What about that line of hoofprints we came upon earlier?" asked Earl.

"What about them?" Hopper responded, still looking back and forth along the street, seeing the townsmen begin to shovel snow from the front of businesses and into piles along the boardwalks.

"Think it might be that posse?"

"So what if it is, brother?" Hopper raised his pistol and began checking its loads as well. "It was over an hour ago when we saw them. They're long gone up into the hills. Forget about them . . . we've got to get ourselves some pocket money."

"I'm ready when you are," said Earl.

"Good," said Hopper. "Get back there with the horses. Be ready when I come busting out through the back door." He reached over and picked up the shovel they had found in the livery barn.

"I'll be ready," said Earl. "Just get to it." He stepped back, away from his brother and toward the rear of the bank building where their horses stood hitched to the side of a woodshed.

Once Earl was out of sight, Hopper Ganston stepped boldly out onto the boardwalk, shovel in hand, and walked over to the front door of the bank.

He took the door handle in his gloved hand and
shook the door, looking in past the CLOSED sign hanging down on a thin bead chain. "Open up here,"
Hopper said, standing close to the door. He could
see the two men inside, a portly old man with a bald
head, and a younger man wearing a green clerk's
visor and a pair of sleeve garters on his boiled
white shirt.

The young man stepped quickly over to the door
as if he feared it might be shaken from its hinges.
"We're not open yet . . . come back in twenty minutes—"

"I know you're not open yet," said Hopper, cutting
him off. "If you want this snow piled away from out
front, you better let me in and talk about it."

The young man turned and relayed the message
across the room to the older man who stood with a
canvas bag hanging in his right hand. The older man
replied, but through the glass door, Hopper Ganston
could not make out his words. Then the younger
man turned back to Hopper, saying, "Mr. Vittitow
says wait just a second. He's got to put the bag
away."

"Mr. Vittitow better hurry up," said Hopper, feeling better about this by the second. "It's cold out
here. I've got other things that need doing." Staring
through the glass, Hopper watched Vittitow, the
bank owner, step into a back room.

"Oh, all right," said the young man, sounding put
out. "Hold your horses. I'll let you stand right inside
here." He reached up and slipped the safety bolt,
then turned the key in the door and swung the door
open. "I'm not really supposed to be doing this . . ."

"It's neighborly of you," said Hopper, stepping in
while glancing back over his shoulder to see if any-

one was watching. He turned back to the young man and looked past him, saying with a shocked look in his eyes, "My God! What's that?"

"Huh?" The young man swung in the direction of Hopper's pointing finger. The last sound he heard was the loud twang on the shovel smacking him in the back of his head. He crumbled forward onto the floor. Hopper slipped the safety bolt on the door and hurried across the floor, dropping the shovel on his way.

"Timothy?" Darton Vittitow called out, hearing the noise. "What's going on out there?" He started forward, stepping away from the open vault door, the bag still in his hand. But before he could get through the doorway into the next room, Hopper Ganston met him with cocked pistol.

"I'll take that!" Hopper snatched the canvas bank bag from Vittitow's hand as he poked the gun barrel into his soft belly and shoved him back against the open door of the vault. "What else have you got for me while I'm here?"

Sam and Tinnie left Hattie Odle's room. Once they had descended the stairs, Sam asked in a quiet voice, "Do you think she means it, what she said about quitting the business?"

Tinnie turned toward him, a serious look in her eyes. "I hope so, Sam, for her and the boy's sake. Hattie should have never took up this profession. She wasn't meant for it."

"That's the second time you've said something like that. It sounds like you think some women are born to—"

"No," she said, stopping him, "that's not what I mean. I don't think anybody was born to be any one thing or another." She tossed her wool muffler in place around her neck and drew the coat around her, then moved toward the door, motioning Sam along with her. Sam stepped ahead and opened the door for her as she continued, "I think it's a matter of what road life leads you on and what turns and side roads you take along the way. But there are some women who are more suitable to this sporting life than others. Hattie had already settled into having a husband and a child. This was never something she would have imagined for herself." Outside on the boardwalk, she slipped her arm into Sam's and asked, "Walk me to the saloon?"

"My pleasure," Sam nodded. As they began walking along, staying close to the front of the building where the snow had now drifted in, Sam said, "What about you, Tinnie? Is this life something you would have ever imagined for yourself?"

She shrugged, as if having never thought about it. "No, not really. Most of the girls say they were forced into this life—usually it's not true," said Tinnie. "But in Hattie's case it really is. Now that she's in it, look what it's doing to her and her kid. Billy wasn't bad until his pa went to jail and his ma took to the life."

"If he wasn't a bad kid before, I doubt if he's a bad kid now," said Sam. "Not yet, anyway. Right now he's just following bad examples."

Tinnie nodded, looking into Sam's eyes, agreeing with him. "And he's sure found it in this Indian and the Ganston Gang."

"Yep," said Sam. "Give him a little time with that bunch he'll be meaner than a snake—and whatever is wrong won't be wrong with him to his way of thinking."

"It'll be the rest of the world's fault," Tinnie added.

"That's right. I've seen enough this past year to know that once a man throws in with the likes of Willie John and the Ganstons, if he wasn't rotten before, he soon will be."

At the edge of the hotel where an alley led out onto the street, Tinnie started to step down from the boardwalk, but Sam stopped her. "Hold it," he said, looking down at the snow. The fresh hoof prints of a single horse snaked from the alley and crossed the street behind the bank building.

"What's wrong, Sam?" Tinnie asked, seeing the wary look on his face.

"Nothing, probably," Sam said, slipping his arm from hers. "Move back to the hotel . . . I want to check something out." He nodded at the prints in the snow as he stepped back, his hand brushing the edge of his coat back behind his holster.

Tinnie got the idea and whispered, "Be careful, Sam." She inched backward a little as Sam made his way across the snow-covered street. But Tinnie did not go to the hotel. Instead she stepped into a doorway and watched intently, seeing Sam disappear into the alley. "Please . . . be careful," she murmured under her breath.

In the longer alley at the rear of the bank, Billy Odle managed to step down from his horse with both hands raised above his head. Earl Ganston stood with his pistol cocked and aimed at Billy's chest.

"You sure picked yourself a bad time to be passing through here, boy," said Earl Ganston, stepping closer and taking the reins to Billy's horse.

"Mister, please," Billy pleaded. "I came here to get

help for one of your men—Willie John!" He nodded toward the back door of the doctor's office farther along the alley. "Willie's wounded bad and ain't going to make it unless I bring him back some medicine!"

Billy's words caught Earl by surprise. "How'd you know I'm one of the Ganston Gang?" His gloved hand tightened on the pistol butt, demanding an answer.

"I—I saw you with them the day they started to ride into town! The day the posse ambushed them! Mister, I'm not lying. I helped Willie John get away. I'm one of you now . . . and I've got to get Willie John some help!"

Earl got a picture of what was going on and chuckled. "Willie John always had a way of lucking out on something. But you can forget about him, boy. You ain't going anywhere. Get over against that wall and keep your mouth shut. Bad enough I got snow to deal with, let alone a snot-nosed kid."

"Drop the gun!" said Sam Burrack, his voice seeming to come from out of nowhere, only the barrel of his big Colt visible at the edge of the building. "This is Ranger Sam Burrack. You're under arrest."

Earl had started to swing his gun around, but the calmness in Sam's voice stopped him. This Ranger had him cold. Earl's eyes cut to Billy Odle as he lowered his pistol, already scheming for a way to use the kid as a bargaining chip. "Take it easy, Ranger, you've got me," Earl said, his thumb still over the cocked pistol hammer as he took a step toward where Billy stood with his back against the building.

"Don't even think about it, Ganston," said Sam, stepping out into full view now.

Earl sneered, then said, "It's about time we met, lawdog. Seems like you've been dogging us forever."

"It *will* be forever," said Sam, "if you don't uncock that gun and drop it like I told you to."

"Oh, I forgot," Earl grinned. He eased the hammer down and let the pistol fall to the snow at his feet.

Billy Odle stood staring wide-eyed, liking the way Earl Ganston handled himself, taking his own time even with the Ranger's pistol pointed at him. "Now what, Ranger?" Ganston asked, wanting to keep Sam's back to the rear door of the bank, knowing that any second Hopper would come busting out.

But the Ranger stepped sideways to the rear door, already figuring out the robber's plan. "Now we wait."

"Well, hell . . ." Earl let out a long breath, still wondering how to get his hands on Billy Odle, snatch him forward and use him as a shield when the right moment came. "Looks like you're having yourself a good day. I don't suppose it would do a bit of good to remind you that you ain't got a lick of jurisdiction here, would it?"

"Nope, none that I can think of," said Sam. "Now shut up and stand still." He looked at Billy Odle and wanted to say something, to let the boy know that he needn't worry, that his wasn't about him. But Sam didn't want the other robber to hear a strange voice as he came out the back door.

Inside the bank, Hopper Ganston hefted two bags of money up over his shoulder and jerked his pistol barrel toward the rear of the building. "Come on, sport, I'm leaving by the back way."

"There is no back way," said Vittitow. "The back door was sealed and cemented three years ago, as soon as we installed this new vault!"

"You're lying!" Hopper growled, stepping forward and leveling the pistol between the bank owner's eyes.

"No, sir! So help me God! Come, I'll show you! There's no rear way out of here! I swear!" Fresh beads of sweat appeared on his forehead.

"Damn it to hell! Go on then!" He stomped out of the back room, raising a boot and kicking Vittitow ahead of him. "If I get back there and see a door, I'll come back here and shoot your ears off."

"There is a door back there, sir!" Vittitow shook uncontrollably. "But it's sealed, like I told you."

On the floor, the clerk raised up onto his palms with a painful moan. "All right, then," said Hopper, needing to move quickly. "Both of you get back there in the vault."

"In the vault? Sir, you can't leave us in there," Vittitow pleaded. "It could be hours before somebody finds us!"

"Now you're getting the drift of it," said Hopper with a nasty smile. Then the smile faded and his voice rose into a rage as his pistol extended out at Vittitow's sweaty forehead. "Get the hell in there!"

"Yes, sir!" Vittitow lowered his trembling hands long enough to help the clerk struggle to his feet. "Come, Timothy, quickly . . . we'll be all right."

"What's . . . happening?" the clerk asked in a weak voice.

"Jesus!" Hopper shouted. "You're being robbed, you stupid peckerwood!" Swinging the money bags off his shoulders and swiping them at the backs of the two men, forcing them on, Hopper Ganston followed until they stepped inside the big vault. Then he rolled the big steel door shut, turned the handle into place and spun the dial. So far so good, he thought, hurrying back through the bank, picking up the shovel on his way. At the front door he looked through the glass, sweeping his eyes back and forth along the empty street. Then he hefted the tied bank bags over his shoulder, opened the door and stepped out, carrying the shovel in the same hand as he carried his pistol.

He froze for a second, stepping down into the alley, seeing both the hoofprints left by Billy Odle's horse and the bootprints left by the Ranger. "What the—?" He ducked into the shelter of the alley and slung the shovel away. "This place has gotten awfully damn busy," he whispered to himself. He moved in a quiet crouch along the wall toward the rear of the bank. At the back edge of the building he froze again at the sound of Earl's voice speaking in a lowered tone. "What if I told you me and Hopper had nothing to do with shooting that Ranger? If it was all the Injun's doing? Would it make you any difference?"

"None at all," said Sam. "Now shut up. I'll deal with Willie John when I get to him."

Billy Odle's chin grew taut at the Ranger's words. But he stood in silence, watching, listening, his knees shaking inside his trouser legs, but his mind working, trying to keep things in order. He wasn't about to see his friend Willie John get taken by this lawman. He couldn't believe what he'd just heard Earl Ganston say, jackpotting Willie John for murder. Somehow Billy Odle had to get away from here. He had to get the medicine and get back to Willie and warn him.

At the edge of the building, Hopper Ganston cocked his pistol slowly and quietly. Peering ever so carefully around the corner, seeing how the Ranger was concentrating on the rear of the bank building, Hopper raised his pistol to fire. But as his sights drew down on the Ranger and his finger began squeezing the trigger, from the far end of the alley, Tinnie screamed loud and shrill, "Sam, look out!" and Hopper Ganston's first shot went wild as he flinched and spun around toward her.

Hopper's bullet whistled past the Ranger's head. Sam jerked sideways instinctively. As he spun toward the sound of Hopper's second shot, Sam caught a glimpse of Earl Ganston making his move. Earl dropped down, snatched his pistol from the snow and hurled himself toward Billy Odle all in one single motion. Sam aimed at Earl Ganston, but then held his fire as Earl jerked Billy Odle forward and hid behind him. Earl fired, his shot hitting the Ranger high in the shoulder.

Sam staggered a step backward, then dropped to one knee, turning his pistol away from Earl and Billy Odle and at Hopper Ganston who came charging forward, his pistol blazing. Two shots exploded from Sam's big Colt, both of them picking Hopper Ganston up and slamming him back even as another shot from Earl's pistol hit Sam in the hip. The two bags of money flew from Hopper's hand and spilled open in the snow. Sam scrambled away a few feet as another bullet nipped at his heels. He rolled behind the cover of a snow-topped rain barrel and yelled out, "Let the kid go, Earl!"

"Ha! You've got to be crazy, Ranger!" Another shot thumped into the rain barrel. "He's my ticket out of here! You kilt my brother, you sonuvabitch, but you ain't killing me!"

"You're not leaving here with him, Earl. You might as well face that fact." Sam peeped around the barrel enough to see Earl Ganston sidestepping toward Billy Odle's horse, still using Billy as a shield.

"Don't shoot, please!" Billy Odle cried out.

"I'll kill him dead as hell, Ranger!" Earl bellowed. "If you don't believe me, just try following me and see!"

Earl forced Billy up onto the saddle, climbing quickly up behind him so that the Ranger couldn't get a clear shot at him. The horse tried to bolt at the feel of Earl Ganston's spurs digging into its sides, but the deep snow caused the animal to stall for a second. When the horse did manage to get its start, it lunged forward in a halting gait, a cloud of frosty white powder flurrying up around it.

Before the horse had gone ten yards, Sam hurried out from behind the rain barrel and watched Earl and the boy ride away. The wound in his shoulder throbbed with the beat of his heart. He lowered his Colt, not about to risk hitting Billy. They wouldn't get far, not riding double in this kind of weather. He turned and ran limping into the alley. Seeing Tinnie lying slumped against the bank building, he hurried to her and tried raising her from the snow. But the wounds in his shoulder and hip wouldn't allow it. He sank down with her across his lap. "Hold on, Tinnie, you'll be all right," he said. He saw the blood on her side.

"I . . . I know, Sam," she rasped. "Don't . . . worry about me. Take care of . . . yourself."

"What's going on in here?" one of the townsmen cried out as the whole street-cleaning crew came running into the alley. They gathered quickly around Sam and Tinnie, some of them bending down for a closer look. Selectman Collins pointed back at the bags of money on the ground and said, "Somebody gather that up and take it inside. Check on Vittitow and his teller."

One of the townsmen moved over to the body of Hopper Ganston lying crumpled in the snow. "Damn!" He nudged Hopper's head to one side with the toe of his boot. "It's one of them blasted outlaws! Collins, come look at him!"

"I see him," said Collins, stepping over and looking down at Ganston's dead face. "It's one of them, all right." He lifted a long searching gaze out across flatlands toward the hills. "It's like we've been set upon by starving wolves. Will we ever get shed of these men? What keeps them coming back?"

"Money," said Sam. He struggled to his feet and nodded down at Tinnie, who had her hand clutched to her side. "Get her up and get her to the doctor's office. Hurry!"

Three men cradled Tinnie between them and hurried away with her. Sam staggered unsteadily in place. "What about you, Ranger?" Collins said. He stood with a rifle in his hands, having run inside the sheriff's office and grabbed it at the first sound of gunfire. "We better get you to the doctor's, too!"

Sam grabbed Collins by the shoulder to steady himself. "In a minute," he said. He looked down at the big Spencer rifle, then nodded toward the back of the bank building and said, "Come on, follow me."

Chapter 12

As they headed away from Hubbler Wells, Earl Ganston had been riding behind Billy Odle. But to keep the Ranger from getting a shot at his back, Earl had dragged Billy around behind him before the horse had gone fifty yards. Halfway across the stretch of flatlands, Billy Odle said, "All we got to do is get to the hills. I'll get us hidden where they'll never find us."

"Huh?" Earl Ganston looked over his shoulder at Billy in surprise. "Hey, kid, I don't know what's going on in that empty head of yours, but don't make the mistake of thinking I won't kill you if you try something—"

"I know, I know," said Billy Odle, cutting him off. "You still don't believe I'm on your side. But I wasn't lying, mister. You've got to trust me! Willie John is hiding up there in the hills, and he's needing help bad!"

"How do you know the posse ain't there on him right now, boy?" asked Earl, starting to wonder if maybe the kid was his only key to getting out of this mess.

"It's a secret hideout," said Billy Odle. "Only Willie and me know about it. I took him there. I'll take you there, too. But first I've got to get some *haga creer* for Willie's wounds."

"Some what?"

"Some *haga creer*," Billy said, talking fast as the horse struggled on in the snow. "It's a Mexican herb . . . Willie said he hated using it, but sometimes it's the only thing that works."

Earl let out a low, dark chuckle. "Hell, boy, you don't have to tell me about *haga creer*—I speak the language. How do we get to this hideout you're talking about?"

"Huh-uh," said Billy. "I'll show you but I won't tell you."

"Wise little peckerwood," Earl growled, lashing the reins back and forth across the horse's sides, pushing it hard. "If you think you're going to be one of us, you best get to telling me how to get there. What if something happens to you? You plan on leaving me at that Ranger's mercy? Now give me some directions, damn you!"

"All right, then," said Billy Odle, "but promise you won't double-cross me. Willie's counting on me."

Atop the crest of a snow-covered cliff, Colonel Fuller's men gathered close and watched him wipe the lens of his telescope and expand it out toward the horse and its two riders coming across the stretch of flatlands. They had all heard the gunfire echo up from across the flatland and hurried down the hill trail. They had spent the gray hours of morning scouring the hills for any sign of the Ganston Gang. The hunt had left them cold and wet and disheartened. Until now.

Fuller flinched back away from the telescope for a

second as if he couldn't believe his eyes. Then he peered back through the lens, saying to Red Booker in an astonished tone, "As I live, Red! It's Earl Ganston in the flesh!"

"What are the odds of it?" Red Booker looked stunned, watching the riders with his naked eyes, seeing only the small black figures atop the horse, the horse leaving a wash of white above its tracks in the otherwise smooth and untouched snow. "We drag up here before dawn, search every crack . . . then meet a Ganston riding out of town toward us?"

"Let's not question good fortune." Fuller snapped the telescope down from his eyes and collapsed it between his palms with a clap. "Men, ready your rifles! As soon as Ganston gets within range, let him have it."

"What about the man riding behind him?" Red Booker asked.

"What about him?" Fuller asked in reply, slipping the lens inside his greatcoat and drawing the rifle from his saddle scabbard.

"Are we just going to kill him, too? Not even knowing if he's one of the gang or not?" asked Red Booker.

"He's guilty of something, whoever he is!" bellowed Fuller. "Why else would he riding with a Ganston? Now ready your rifles, and prepare to fire! At least we'll get one of the gang before that blasted Ranger gets to him."

"Yes, sir!" Red Booker stepped down from his saddle, slipped his rifle from its boot and levered a round up into the chamber. "You heard the colonel, men. Get ready to cut them both in half."

Out on the flatland, Billy Odle held on to the back of Earl Ganston's coat with one hand, his free hand firmly holding his hat down atop his head. Now that Billy had told Earl Ganston how to get to the old cliff ruins, Earl was beginning to see his chances of escape grow better by the minute. But now that he knew the way to the hideout on his own, he wasn't about to have this kid holding him back. He turned his head, looking back past Billy Odle as the horse trudged along in its hopping, lunging gait. The town had grown tiny in the distance.

"Boy, this ain't going to work, This horse will break down before we go another mile." Earl brought the horse to a halt. "Sorry, boy, this is where you get off."

"What?" said Billy. "You said you wouldn't double-cross me!"

"Did I sure enough?" Earl reached around and grabbed him by his coat. "Well, I must've misunderstood." He slung Billy to the ground and watched him roll in the foot-deep snow. As Billy caught himself and wiped his face, blowing snow from his lips, Earl raised his pistol from his holster and cocked it.

"What about Willie?" said Billy Odle. "You can't just leave him up there to die! He's a part of your gang!"

"You just don't get it, do you, boy?" Earl said. "I don't give a damn about Willie John or anybody else. Sorry, kid," he chuckled, drawing a bead down his pistol sights.

The reality sunk in and Billy Odle trembled. "You're going to shoot me?"

"Oh yes," said Earl Ganston.

"But why?" Billy Odle cried out.

"Because I ain't leaving you here to tell that Ranger how to get to the hideout," Earl growled.

"I won't tell him, I swear! Why would I? I'm a

friend of Willie John! I'm just like him, an outlaw! I wouldn't tell on nobody for no reason. That's my code." His voice had started to break down into a pleading sob.

"If that's true," said Earl Ganston, "then you're too damn stupid to live." He grinned. "So long, boy."

Billy Odle screamed at the last second and squeezed his eyes shut. The shot sounded louder than anything he'd ever heard in his life. He jerked, feeling the bullet going into his chest, slicing hot and deep while the blast still rang inside his head. Something wet and warm slapped him in his face—his life's blood, he thought, for one terrible instant. Then he began to realize that he hadn't really felt any pain at all, only the dread of it. He blinked and ran his hand down his face, feeling the warm blood as he wiped it from his eyes. When he looked up, he saw no sign of Earl Ganston, only the empty saddle, and the tired horse stepping back and forth nervously in the snow.

"Oh my God!" Billy exclaimed, looking to his right and seeing the body of Earl Ganston lying facedown in the snow, a gaping bullet hole in the center of his back. Steam curled up from the bloody wound. Billy scooted back quickly away from the body and sat staring at it. Gathering his knees up against his chest and wrapping his arms around them, he rocked back and forth in the snow, letting out a long, strained whine through his clenched teeth. On the cliff line, Red Booker lowered the rifle from his shoulder and looked at Colonel Fuller in bewilderment. On either side of Booker, the rest of the men did the same. "What the hell happened, Colonel?" Booker asked.

"What happened?" said Colonel Fuller, barely controlling his rage. "I'll tell you *what happened*! Somebody just shot that sonuvabitch dead, right under our damned noses!" He jerked his horse around and heeled it away.

In the alley behind the bank building, Sam Burrack let out a breath. Seeing Earl Ganston fall from the saddle, Sam let the Spencer rifle drop from his hands onto the top of the snow-covered rain barrel. "Somebody ride out there and get the boy," he said. Then he let himself slump forward against the barrel and succumb to the weakness that crept up around his chest and shoulders. Blood ran freely down his arm and dripped from the fingertip of his glove. He took a labored breath and said to Selectman Collins in a waning voice, "Let's get on over to that doctor's office now."

Collins and the townsmen stood staring out across the snowy flatland with their mouths agape. "Carl," said Collins without turning to face the short blacksmith standing nearest him, "why don't you and Ronald ride out and bring Billy Odle back here for the Ranger?"

"Uh, yes, we surely will," the blacksmith replied, gazing out across the flatlands with him.

Billy Odle had no idea how long he'd sat in the snow, but it had to have been long enough for Earl Ganston's blood to dry on his face. Billy had gone into some sort of trance, until the sound of men and horses came lurching through the snow toward him from the hills on his right. Two more riders approached from Hubbler Wells on his left. Only then did he manage to shake himself back to consciousness and stand up, dusting himself off. Without taking the time to pick up Earl Ganston's pistol from the snow where it'd fallen, Billy Odle snatched up the reins to the horse and climbed up into the saddle.

He batted his heels to the horse's sides and headed west across the long snow-filled basin.

"Collins and that Ranger were right," said Carl Yates to his apprentice, Ronald Andrews. "That's Billy Odle all right. I'd recognize that little knot-head anywhere."

"Yeah," said Ronald, "but look who's coming from the hill trails." He nodded toward Colonel Fuller and his men. "Billy better hope we get to him before they do."

"Come on," said Carl, reaching back with his reins to slap his horse's rump. "Let's get between him and that posse . . . keep them from shooting his fool head off." Even as he spoke, he saw the rifles in the hands of Fuller's men, who were getting closer every second.

Ronald paused. "What if they think we're part of the Ganston Gang?"

"Why would they think that?" asked Carl. "They all seen us in the saloon back in town.

"I know they saw us, but I don't know how good their memory is, coming on at a run. I don't want to get shot over it," said Ronald.

"Then stay here, Ronald," said Carl. "But I couldn't live with myself if I just sat still and watched them buzzards kill that stupid kid." He slapped the reins and sent the horse loping forward.

"Aw hell," Ronald mumbled, "neither could I." He batted his heels to his horse's sides and fell in behind the blacksmith, both horses struggling to get up a running pace in the deep snow.

Billy Odle's horse was nearly blown from carrying double weight at a hard run all the way from Hubbler Wells. He hadn't gone two hundred yards when he looked back and saw the posse gaining on him as if he were sitting still. He also saw Carl and Ronald cutting in behind him and taking up his trail. He looked back and forth wildly for any way out. Beneath him, the horse slowed more and more with each labored yard it gained. Finally it stopped altogether and stood spraddle-legged and heaving, Billy's boots batting its sides to no avail.

Finally, Billy ceased goading the worn animal and slumped in his saddle. "I tried, Willie, I swear I did," he said to the empty sky, his eyes welling up. As Ronald and Carl advanced on Billy Odle, calling out his name, Colonel Fuller raised a gloved hand to his men, signaling them not to fire. Fuller slowed his horse to walk the last fifty yards, seeing that neither the boy or the other two riders were going anywhere. "So, Billy Odle . . . at last we meet," Fuller said, stepping his horse wide of Carl and Ronald for a better look at the boy.

Carl stepped his horse alongside Fuller's, saying, "I'm telling you right now, the Ranger asked us to bring this boy to town. I'm not letting nothing happen to him whilst he's with us. Ain't that right, Ronald?" He glanced at his apprentice for support.

"That's right," said Ronald. "We as good as gave our word on it."

"Don't worry," said Fuller, giving them a look of disdain. "We wouldn't want to do anything that might upset the Ranger, now would we?"

Billy Odle had stepped down into the snow and stood beside the tired horse. He stared at Colonel Fuller as the possemen formed a half circle around them. "You might as well not ask me nothing," said Billy. "I ain't telling you a thing about the Ganston Gang."

"The Ganston Gang." Fuller and his men chuckled.

"I saw Earl's body back there. All that's left now is Hopper and that Injun. There *ain't* no more gang."

"The Ranger shot Hopper Ganston dead," Carl cut in. He felt himself shrink back as all eyes turned to him.

"Damn it to everlasting hell!" Colonel Fuller's expression soured for a second. But then he collected himself and turned back to Billy Odle. "There, you see? No more Ganston Gang. All that remains is the Injun. So you just point us in his direction and we'll be on our way." Fuller had brought his horse within a foot of Billy Odle and stopped. He sat glaring down at him.

"I already told you, I ain't—"

Billy Odle's words stopped short as Fuller reached down, and with a powerful backhand, sent Billy flying backward to the ground. "I'm through being nice to everybody!" Before Carl or Ronald could stop him, Colonel Fuller jumped down from his horse and advanced on Billy Odle. When Billy shook off the slap and tried to struggle to his feet, another hard swing knocked him down again.

"Leave him alone!" shouted Carl, jumping down from his horse and stepping forward. "We're taking him back to town in one piece!"

He started to reach out and grab Fuller's arm, but the sound of the possemen's rifles cocking caused him to stop cold.

"Look like you just stepped into something over your head, don't it, shorty?" Fuller said with a dark grin. "Make a false move now, see if these boys won't eat you alive."

"They might, but you won't live to see it," said Ronald from atop his horse, a sawed-off shotgun cocked and pointed at Colonel Fuller's face, only ten feet away. "Now tell them to lower those rifles."

Fuller stared at him for a second trying to read the seriousness of the apprentice blacksmith's intent. "If you think I'm bluffing, mister, just say the words and let the killing commence."

"Easy, Ronald!" Carl said, trying to calm the young man. "Colonel Fuller ain't going to do nothing that foolish, are you, Colonel?"

Fuller looked back and forth between the two men, then at his own men who stood twitching, ready to start shooting. "The fact is, Colonel," said Carl, "ole Ronald here ain't got but about half sense once he gets his bark on. Don't do something to set him off . . . for all our sakes."

"You men ease down," Fuller said, raising a hand and watching the men slowly lower their rifles. He looked back at Ronald. "All right, young man . . . take that scattergun off me. You made your point. We'll all ride in together and take this boy to Hubbler Wells." He waited until he saw the shotgun lower an inch, then he let out a tense breath and took a step back. "No use in us fighting among ourselves. We're all after the same thing here." He collected himself, leveled his hat on his forehead and walked back to this horse as Carl walked over and helped Billy Odle to his feet.

"That critter will never make it to town," said Red Booker, drawing attention to the horse Billy Odle had been riding. "You might as well put it out of its misery."

Carl looked at the exhausted animal and recognized it as one of Old Man Renfro's. "Billy, what are you doing on one of Renfro's horses?" His voice had a flatness to it, as if he already dreaded what the answer would be. "Renfro never lent his horses. He hardly ever left them out of his sight."

Billy Odle stood looking down at the ground.

"You stole it, didn't you?" Carl accused. When Billy didn't reply, Carl eyed him closely, then asked, "Is Old Man Renfro all right, Billy? Has harm come to him?"

"I didn't steal any of Renfro's horses," Billy blurted out. "They were running loose . . . all me and Willie John did was rounded them up."

"Oh Lord," said Carl shaking his head, getting a bad mental picture of what terrible thing had befallen the old man. "You and that Indian killed him and stole his horses."

"No, we didn't," said Billy through his swollen bleeding lips. "I swear we didn't. We found the horses wandering out behind his place and took them, that's all!"

"See why I show no mercy?" Fuller said to Carl. "It makes no difference, young or old . . . an outlaw is an outlaw. And the only good one is a dead one. If you're smart, you'll turn him over to me and I'll see to it he—"

"He's no outlaw," said Carl, cutting him off, "he's just a dumb kid!" His gaze narrowed on Billy Odle as he spoke. "And if his daddy was here and could see how he's acting, he'd box his jaws for him." He grabbed the reins to Billy's exhausted horse and pulled it forward alongside his own horse. "Come on, Billy, you're riding double with me. I'm leading this horse back to town, if it'll make it that far. We'll have to get to the bottom of this."

When Fuller and his men had pulled back and given Ronald and Carl room to turn their horses and head back toward Hubbler Wells, Ronald sidled his

horse in close to Carl and whispered just between
the two of them, "How'd I do, Carl?"

Carl returned his whisper, "You did fine, Ronald,
but you nearly scared the be-jesus out of me. I know
as well as you do that old shotgun hasn't been fired
in years. I hate to guess what would have happened
if you'd pulled the trigger. Like as not it would have
exploded in your hands."

"No danger in that," Ronald whispered. "It ain't
been loaded since last Christmas."

Carl's face turned stark white for a second. "Lord
God!" He rode a few steps forward, then stopped
his horse in its tracks and said to Ronald, "I've been
thinking lately, Ronald . . . business is real good. It's
about time I gave you a raise."

"That's what I've been thinking, too," Ronald replied, gazing ahead with a blank look on his face.

Chapter 13

Once the Ranger's wounds were cleaned and dressed, and he saw that Tinnie was doing all right, he fell asleep on a gurney set up in the back room of the doctor's office. Tinnie had been taken upstairs where the doctor's wife could attend to her. Luckily, Tinnie's wounds were not life threatening. Neither were Sam's. One of the bullets had gone clean through his left shoulder. The other shot had grazed his hip. By the time Carl, Ronald and Fuller's posse arrived with Billy Odle and the worn-out horse, Sam had sat up on the gurney with two large pillows propped behind his back. His shirt lay across a ladder-back chair where his gun belt hung, his pistol butt close at hand. The big pistol was the first thing Billy Odle took notice of when he entered the room.

"Here he is, Ranger," said Carl, and he and Ronald nudged Billy forward a step. "Maybe you can get something out of him. We can't." They had found a pair of handcuffs at the sheriff's office and had put them on Billy's thin wrists. "I don't mind telling you it was no easy job, getting him back here and away from Colonel Fuller and his men. Fuller said if there's any reward on Billy, he gets it."

"Reward?" Sam asked as he looked Billy Odle up and down. "Reward for what?"

Carl shrugged. "I'm just telling you what he said. I reckon he keeps rewards on the brain in his line of work." Carl looked down and scratched his head up under his hat brim. "There's one thing I told Selectman Collins . . . and I need to tell you, too. We caught Billy here on a horse belonging to a man who lives just outside of town between here and the hill country. His name's Renfro and he's awfully partial to his horses. Billy said him and the Indian found them running loose. But I've got serious doubts about it. It'll have to be checked out."

"Oh?" The Ranger's gaze went back to Billy Odle as he said to Carl, "Why don't you and your helper go have a drink on me. Looks like you could both use one."

Carl glanced at the gun belt on the chair. "Are you sure you'll be all right, Ranger?"

"I'm sure," said Sam, eying Billy Odle who stood staring down at the floor.

"What if he tries to make a run for it?" Carl asked. "Think maybe one of us ought to stay outside the door here just in case?"

"Much obliged for all you men have done," said Sam, "but I'll be able to take care of things from here."

"All right, then," said Carl, him and Ronald both taking a step back. "Collins will be wanting Billy as soon as you're through with him."

"I understand," said Sam. "Tell Collins that Billy will be along shortly." His left arm lying cradled in a sling, Sam raised his right hand and motioned Billy Odle forward. "Come on over here closer, young man. We've got some things to talk about."

Carl and Ronald hesitated near the door until they

saw Billy Odle walk forward. Then the two stepped back through the open doorway and closed the door behind them. Billy stopped at the side of the gurney and stared down at his cuffed hands. "If you're going to ask me to tell you where my friend Willie John is hiding, you'll just be wasting your breath," he said without raising his eyes to the ranger.

Sam seemed not to have heard him. "Look up here at me, Billy Odle, like a man, not down at your boots."

The Ranger's tone was not harsh, but it was firm. Billy raised his eyes grudgingly. "It won't make any difference, I still won't tell you."

The Ranger nodded. "So far I don't recall asking you where he's at. When it comes time to find him, I'll find him. Meanwhile, I'm concerned about what it's going to take to get your head cleared and get you on the right track."

"Don't worry about me getting on track," said Billy Odle. "I know what it is I want . . . ain't you or nobody else going to stop me."

"I see," said Sam. "You've been gone from home all this time, your mother worried sick about you. All you can think of doing is picking an argument with me? Young man, you don't have the slightest idea how close you probably came to getting your throat cut by your best buddy hiding in the hills."

"I was going to ask about Ma," said Billy Odle, his eyes dropping again, ignoring what Sam said about Willie John. "Besides, Ma's okay, so long as she can get her drink and her drugs."

"Look at me, Billy," Sam said, more firmly this time. "Your mother has quit all of that stuff. She's been sweating it out of her system ever since she found out you rode away with Willie John."

"Really?" Billy Odle raised his eyes now, looking a bit surprised. "She was that worried?"

"That's right, and with good reason," said Sam. "Willie John is on the run from the law. That puts him and anybody with him in danger. He's got to say and do whatever he has to to keep the law from closing in on him. If he has to give up a friend who's riding with him, then that's how it's got to be." He studied Billy's face for any telling response. When none came, Sam added, "You've been playing a dangerous game, Billy. It's time to stop and get straightened out before it goes any further."

Billy shook his head. "This hasn't been no game for me. Willie never gave me up," Billy said. "And you're wrong about him, lawman. Willie and me are best of friends, and he would never give up a friend, not for any reason."

"Yeah? Then why are you standing here in handcuffs instead of him?" Sam asked.

Before Billy Odle could answer, the doctor came into the room, having heard the Ranger's voice. "I see you're awake," he said, standing inside the doorway with his hands on his hips, the front of his white apron stained with blood.

"Yes," said Sam. "How's the woman doing?"

"I gave her something to make her sleep," said the doctor. "It was a close call for her, but that bullet managed to slip past every vital organ. She's in a lot of pain . . . she's going to be all right, though. I'll be giving her something to stave off any infection. You, too." His eyes went to Billy Odle. "Well, young Billy, you appear to be no worse for the wear. Should I take a look at you?" As he asked, his eyes went to the cuffs on Billy's wrists.

"No, I'm fine, Dr. Blanton," said Billy. "Are you talking about Tinnie, from the saloon?"

"Indeed I am, Billy," said Doc Blanton. "She took a bullet wound in—"

"What will you give her for infection," Billy cut in with no hesitancy, "some kind of herb medicine?"

Noting Billy's keen interest in what the doctor had to say, Sam listened and observed.

"Well, there are several things I use, depending on what's available," said Blanton, bemused by Billy Odle's sudden interest in the healing arts. "Why do you ask?"

"Nothing," said Billy Odle, shrugging, looking back down at the floor. "Do you ever keep any *haga creer* medicine on hand?"

The doctor turned his gaze to the Ranger as he said to Billy with a curious expression, "*Haga creer?* Why, I believe that's Mexican isn't it, Billy? If I'm not mistaken, it means—"

"Yes, it's Spanish," the Ranger cut in, before the doctor had a chance to offer any further comment. He saw something at work here and wanted to know more. He looked at Billy Odle, knowing how young and pliable this boy was. "What would you need with something like that? Is that something for Willie John? Something he sent you here to get for him?"

The doctor chuckled under his breath, saying, "But, Ranger, you can't be serious."

"Doc, would you leave us alone here?" the Ranger asked in a sharp tone.

Doctor Blanton's smile melted. "Certainly . . . I'll just go check on the woman."

When Doctor Blanton had left the room, the Ranger turned back to Billy Odle. "I see what this is now, young man. It's not going to work. You're not going anywhere. Even if you did, Willie John is long gone."

Billy started to protest, but he caught himself and said, "I never said he was anywhere waiting for me."

"You don't have to. I can tell by the look on your face that you think he is. But you're wrong." The Ranger swung his legs off the side of the bed and sat up. He grunted slightly at the pain in his shoulder but then pushed himself to his feet. "Willie John's not there. He gave you something to do to get rid of you . . . so he could cut out on you."

"No he didn't! That's a lie!" Billy shouted.

"Do you know what *haga creer* means, Billy?" Sam asked.

Billy Odle didn't answer.

"In Spanish it means 'make believe,' " Sam said, his voice softening to take some of the sting off of his words.

"Make believe?" Billy Odle looked stunned. There was hurt in his child's voice. "That can't be right. Willie John didn't double-cross me!"

"I didn't say he double-crossed you." Sam picked up the bloodstained shirt hanging across the chair back. "I said he gave you something to do to get rid of you. He knew if you came here asking for *haga creer*, somebody would see it was just his way of sending you home. You're lucky, kid. He must've taken a liking to you." Sam slipped his good arm through the shirtsleeve, then said to Billy, "I'd appreciate it if you'd hold my shirtsleeve out so's I can stick this arm into it."

Billy hesitated for a second, trying to get a mental grip on what Willie John had done. "Well . . . then all that means is that Willie was looking out for me. Ain't that what real friends do for one another?"

"The sleeve?" said Sam, not offering an answer.

"Oh all right." Billy reluctantly stepped forward when he saw that the Ranger was not going to take his sharp stare off of him until he helped him with the shirt.

Sam slipped his arm from the sling, and saw how Billy's eyes went to the gun belt on the chair as he held the loose shirt sleeve up for him. "*Gracias*," said Sam, working at buttoning his shirt with his free hand, keeping his sore left arm at an angle until he could get the sling back around it. "You know, there's nothing hurts worse than a shoulder wound," he said matter-of-factly. Nodding at the gun belt he added, "Want to hand that shooting iron over to me, Billy?"

Billy stared at the big Colt before reaching for it. Sam could see the wheels turning in the boy's mind. When Billy's cuffed hands reached out to lift the holster belt, Sam said, "Not the whole rig, just the Colt . . . so I can check it."

Billy looked at him and swallowed back the tension that formed quickly in his throat. Sam appeared relaxed, yet he was ready for whatever Billy Odle might decide to do. Billy closed his hand around the pistol butt, and lifted it slowly. He stared at it closely, then handed it to the Ranger. "Is . . . is it loaded?" he asked.

Sam offered a thin smile, slipped the cylinder out from the side of the Colt, turned the back end of six unfired cartridges toward Billy Odle and said, "Yep, see? As loaded as it's ever been." He snapped the cylinder shut, spun it with the hammer cocked, then lowered the hammer and handed it back to Billy butt first. "Ever handled a Colt that feels that well balanced?"

Billy had not handled enough Colt pistols in his life to be able to tell the difference, yet he hefted the weight of the gun on his hand as if judging it. "I can't say as I have. She's a beauty, all right." He turned the Colt back and forth while the Ranger watched intently. Billy's thumb even went across the hammer, but Sam appeared not to notice. Then Billy turned the big pistol in his hand and offered it back to the Ranger butt first, the same way it had been handed to him.

Sam took the pistol, holstered it, and said to Billy Odle, "If you had anything to do with stealing those horses, you better tell me now. It'll go bad on you if anything's happened to the old man who owned them."

"We didn't steal them . . . we found them running loose just like I said."

"I see," said Sam. "If that's the truth, then you tell it to Selectman Collins, and be prepared to stick to it. If it's not the truth, then you be prepared for whatever this town will do to you. Willie John won't be here to face the charges. It'll all be on you."

"But—but what if something had happened to the old man before we found the horses, something me and Willie didn't even know about? Won't they have to prove we had something to do with it? They can't do nothing to me without any proof!"

"Listen to me Billy," said Sam. "It's time you step into some grown-up boots. This is not a child's game with wooden guns and mop-stick ponies. If anything's happened to that old man, and you're riding one of his horses, that's all it takes to tie you to it. Whatever explanations you have better be good."

"Would they—" Billy's words stuck in his throat

until he swallowed hard. "Would they hang me for it?"

"I can't say, Billy. All I can say is, whatever part you've played in it, you best admit to it and hope for the best. Don't be holding nothing back to protect Willie John."

Billy's face turned ashen as he ran the Ranger's advice through his mind. Then, in a quiet voice he asked, "Do you want me to tell you about the horses . . . about what happened?"

"Only if you want to, Billy," said Sam.

At the saloon, Selectman Collins tossed back a shot of rye and tried to avoid the eyes of Asa Dahl and the other men gathered around him. "If the Ranger had any jurisdiction here it would be different," said Dahl, "but he has no right to keep you waiting. If anybody has a right to question that boy first, it's you, Collins. Am I right, boys?" Dahl turned to the bar crowd for support and got it.

"Damn right," said one voice above the others.

"We know how to handle lawbreakers of all ages," said another voice.

Collins looked nervous for a second, then he shook it off and said, "All right, I'm not waiting on the Ranger. Billy Odle is our problem . . . we'll handle it."

Seeing the tension of the crowd swell, Carl spread his hands, trying to settle them. "Listen to me! The Ranger said he'd turn Billy over to Collins as soon as he's finished talking to him. Let him do this his way. He knows more about this sort of thing than the rest of us!"

"Carl," said a man with a bristly beard who stood

close by with a bottle of rye in one hand and a glass in the other, "you're a good man and a fine blacksmith. But you don't know *squat* about dealing with criminals."

"Massey," said Carl to the man. "You're a mule skinner and a fall-down drunkard. Does that qualify you?" He looked at the others in turn then added, "Besides, boys, this isn't a criminal we're talking about. This is Billy Odle. He's one of our own, and he's just a scared kid who doesn't know what the hell he's doing."

"Scared kid? Ha!" said Asa Dahl. "I'll tell you what he is. He's the son of a town whore. He's a thief, a liar and a troublemaker. He's taking up with outlaws, and if you don't stop him hard and cold right here and now, he'll go on to worse things, I can promise you that."

Carl Yates stepped forward. "You're just trying to stir things up worse than they are, Asa. Ronald and I brought the boy in. He said they found the horse running loose . . . maybe he did."

"Oh really?" Asa Dahl's voice was sarcastic. He stepped in almost nose to nose with Carl Yates and said, "Look me right in the eyes, Carl, and tell me you believe that hogwash."

"Damn it, Asa," said Carl, his face reddening, "it's not my place to believe or disbelieve it. If it comes down to a matter of the law, only a jury can decide if the boy's story is true or not."

"It's not going to come down to a matter of the law," said Asa Dahl, "not over a lying little whelp like Billy Odle. I'll personally take him out behind the livery barn and tan his hide with a snake whip. We'll get to the truth of it right quick."

"Now you're talking crazy, Dahl," said Carl.

Asa Dahl ignored him and turned to Selectman Collins. "Are you ready to go get Billy Odle and tell that Ranger who's in charge here?"

Selectman Collins looked unsure of himself, but only for a second. He reached into his pocket, pulled out a sheriff's badge and pinned it to his vest. "As a selectman, I have a right to assume the duties of sheriff." Then he took a deep breath, smoothed the front of his vest down and said, "All right, let's go get it done."

Asa Dahl lagged behind as the group of men left the saloon and advanced on the doctor's office across the street. In the open doorway of the livery barn, Red Booker stood kicking snow from his boots. When he saw the townsmen, he called over his shoulder to Colonel Fuller, "Here they come, Colonel, just like you said they would."

"Splendid," the colonel grinned. He stepped in beside Booker with a long cigar between his lips. He puffed a few times as the townsmen gathered in a tight group in the street outside the doctor's office. "Now we stand back and let the law take its course. Once the town has that boy in custody, I'll make him sing a different tune."

Chapter 14

Sam and Billy Odle stepped out of the doctor's office onto the boardwalk, only to be met by the group of townsmen in a half circle in the street. Before Sam could say a word, Selectman Collins stepped forward and called out his name. "Ranger Burrack. I want that boy, and I want him right now. I have reason to believe he stole some horses."

"Easy, Collins," Sam cautioned. He took his time looking back and forth across the hardened faces in the crowd. "The fact is, I was just on my way, bringing him to you. He wants to explain—"

"Then I'm saving you the trouble, Ranger," Collins said in a clipped tone, not letting Sam finish. "Hand him over."

Sam finished scanning the crowd, the shoveled street, the piles of snow along the boardwalk. Then he said in a calm voice, "I don't like your attitude or your tone, Collins." His eyes met Collins's. "Be careful we don't lock horns here."

"In case you haven't noticed, Ranger," Collins said, trying not to wither in the Ranger's harsh glare, "I'm wearing a sheriff's badge." His fingers tapped the badge on his chest.

"Believe me, Collins," said Sam, "I saw that badge the first thing when you called out my name." He took a step forward from Billy Odle and added, "There's more to wearing it than just pinning it on and keeping it shined. I hope you haven't let somebody talk you into doing something foolish."

Collins stood rigid. "As the town council's selectman, it's my right, my *duty*, to fill the position of sheriff until such time as we appoint someone through the appropriate procedure." As Collins spoke, Colonel Fuller and his men left the livery barn and drifted in slowly behind the townsmen. Sam took note of this out of the corner of his eye.

"I've already questioned young Billy about those horses," said Sam. "Apparently, Willie John stole those horses while he was holding Billy captive."

Billy Odle was surprised to hear Sam say such a thing. Only moments ago he'd come clean and confessed what had happened to the Ranger. Now the Ranger was lying, changing the story around to save him. Billy couldn't believe his ears.

"Nice try, Ranger," said Colonel Fuller, shoving his way to the front of the crowd beside Collins, "but if it's all the same with you, *Sheriff* Collins here would like to question the boy anyway. Right, Collins?"

Collins's face reddened as he stared at Fuller, not expecting Fuller to come forward and butt into town business.

"Well, Sheriff Collins," said Sam, "now that this bounty hunter is doing your talking for you, tell him I said it's not all the same with me." His eyes went from Collins to Fuller. "I'm not turning this young man over to anybody as long as I think you're still in the mix of things, Colonel. I saw what you were going to do to his ma."

"What about my ma?" Billy Odle said, taking a step forward beside the Ranger.

"Keep your mouth shut," the Ranger said in a harsh whisper, swinging a cold stare at Billy Odle. Billy shied back. Sam turned his gaze back to Collins. "This young man is in my custody. Any questioning will have to be done with me present."

"You have no jurisdiction here, Ranger!" Collins shouted.

"I heard that enough to know it by now, Collins," said Sam. "But the fact is, Billy's father is a prisoner in Yuma, Arizona. That makes Billy here a ward of the territory until his pa's released."

"What the hell are you talking about?" Colonel Fuller raged.

"It's federal law," Sam said with a slight shrug. "Go look it up if you don't believe me."

"Collins," said Fuller, "that's nothing but a sack full of pure bullshit!" He pointed a finger at Sam as he spoke to the townsmen. "This Ranger is making a mockery of the law, and he's treating all of you like a bunch of idiots to boot!"

"No," said Carl the blacksmith, stepping around from the edge of the townsmen. "The Ranger's telling the truth. I've heard of that law myself."

"You're a damn liar!" shouted Colonel Fuller. He stepped toward Carl Yates, then stopped short when Ronald Andrews swung the sawed-off shotgun up off the crook of his arm and cocked it toward him.

"Don't call my boss a liar," Ronald warned. "Now back off before I chop one off at the knee for you. I've had enough of your guff to last me the winter."

Fuller looked to Red Booker and his men for support. Red Booker gave him a nod, yet Fuller knew that having his whole force present wouldn't help him one bit once the hammer fell on the ten-gauge. "All right, blacksmith, I'm stepping back, see?" He took a slow step back, then let out a tense breath and said to Collins, "Sheriff, you're well within your right to take that boy to jail."

"I know." Collins bit his lip in deep consideration, seeing the way the Ranger had let his right hand fall back near his pistol butt. Whether there was such a law or not really didn't make any difference. The Ranger was just letting him know that the boy wasn't going to be taken from him. "I'm not an attorney, Ranger," said Collins, "and I'm not all that familiar with federal law. But I do want to know what went on out there with Renfro's horses. I've got a right to question Billy Odle."

"Indeed you do, Collins," said Sam, "and I'll be right there watching just in case I can help."

"He doesn't need you there, Ranger," said Colonel Fuller. "If he needs help, I'll help him."

Collins shot Fuller a hard look. "It's time you butt out, Fuller. Nobody asked for your two cents."

Fuller fell silent under Collins's stare.

"Ranger," said Collins, "I'll question this boy when I think it's time to question him." He looked a bit embarrassed. "My main concern now is whether Old Man Renfro is dead or alive." He looked around at the men in the street.

"If it'll help Billy here," said Ronald Andrews, "I'll ride out and take a look around at Renfro's place."

"We both will," said Carl Yates. He turned to Sam. "And don't worry, Ranger, we'll give everybody a fair shuffle." He passed a look of disdain to Colonel Fuller, then returned his gaze to the Ranger.

"Much obliged, blacksmith," said Sam. "It's time somebody in this town came forward to help one of their own." He stared at Fuller, then back at Collins. "Billy and I will be at the jail if anybody wants us."

"Carl and me will escort you there before we leave," said Ronald Andrews, the shotgun still over the crook of his arm. "Just to make sure everything's jake."

"Thanks," Sam nodded. He reached around and took Billy Odle by his cuffed wrists and said, "Come on, Billy, don't be afraid; I'm right beside you." From the swollen gray sky, fresh snow began to fall.

Making their way through the parted crowd toward the jail, Billy Odle stuck close to the Ranger's side, feeling pressed by the looks of hatred and anger on the hard faces surrounding them. On the boardwalk outside the jail, Billy asked in a lowered voice, "What about my ma, Ranger? Is she really doing all right?"

"She's at the hotel, Billy," said Sam, swinging the door open and stepping inside the plank and stone jailhouse. "The women from the saloon are taking turns looking after her." He looked all around for Kirby Bell, but Bell wasn't there.

Inside the jail, Billy turned and faced the Ranger, Ronald Andrews and Carl Yates. "Can I see her?" Billy asked.

"Not yet, Billy," replied Sam. "We've got to let this town settle down some. It might not look it, but the least little thing right now could send these men into a hanging frenzy." He looked past Billy Odle and saw Bootlip Thomas through the bars of one of the cells along the wall. "Nobody wants that to happen, do they, Bootlip?"

Bootlip stood clinging to the bars, blood-stained bandages wrapped around him from the waist up.

His voice wheezed as he said, "Nobody I can think of."

"Where's Bell?" Sam asked Bootlip.

"He went to bring back some grub," said Bootlip. "Now that I'm mending I could eat a quarter of beef just while I'm waiting on supper. Are you the same way after getting shot, Ranger?"

Sam didn't respond to Bootlip. Instead he nudged Billy Odle toward an empty cell. "For the time being we're going to have to keep you in here, Billy."

"Huh-uh!" Billy hesitated, getting excited, planting his feet firmly on the floor. "I want to see my ma and make sure she's all right!"

Sam knew that what he heard was just Billy's way of calling out for his mama the way any scared child might do. "Sorry, Billy, not right now." He gave an extra nudge, sending Billy though the open cell door before the boy had a chance to get any more frightened by the looming iron bars or the black slices of darkness lurking in the corners of the cell. Sam closed the iron door and locked it. Billy stood with the terrified look of a trapped animal.

"Step over here, Billy," said Sam. "Let me take the cuffs off."

With his head bowed, Billy held his wrists forward to the bars, allowing Sam to reach through and remove the cuffs.

"Don't worry, Billy," Ronald Andrews offered, seeing the look on the boy's face. "I'll go look in on your ma, tell her you're here and—"

"You stay away from her!" Billy warned, throwing himself forward, grasping the iron bars with both hands. "You've looked in on my ma for the last time!"

"That ain't the way I mean, Billy." Ronald Andrews's face reddened in embarrassment.

"Easy, Billy," said Carl. "Ronald just wants to help."

Sam watched in silence.

"He wants to help?" Billy shouted through the bars. "I've seen how Ronald wants to help my ma!"

"Billy, I'm sorry," said Ronald Andrews, sounding ashamed. But Billy Odle didn't seem to hear him.

"Did you think I was blind, or stupid?" Billy raged. "Or did you think it was all just fine with me . . . seeing all you drunken bastards come and go in the night? Did you think it was all forgotten the next day? That the few dollars you left behind made up for everything?" As he shouted and sobbed, he began banging his forehead on the bars until the Ranger stepped forward, reached through the bars and stopped him.

"Billy! Stop it!" ordered Sam. "What's done is done. Get a grip on yourself." He turned to Ronald Andrews and Carl Yates. "Maybe it's best you two get going. I'll take care of everything here."

"Yeah, you're right," said Ronald Andrews, avoiding the Ranger's eyes.

"Don't worry, though, Ranger," said Carl, "anything we learn out there, we'll bring to you first . . . make sure you decide how to tell the town about it."

"Much obliged," said Sam. He watched them turn and walk through the door. As soon as they closed the door behind themselves, he said to Billy Odle, "Settle yourself down, young man. I don't know what's gone on here in the past, but those men are doing the best they can to help you out."

"I don't want their help," Billy said, his red-rimmed eyes still welling with tears. "They're not friends of mine or my ma or pa. All they wanted was what they could get, once my pa was hauled off to jail."

Sam didn't know what to say. He stood and listened and let the boy get it off his chest.

"Willie John is the only friend I've got. He's the only one who ever helped me and ma without wanting something in return. That's why I helped him . . . that's why I'd do it all again if I had the chance." As he spoke, he reached into the pockets of his outgrown trousers, took out the twenty-dollar gold piece Willie John had given him and held it up for the Ranger to see. "There, see that? That's twenty dollars Willie John gave me, said give ten of it to my ma and tell her 'no strings attached.' " He jutted his chin as he flipped the coin, snatched it out of the air and pocketed it.

Sam shook his head slowly. "Billy, I don't know why folks mistreat one another the way they do sometime. I see what happened to you and your ma, and I wish to God things had gone different for you. But no matter what brought you to where you are, you're here now and things have to be made right. You're wrong about Willie John being the only friend you've got. There's people in this town who care about you and your ma."

"Then they've had a strange way of showing it," Billy said, his voice lowered to a murmur as he plopped down on the wooden cot on the back wall of the cell and rubbed his freed wrists. Sam turned away and walked to the front window where he stood looking out at the group of men as they slowly broke away from one another and walked off in different directions through the falling snow.

"I find that most people want to do the right thing,

Billy," Sam said over his shoulder. "Sometimes it just takes a little prodding to get them started in the right direction."

"Not here," Billy Odle said. "This town is full of nothing but rotten no-good sonsabitches. I wish the Ganston Gang had shot it to the ground."

Bootlip Thomas let out a low wheezing laugh, then coughed against the back of his hand and said, "Boy, this town is no different from the next. They're all the same when you're looking up at them from the bottom. I found that out when I was no more than a pup like you. That's what made it easy for me to do the things I done."

"Quiet down, Bootlip," Sam said without turning from the window. "This young man already has a bad enough attitude. We don't need you making it worse."

"This here's the one what cut out with Willie John, eh?" said Bootlip, trying to look sidelong through his bars over at Billy.

"Yep, he's the one," said Sam. "Tells me him and Willie John are good friends."

"Good friends with that wild Indian outlaw?" Bootlip shook his head. "I've known Willie John longer than I wanted to. If he's ever befriended anybody, I never saw it."

"Maybe you don't know everything," Billy shot back, as he rushed up to the bars.

When Bootlip Thomas fell silent, Sam turned from the window and looked at Billy Odle. "Easy, kid. Bootlip here might not be the best example for a young man to follow, but when it comes to knowing outlaws he could write the book on it."

Billy stepped back from the bars and slumped once again on the edge of the cot. "I didn't mean anything by it, Mr. Bootlip," he said. "We're both in the same fix here. I guess we ought to stick together."

"Stick together? Ha!" Bootlip Thomas and Sam Burrack passed one another a glance, then Bootlip said, "Son, we ain't in the same fix here at all . . . I figure I'm good for a hanging, soon as I get well enough to die and Fuller can talk the townsmen into lending him a rope." He grinned. "But you're just a boy. All you got to do is act sorry, tell them whatever you can make up about the Injun, and you're back out there busting windows with a slingshot before suppertime."

"I ain't telling nothing about Willie John," said Billy.

"Then you're plumb *loco*," Bootlip wheezed. "Part of knowing this business is knowing when and who to trade off for yourself, if you're lucky enough to get the chance. If Willie John was around when those horses were stolen, I can tell you, straight up, that old man is dead. Willie never liked to leave somebody fanning his trail."

Sam looked back and forth between the two cells. Noticing that Billy Odle seemed to be paying attention to Bootlip Thomas, Sam offered in a quiet tone, "I'm not asking him anything about the Indian, Bootlip. Besides, he might not be so lucky, not if Fuller and a couple of the town leaders get their way."

"What?" Bootlip Thomas gave the Ranger a surprised look. "You don't think they'd try hang him do you . . . him being just a lad and all?"

"Who knows what they'll try?" said Sam. "The whole town's been milling like cattle before a storm. If anybody ever steps forward and takes control, there's no telling where he could lead them."

"I know," said Bootlip. "I've seen it a hundred times. Let the weather set in hard, least little thing, a town turns into a powder keg—all it needs now is something to light the fuse."

"I know," said Sam, running faces through his mind—Meigs, Colonel Fuller, Asa Dahl, Selectman Collins. He considered each man in turn.

"You best hope it ain't that Colonel Fuller that takes charge," Bootlip said, as if sharing the Ranger's inner thoughts. He jerked his head sidelong toward Billy's cell. "Fuller would just as soon hang a young boy as look at him. It wouldn't be the first time, either."

Sam saw the look of fear sweep over Billy Odle's face at the sound of Bootlip's words. "Don't worry, I won't allow it, Billy," Sam said. "I give you my word on it." He looked back out through the window at the falling snow, and saw Kirby Bell come toward the jail with a covered basket of food. "Looks like this snow is going to get worse before it gets better," he said to the quickly frosting windowpane.

PART 3

Chapter 15

Throughout his first day traveling, the snow had fallen thick and steadily. Before slaughtering the mule, Willie John had waited until he was two miles up the switchback trails into the shelter of the hills. Tethering his horse, he led the hapless mule a few yards off the swollen snow-covered trail into a narrow crevice. He'd killed the mule slowly by bleeding it out, as much to keep it quiet as to create for himself as little activity as possible. Had the mule felt the sharp pain of death and struggled against it, Willie knew he could not have held it still. So, he'd taken his knife and slit a long artery high up in the mule's shoulder and watched its blood spill into a hoof-deep puddle of red slush. As the mule sank to its knees, Willie sat back and drank two tin cups of its steaming blood, to both warm and sustain himself. When the animal had rolled over onto its side and its breathing slowed to a halt, Willie John moved in with his knife and began his task.

Willie knew he needed to find a place to rest in order to regain his strength. But rest was still a long time coming. In his fevered condition and still weak from his wounds, it took him longer than it should have to butcher the mule. But by nightfall he had cleaved off nearly fifty pounds of red flesh and cold-packed it by covering it in a thin layer of snow and wrapping it in a ragged blanket. It was past midnight when the snow stopped. He found shelter beneath the skeletal remains of some tangled cedars whose roots had loosened their grip on the shallow soil and had toppled over in such a manner as to form a natural lean-to across the narrow trail. Beneath this snow-laden canopy, Willie made a cold camp for himself and ate the raw mule meat. He slept wrapped in his coat and a thin blanket; at the first trace of silver sunlight beneath the dome of the earth, he stood up shivering beyond his control, mounted his horse, and rode on.

The second day he spent in the saddle, stopping only long enough to relieve himself and check on his wounds. By late afternoon Willie John rode slumped forward in his saddle, being led by the horse. Only when the horse came to a halt and had stood still for a few minutes did Willie John stir from his half-conscious stupor and look around in the gray shadows of evening. The trail he was on had ended at a boarded-up mine shaft.

Willie stepped down from his saddle, kicked away snow and empty tins and whiskey bottles until he could get both hands around the edges of brittle pine boards and yank them free. When he'd ripped an opening large enough for him and the horse, he turned gasping for breath, feeling a trickle of fresh blood begin to seep down his side. "We're . . . home," he rasped wryly, in the direction of the tired animal. Within minutes he'd cleared a circle on the dirt floor inside the mine entrance and tied the horse to a timber. He gathered broken boards and kindling and soon had a fire licking upward. He slept the sleep of the dead.

Most of the next day he spent lying huddled close to the fire inside the timber-framed entrance to the mine shaft, the only place large enough for both himself and the horse. What little time he was awake he spent attending to his wounds and eating roasted mule meat from the end of his knife blade. In the afternoon Willie led the horse outside to a nearby hitching post, then dragged more wood back into the mine. He boiled water in a discarded metal bucket he found and bathed himself. He fed the fire until waves of heat shimmered off of the rock walls around him. Then he sat sweating with a blanket wrapped around himself for over an hour until the heat became unbearable an his own sweat felt scorching hot against his flesh.

By nightfall, Willie John could feel himself growing stronger. With his strength returning, his mind cleared. He thought about Hubbler Wells and realized that he had to go back there. He thought about Billy Odle and shook his head. He told himself that Billy Odle had nothing to do with his reason for going back . . . or did he? *Cut it out!* He chastised himself for even thinking that way. This was business, nothing more. With the fire lowered and a hot cup of mule broth in his hands, Willie sat near the fire with his head bowed. *That dumb kid . . .*

He relaxed and drifted in the silence and the crackling fire. Then, like a creature of the wilds whose seclusion was about to be encroached upon, he lifted his dark eyes and directed his senses toward the cold white world beyond the mine's entrance. A presence was out there now, someone moving ever closer along the trail. There was no sound, but there didn't need to be. In place of sound there was premonition. A presence loomed somewhere just beyond the outer circle of sound, and when it finally moved into hearing range, the faint neighing of a horse came as no surprise, but rather as an affirmation.

In his mind's eye, Willie saw tired horses struggle upward through the thick, heavy snow, just off the trail on a dangerous rocky slope. They were lost, whoever they were, Willie John thought. He stood up and walked to the front of the mine entrance, and stared through the moonlight along the trail until a faint waft of steam from a blowing nostril billowed up and drifted on the air. Then he slipped out silently and circled wide of the trail and down the sloping hillside.

At the upper edge of the trail, forty feet from the mine entrance, Texas Bob Mackay pulled his horse forward by its reins, then turned and said down to the others in a lowered voice, "Come on, boys, it ain't that much farther."

He stood waiting, catching his breath until the other three topped the edge on foot, leading their tired horses. "Lord have mercy! That was a hell of a climb," said Morgan Aglo, the first man to step beside Texas Bob. "I thought you said you knew this country. If I'd figured you'd get us lost, I'd never let you throw in with us."

"Keep your voice down, Morgan," Texas Bob said. "You were lost when I ran into you." He nodded toward the glow of firelight flickering beyond the mine entrance. "There's a warm fire just ahead. If it's not Willie John's, we might just have to kill somebody to get to it."

Morgan looked toward the licking flames coming from the mine-shaft entrance. He took Bob's warning and replied in a gruff whisper, "Hell, whatever it takes." As he spoke he drew a pistol from his waist. Two more men led their horses up over the edge of the trail. They looked at the pistol in Morgan Aglo's hand, then at one another. The thinner of the two, Joe Shine, said to Aglo in a loud panting voice, "If you're holding that pistol on me I wish to hell you'd go ahead and shoot . . . I'm too tried and cold to care."

"Shine, shut up, damn it!" Morgan Aglo hissed. "You're louder than an army bugle!"

"Why all the whispering?" asked Joe Shine, his blaring voice unchanged.

"Jesus . . ." Texas Bob shook his head in disgust and pulled his horse away from the others.

"You'll know why when you go grabbing at a bullet in your belly," Morgan Aglo said to Joe Shine. "Texas Bob says that might be Willie John's fire . . . that Injun's liable to commence shooting, not knowing it's us."

"He might start shooting even if he knows it *is*," said Tack Beechum, the fourth man, moving his horse back a step as if in wary anticipation. "He's one bad Injun, as I recall."

Morgan Aglo scoffed. "He ain't that bad, and he ain't all Injun. There's a good deal of backwater Louisiana, bale-tottin' Negro in him if you ask me."

"He never looked like it to me," said Beechum.

"How do you know who's part Negro and who ain't?" said Morgan Aglo. He grinned. "Someday we'll shake the branches of your family tree, see what falls out scratching its belly."

"That ain't no way to talk to me," said Beechum.

Morgan Aglo ignored him, jerked his horse forward, saying over his shoulder, "Come on, boys, if it's Willie John and he gives us any sass, I'll shake him by his neck like a little black rag doll."

Tack Beechum looked dubious as Joe Shine led his horse past him and fell in behind Morgan Aglo. Shine snickered. "He ain't kidding, either, he'll do it. Injuns, Negroes, hell he don't care. He never liked nothing but his own kind . . . and I'm just like him."

"What do you think?" Tack asked Texas Bob.

Texas Bob stooped down and raised his horse's left front hoof, as if to check it. He brushed snow from the hoof, saying to Tack Beechum, "Do what suits you . . . I'll be along in a minute."

Beechum looked all around in the moonlight then ventured forward, hiking his coat collar up against the chill of night. Texas Bob waited until the others were almost at the entrance of the mine before leading his horse along behind them, his hand resting on the pistol at his hip. From beneath the edge of the trail where Willie John lay listening in the snow, he raised himself up and watched until Texas Bob had covered half the distance to the mine entrance. By then, Morgan Aglo, Joe Shine and Beechum had already crept inside. Willie John could see their dark figures move back and forth in the firelight.

Inside the mine entrance, in the twelve by fifteen feet of dry warm space, the intruders looked around, seeing the horse, the scraps of meat, the tin cup on a stone beside the crackling fire. Against the back wall, the horse watched them nervously and scraped a hoof in the dirt. "By God!" said Morgan Aglo. "Looks like whoever lives here must've stepped out for the evening." He stepped sideways around the small area, his pistol still in his hand. Shine and Beechum circled in the other direction. Morgan Aglo raised his voice as if speaking to the air around him,

"Where oh where would you go on a cold night like this?" He laughed at the way Joe Shine and Tack Beechum looked at him.

"Don't you see?" said Aglo, "Somebody heard us coming and slipped out of here. Left us all the comforts of home."

"Without their horse?" Beechum cut in. "I doubt it." He lifted his pistol and cocked it, taking on a wary expression, his face looking lined and frightened in the flickering firelight. "Let's get back out of here, see what's going on.

"Damn it, Beechum," Morgan Aglo chuckled, "you're getting as fretful as that ole Arkansan wife of mine. Whoever's out there will either leave or make themselves known." He continued by raising his voice and calling toward the outside of the mine entrance, "Ain't that right, pilgrim?"

There was a moment of silence, then Willie John's voice said from just beyond the front opening, "Aglo, you old snake." Texas Bob came through the door without his pistol in his holster, Willie John shoving him from behind. "You were supposed to meet us on the way to Hubbler Wells over a week ago," Willie John continued, stepping in behind Texas Bob. "What happened, did you get lost again?"

"I've never been lost," said Aglo, looking embarrassed. "But I have been misdirected on occasion." He shot Joe Shine a cold stare, then looked back at Willie John. "Where was you just now? Breathing right down our shirts?"

"Yep, just about," said Willie, stepping in close to the fire, reaching down and picking up a piece of cooked mule meat.

"Then I reckon you heard some things said?" Aglo gave a sheepish expression.

"Nothing I hadn't heard before," said Willie John, holding no grudge over what he'd heard these men say outside while he lurked beneath the edge of the trail. He'd already decided he could use Morgan Aglo and these others for his trip back to Hubbler Wells. Uncocking the pistol in his hand, Willie pitched it to Texas Bob, saying, "This hammer feels a little stiff, mister. You might want to check it."

"Much obliged," said Texas Bob humbly as he looked at his pistol, then put it in his holster.

Willie John seated himself near the fire and crossed his legs. Aglo and the others waited for an invitation, but when none came, they shrugged at one another and sat down anyway as Willie handed Morgan Aglo his knife, butt first. "What are we having here? Buffalo? Elk? New England pheasant?" Aglo asked as he carved a piece of meat, stabbed it and held it over the fire.

"Yep," said Willie John, without sharing in Morgan Aglo's humor, "nothing but the best for my *amigos.*"

"Sounds like you was expecting us," said Aglo.

"I'm always expecting somebody," Willie John replied.

The other three brought out knives of their own and went to work carving out portions of the red meat for themselves. Beechum held up his piece of meat and examined it. "This don't look like elk or buff either one to me," he murmured.

"Then look at it from a different direction," Joe Shine snickered. "Use your imagination."

"No offense, Willie John," said Aglo, "but you sure enough look like hell."

"I've had a rough week," said Willie. Then he

added as he passed a glance at the faces around the short licking flames, "But I'm feeling fine now."

"Yeah, I heard how things went wrong at Hubbler Wells," said Aglo. "I just wish I'd been there . . . maybe things would've gone different. I've always been a real red-balled wolf when it comes to a shooting scrape."

"How'd you hear about it?" Willie asked.

Morgan Aglo pulled the knife blade back from the fire, blew on the sizzling meat, touched his tongue to it, then blew on it again. He jerked his head toward Texas Bob. "He was there." Aglo grinned, tore off a bite of meat with his teeth and chewed as he watched Willie John look Texas Bob up and down. "This here's Texas Bob Mackay," said Aglo, getting a chuckle out of it for some reason. "He used to ride with us, then he dropped out of sight for a while."

"I've heard his name," said Willie. "What were you doing there, Texas Bob?"

"I was one of—"

"He was with that *killing* posse," Aglo blurted out, laughing, chewing, shaking his head at the same time. "The ones shooting the hell out'n you and the gang!"

Willie John's nostrils flared a bit, enough that Texas Bob raised a hand in a show of peace and said quickly, "But I never shot you Willie . . . I swear I never! I rode up with that posse because I needed a stake to get me here. I've been two years drunk and drying out—hell, my hands shook so bad I couldn't piss without abusing myself. Fuller's posse was my only chance at catching up to everybody, getting back to work. I never would have done it if I hadn't needed money something awful, that's the truth, so help me God. It broke my heart seeing ole Nian the Swede get shot to pieces, me not able to do a thing about it. I even said a little prayer that you made it out of there safe. And now seeing you did, it's enough to make me want to praise the Lord."

Willie looked him up and down again. "Two years, huh?"

"Yep, two years give or take. But I'm on the mend now," said Texas Bob. "Hope there's no hard feelings."

Willie John shrugged stiffly, his shoulder wound still troubling him. "No, I reckon not. A man needs a stake, he has to get it where he can."

Texas Bob relaxed and held his meat back into the fire. "The main thing is I'm back where I belong," he said.

"Yeah," Willie said in a wry tone, "that's the main thing, Texas Bob."

"If you don't mind telling me," said Bob, "how'd that whore's boy get you out of town and do such a good job of hiding you?"

Willie offered a weak smile. "A stroke of luck. That boy saved my life. Talk about something strange, that's the second time. The first time was when he and his pa found me shot all to pieces."

"I always said, getting shot is the worst part of this robbing business," Morgan Aglo said, smiling. "You sure have caught your share of bullets lately, Willie."

"Yeah, I know." Willie fell quiet for a moment, staring into the fire in contemplation. "I'm wondering if maybe it ain't time I hang it up."

"Hang it up?" Morgan Aglo looked astonished. "You can't quit now, Willie. I was just getting ready to ask you if you wanted to hit that bank with us. I figure they won't be expecting nothing right now."

This was just what Willie had wanted to hear, but he wanted to sound hesitant. "I don't believe so, Morgan. I've been doing some serious thinking. That kid helping me and all. I figure it might be a sign."

"A sign? I never thought you was the kind of Injun to believe in signs," said Aglo.

Willie nodded in consideration. "Well, even so, maybe it's time I cash my chips and call it a game."

"I need you awfully bad, Willie," said Morgan. "Same deal as you got with Earl and Hopper—go in and scout things out. Of course you'd have to be careful now not to get recognized. What do you say?"

"I already told you, Morgan." Willie John stared at him. "Count me out. I'm heading on down to Old Mex. If you run across Earl and Hopper, tell 'em I said *adios*."

"Hell, you don't mean it, Willie," said Aglo. "I know you're good at squirreling away money, but damn, you don't have that much hidden away that you can afford to quit, do you?"

Willie knew better than to mention how much money he might have stashed to the likes of these so-called friends of his.

"Right now I don't have any money at all," Willie said, seeing a sharpness fade into disappointment in Morgan Aglo's eyes. "But like they say, money ain't everything." He gestured a hand at his bandaged wounds and gave a weak smile. "I've got my health."

Dark, low laughter drifted across the men as they ate the sizzling mule meat from their knife blades. After a moment Willie asked Texas Bob, "So, how's the kid doing? Did they give him a hard time?"

Texas Bob Mackay had already left Fuller and his

men before Billy Odle had returned to Hubbler Wells, but Willie John had no way of knowing that. Texas Bob considered his words before he answered, shooting a gaze at Morgan Aglo for some sort of direction. Then he lied, saying, "When I left it looked like they was getting ready to hang him. They will, too, if Fuller gets his way—and he most always does." He watched Willie John's expression turn grim as the Indian stared into the fire without facing him.

"That poor dumb kid," Willie whispered to the licking flames.

Morgan Aglo leaned in grinning near Willie John. "Wanted to be an outlaw, did he? I've seen them kind. Best thing you can do is forget him. You got away, that's all you needed him for. I always said, use people so long as it suits you, then drop them quicker than a hot pot handle." He laughed and slapped his leg, the others joining him.

Willie John looked at each of their faces in turn, fingers of flame dancing in their eyes and across their faces, turning them into laughing demons. Men without souls or purpose, he thought, and his insides suddenly felt cold and ill knowing he was one of them.

"Maybe I will ride in with you after all, Morgan," Willie John said.

"Wait a minute, Willie," Morgan Aglo replied. "If you go along with us, I want you going for the right reasons . . . I want all your attention when we hit that bank. I don't want you riding in there because you got some foolish notion about helping some knot-headed kid."

"Never mind my reason, Aglo," said Willie John.

"I said I'd go. Let's say I just remembered something I left there. I'm ready to go get it."

"Yeah, and what was that?" Morgan Aglo asked, giving him a distrusting look.

"My horse," Willie smiled thinly. "I always was partial to that dapple-gray." Yes, he was going back to Hubbler Wells. But there was no question he needed the others' help. He couldn't risk it alone in his current condition. He thought about Billy Odle and shook his head, reminding himself once again that this had nothing to do with the kid . . . nothing at all.

Chapter 16

"Is that you, Billy?" Hattie Odle asked, rubbing her sleepy eyes as she raised up against the pillow behind her back. She looked at her son, then looked at the Ranger. Then she turned her head away in embarrassment as she said to Billy, "You had us all worried to death, Billy. I don't know what I'm going to do with you." There was a lack of conviction in her voice, as if she felt she had no right to ask anything from her son.

"I'm sorry, Ma," Billy said. "The Ranger here has been helping me understand some things . . . told me how you using that black tar is like an illness that won't heal. I know it ain't made things any better, me running off. I'll be around here now, though, to help you get well."

"Good, Billy," she whispered, her pale hand grasping his wrist and drawing his hand to her cheek.

"Try not to worry, ma'am," said the Ranger. "I'm keeping him in custody for his own good until this weather breaks, and folks settle down a little."

Beside Sam, Tinnie Malone stood supporting herself on a hickory cane. Her face was drawn and she stood stiffly in place, her wounded chest tender and mending slowly. "They found Old Man Renfro," she said quietly and solemnly. "The blacksmith and his helper found him dead in the snow . . . his throat cut."

Hattie let out a faint gasp, and Sam put in quickly, "But nobody is accusing Billy, ma'am. Leastwise not to our faces. The way the blacksmith talks, it took a grown-up to commit this kind of an act." He nodded toward Billy, adding, "Billy here has told me what happened. He's got nothing to worry about."

"Thank you, Ranger," Hattie Odle whispered, her eyes shiny with tears.

"Tinnie and I will step outside," Sam said quietly. "Give you two a couple of minutes alone." He glanced at the second-floor window, where sunlight reached through and striped the floor. He thought about the deep snow engulfing the town as it had for the past three days. Then he said to Billy Odle, "I'll be right outside the door, young man. Just make sure you leave the same way you got here."

"I will, Ranger Burrack," said Billy. "You needn't worry about me. I've learned my lesson."

Tinnie stepped in and said to Hattie Odle, "Don't take long Hattie. You still need your rest."

"Look who's talking." Hattie offered a faint, tired smile.

The Ranger and Tinnie Malone left the room and stood outside the door in the narrow hallway. "He doesn't mean a word of it, does he?" Tinnie whispered, nodding toward the door to Hattie's room.

"Probably not," said Sam, "but with a kid like Billy you have to give them the benefit of a doubt. All we can do is hope he's got enough sense to see we're all trying to help him." Sam looked her up and down, seeing how hard she was trying to mask her pain, but all the same seeing it was obvious in her eyes. "You need to get off your feet, Tinnie; you look bad."

"Thanks a lot," Tinnie replied.

Sam smiled. "You know what I mean. You need to stay down and rest, let that wound heal up some."

"Like you did?" she said in playful defiance.

"That's different," said Sam, "I have too much to do. Besides, I'll rest when this town is back to normal . . . and when I finish with the Indian."

"Don't you figure he's long gone by now, Sam?" said Tinnie, standing close to him. "Don't you think he used this weather to his advantage and cut down to Mexico?"

"No, he's still here," said Sam. "I can feel it. He's got unfinished business here of some kind. He'll be back."

"Unfinished business? You mean with Billy? The bank?"

"I don't know," said Sam, "but he does. And wherever he's at, he can feel me here waiting for him."

Tinnie stood in silence for a moment, then said, "And that's the real reason you haven't rode out looking for him. It's not the weather . . . it's not because you're worried about what the townsmen will do to Billy once you leave. It's because you think he'll be coming back here for some reason."

Sam glanced at the door to Hattie's room. Hearing a floorboard creak on the other side of the door, he said to Tinnie in a hushed tone, "Keep your voice down. It's best that Billy not hear any of this."

The door opened slowly and Billy Odle stepped into the hallway. "Thanks for bringing me here,

Ranger Burrack," he said. "How much longer are you going to have to be with me everywhere I go?"

Sam smiled. "Are you already tired of my company, young man?"

"No, Ranger Burrack, it's not that," said Billy.

Sam cut him off before he could say anything more. "Let's go, Billy. Maybe Carl and Ronald have some hot grub from the restaurant."

As the three descended the stairs to the hotel's small lobby, one of Fuller's men looked up from the counter where he stood, the neck of a whiskey bottle sticking up from his coat pocket. He looked at Billy with a cold, bloodshot leer and said, "Here comes that killing little devil right now." He took a drunken step toward Billy Odle, a rifle clutched in his right hand.

"Back off, mister!" Sam Burrack warned, stepping around from behind Billy Odle and blocking the man from coming any closer.

The man took note of the Ranger's hand resting on the butt of his big Colt. He relented and stepped to the side but couldn't resist saying, "Yeah, that's it, protect that little snake while you can, Ranger . . . it ain't going to last much longer! This town will soon tire of being run by kids and whores! Then you'll be answering to us!"

Sam kept his eyes on him until Tinnie and Billy Odle were out the door. Then Sam closed the door and stalked over to the man, taking his hand off his pistol butt just to prod the man into making a move. "Now why'd you say such a thing as that to my lady friend?" Sam asked, seeing the tip of the rifle come up toward him.

"You son of a—!"

The man's words stopped short as Sam snatched the rifle by the front stock and swung the barrel upward, cracking him in his forehead, then jerking the rifle from his hands. "Better let me keep this for a while before your shoot your foot off," Sam said. The man collapsed against the stair banister and slid to the floor, a long red welt popping up between his eyes and his hairline. He tried to speak but could only mouth the words, gasping like a fish out of water.

"You can thank me later," said Sam. "Right now you need to get a handful of snow against that forehead."

Once outside, Sam stepped over to where Tinnie and Billy Odle stood waiting for him. Sam noted that townsmen on the boardwalk across the street were eying Billy Odle. At the front of the townsmen stood Asa Dahl with his thumbs hooked in his vest behind the open lapels of his heavy winter coat. A black cigar tipped upward between his teeth.

"You've acquired yourself a new rifle, I see," Tinnie said to Sam, leaning on the hickory cane for support.

"Yep," Sam replied. Looking over toward the townsmen as he spoke, he raised his voice for their benefit and said, "There's no need in letting this thing get out of control. This young man is innocent. Now whatever you're thinking . . . put it out of your heads before this thing turns ugly."

On the opposite boardwalk, Asa Dahl and the men watched Sam, Tinnie and Billy Odle walk away toward the jail. To the men behind him, Asa Dahl said, "Don't worry, that Ranger can't stay forever. Once he's out of here we'll take care of everything ourselves."

"What about Selectman Collins?" asked one of the men. "He's the one supposed to be the law here, temporarily at least."

"Yeah . . . well, if he's with us, fine. If he's not, we'll still see to it that whore and her kid are run out of here."

Massey, the old mule skinner, said to Asa Dahl with a drunken laugh, "Damn, Asa, I never seen you so sour on anybody. What did that woman ever do to you, anyway?"

"She's a stupid whore and she plain offends me," said Asa Dahl. "I hate her something awful."

"But you run whores, Asa," said Massey. "What's so different about her?" He pointed across the street at Tinnie walking along with Billy Odle and the ranger. "Look, Tinnie's one of your girls, and she's *helping* Hattie."

"Tinnie's a fool! She's on her own from now on," said Asa Dahl. "As soon as she shows up at the saloon, she's fired!" Rage turned Asa Dahl's face beet red. Veins stood out on his forehead.

"Lord, Asa! I've never seen you in such a shape! What the hell's wrong with you?" Massey's eyes widened, looking at Asa Dahl.

"I don't know!" Asa Dahl snapped. "What the hell's it matter to you? A person doesn't always need a reason to hate somebody! Look at her. She's a lousy whore, her husband's a lousy convict, her son's a . . . a . . ." He hesitated, running out of words for a second. "Well, hell, you can see what he is!" He swung himself around to face Massey. "Tell you what, mule skinner . . . if you don't think like the rest of us, maybe you're not a part of us! Maybe you better keep to yourself and we'll all do the same."

Ash Dahl's words seemed to have a sobering effect

on Massey, and his expression turned serious. "Now, wait, Asa . . . I was just funning mostly. You know that whatever all of you boys say goes, it always has."

"That's good to hear, Massey," said Dahl, "because we were starting to get worried about you, the way you were talking. Like maybe you didn't agree or something."

Massey swallowed and stepped back, looking up at the man beside him. "Damn, I didn't mean no harm."

"We know that Massey, so keep your mouth shut," said Pete Chaney, the town barber. He turned to Asa Dahl and said, "Where is Collins on all this? He's supposed to be our sheriff now. Seems like once the blacksmith and his helper got back and said they found Renfro with his throat cut that bad, Collins has just decided to let the matter drop . . . says the kid couldn't have been capable of doing such a thing."

"I know what he said, Pete." Asa Dahl looked around at the others. "But he said that just because the Ranger said it. I don't agree with either one of them. Collins might be the law here, but when the law doesn't do like the majority wants, it's time to do away with the law, the way I see it." He took the cigar from his mouth and lifted his chin to a proud height. "And we are the majority here! Am I right? Take away the whores, the riffraff, the ones that don't count . . . that leaves us in charge, doesn't it?"

"Damn right it does," said a voice in the crowd.

"We've been tolerant long enough!" another voice called out from the rear of the crowd.

"Too damn long!" cried a third.

On the street, walking along a shoveled path where

piles of snow stood knee-high on either side, Tinnie looked toward the sound of the angry voices, then looked back at Sam walking beside her. She had her free hand resting on his forearm for support, her other hand using the walking cane. "No offense, Sam, but are you going to be able to handle this town once the lid blows off?"

Looking straight ahead, Sam replied, "I've got to. What choice do I have?"

"What choice?" Tinnie looked perplexed with him. "You could always leave. The snow's not that bad, not yet."

"What about Billy and his ma?" Sam asked, still not facing her.

"Hattie will be all right," said Tinnie. "They will bluster and snort, but when it comes down to it, they won't harm a woman, even a whore. Asa Dahl ain't persuasive enough to pull that off. If he could, he would have already. But Billy's a different story . . . they really think he's had something to do with Old Man Renfro's death. So take him away from here."

"We'll see," said Sam.

Tinnie looked him up and down, then as if a light had come on in her head, she said in a hushed tone of disbelief, "Wait a minute, Sam." She stopped and let her hand fall from his forearm. "You're not keeping Billy around here, hoping that Indian shows up for some reason, are you?"

"No," said the Ranger, "of course not. How can you say such a thing?"

She hesitated for a second, seeming to work it out in her mind before saying, "Sam, I believe you *are*. Maybe you don't even realize it yourself. But that's what you're doing."

Sam stopped in the narrow path beside her as Billy

Odle walked on a few feet ahead. "That's crazy talk, Tinnie. I know exactly what I'm doing. When it comes time to go after Willie John, I'll go after him. But I won't take up the trail of an outlaw like him over the welfare of folks like Hattie and Billy. That wouldn't be serving any kind of justice." He continued walking, saying, "Come on, he's getting too far ahead of us."

Tinnie fell silent, glancing back over her shoulder at Asa Dahl and the townsmen. "Maybe you're right, Sam," she said under her breath, stepping forward quickly with the help of the cane. "I sure hope to God you are . . ."

Inside the sheriff's office, Ronald Andrews stood rolling himself a smoke, his shotgun under one arm. When Billy Odle walked in followed by Sam and Tinnie, Andrews looked first at Tinnie and touched his fingertips to his hat brim. "Ma'am," he said.

Looking around, Sam didn't see Selectman Collins or Carl Yates, and he asked Andrews about them. Bootlip Thomas stood inside his cell, clinging to the bars, watching the Ranger intently.

"Carl said he had too much work backing up on him over at the forge," Andrews told Sam, jerking his head in the direction of the blacksmith shop. "Collins and Bell left here a while ago to get some grub—hope they remember to bring some back," he spread a broad friendly grin. "So for now, I'm all you get."

"That's good enough for me," said Sam, stepping over to the empty cell and swinging the door open for Billy Odle. "In you go, young man," he said.

"I've been thinking, Ranger Burrack," said Billy. "I ain't being held on any charge . . . and everybody's having to go out of their way to accommodate me here. Why don't I just leave and slip along the alley out of sight?"

"Where to, Billy—that cold shack?" the Ranger asked. "Naw, you're staying here a little while longer, just until things settle down a bit more."

"While I was talking to my ma," Billy said, "she told me we're leaving here as soon as the weather lifts and a stage makes its way through here. So, don't worry about us, sir, we're going to be all right."

"Where'd she get the money to do that?" asked Tinnie. "She told me she was busted flat."

Ronald Andrews said in a bashful manner, "Me and Carl are chipping in, getting up enough to pay stage fare to the next stop east, over at Pembro Station."

"That's great, Billy," said Sam. "Once all that happens I'll be the first one to step back and wish you both the best. But until then, I'm your shadow . . . so get used to it."

"But I'm not your keep," Billy protested, trying not to sound like a child, his thin voice betraying him. "I'm my own man. The law doesn't make you responsible for me!"

Sam gave him a patient smile. "That depends on which laws you're talking about, Billy. I'd hate to see a time when older folks don't take responsibility for the young. That's not man's written law, Billy. That's common decency. So don't argue with me."

Billy stepped into the open cell and slumped onto the cot. Ronald Andrews picked up a cup full of steaming cocoa from the warmer on the woodstove and walked over and held it out to Billy. "Here you go, son, drink this."

Billy looked away, refusing the cup. "I'm not your

son. And don't expect me and Ma to take your charity money, either. I know about all the times you and Carl came calling.''

Ronald Andrews backed away and left the cell. He avoided the Ranger's gaze and offered the cup to Bootlip Thomas through the bars. ''Hell yes, I'll take it,'' said Bootlip. He cradled the hot cup in both hands, sipped it, then said to the Ranger, ''What's the deal on me? Is Collins going to turn me over to Fuller and his bounty dogs and let them hang me, or what?''

''You're their prisoner, Bootlip,'' said the Ranger. ''I don't think he feels like he's got any choice in the matter.''

''Damn it,'' said Bootlip, ''I know I'm as guilty as any man who ever spit in the devil's eye, and I got no right to complain, but I hate to think about my head riding out of here in a flour sack. That's nothing to show for a whole life on earth, is it?''

''No,'' said Sam, ''it's not. But you carved it out to suit yourself. I won't let Fuller and his boys mistreat you while you're here, neither will Collins, I don't reckon. But once they come for you, ready to leave town . . . it's all between you and them.''

Bootlip sighed, sipped his cocoa, and fell silent, looking down at his stockinged feet.

''Why *are* Fuller and his men still here?'' asked Andrews. ''This weather ain't all that bad headed southwest. That's the way they said they were headed.''

''I think Fuller's still here because of me,'' said Sam. ''I believe he's got me stuck in his craw. He doesn't like the idea of me taking down the Ganstons.''

''But he gets the bounty all the same,'' said Ronald Andrews.

Tinnie cut in before the Ranger could reply, saying to Andrews as she gave Sam a skeptical look, "There's more to these kind of men than just the blood money, Ronald. There's some twisted honor in the hunt . . . pride in the bloodletting. Isn't that right, Sam?"

The Ranger looked into her eyes. "When you say *'those kind of men,'* I hope you're not counting me with the likes of Fuller."

"No, Sam, I'm not. You're a lawman . . . whether we agree with you or not, you're what stands between us and the whirlwind." Tinnie started to say more, but a loud crash came from the direction of the saloon, causing her, Sam and Ronald Andrews to hurry to the window and look out.

One of the large windows on the front of the saloon was shattered on the boardwalk, its wooden frame hanging loose and swinging back and forth. Hoots and laughter resounded from within the saloon. In the street, Kirby Bell stood up dazed. He staggered in place wiping snow and blood from his forehead as Fuller's men gathered in the doorway.

"Lord have mercy," said Andrews. "They've thrown Bell through the window!"

Sam stood silent for a moment, then said under his breath, "Looks like they're starting to come together."

Chapter 17

Colonel Fuller stood at the bar with Red Booker and Asa Dahl while the rest of the posse and the townsmen spilled onto the street doing battle. "How long should we stand back and let them beat the hell out of one another?" Dahl asked, cutting a glance to the large gaping hole in the front of his saloon where the window used to be. As he spoke, a townsman jumped through the window opening, grabbed a wooden chair by its back and hurried out through the window with it. Dahl shook his head. "I don't think I can afford this!"

"You can afford it, Dahl," said Fuller, tipping a shotglass up to his lips, then lowering it to fill it again. "This is what it takes to get the twist out of your stomach over that whore and her boy being here." He winked with a sly grin. "You don't really care what it costs, now do you?"

Asa Dahl's face reddened. "I care about what happens to Hubbler Wells. I want the likes of her and her son out of here!"

"Ha," Fuller scoffed. "No you don't, not really. Once she's gone, you'll have to go looking for somebody else to look down on."

"I don't know what you're talking about, Colonel,"

Asa Dahl fumed. He looked toward the sound of a fistfight in the snow-piled street. Then said to change the subject, "Maybe we better break it up now."

"I'll tell you when it's time we break it up," said Fuller. "You had your chance to whip this bunch into a frenzy, but you failed. Relax. Sit back and let an expert do it."

"I don't get it," said Dahl, looking from Colonel Fuller to Red Booker for some explanation.

"Don't act innocent with us, Dahl," said Fuller. "You've been trying your damndest to work up a mob. But you didn't have the know-how or the guts."

"What the colonel is saying, Dahl," Red Booker cut in, getting a nod of permission from Fuller, "is you didn't know how to pop the cork and get the blood flowing." He jerked his head toward the fighting in the street. "A few minutes of busting one another's head, and they'll be lathered up enough you can lead them to do most anything." Red Booker and Colonel Fuller looked at one another and laughed.

In the jail, Sam Burrack finished checking his pistol and slipped it back into his holster. Moments earlier, Selectman Collins had returned with food from the restaurant. Now he stood behind the Ranger and watched the men brawling in the street. His voice sounded shaky as he said, "I suppose it's actually my job to get out there and stop this . . . I am the acting sheriff."

"Huh-uh," said Sam. "That's exactly what Fuller wants you to do. He figured on you getting out there in the midst of this, and me coming to back your play."

"Fuller?" Collins looked confused. "I thought Asa Dahl is behind all this."

"Asa Dahl is still dancing," said Sam, "but now it's Fuller who's playing the tune. Fuller knows how to make a mob work itself into a frenzy. He'd love to see you and me go out there first and break this up. Then he could step out and say his piece, tell us how wrong we are, demand we turn Billy Odle over to him. But we won't do it. Not until he gets out there first. We're not playing it his way."

"But, the fighting will only get worse, the longer it goes on," said Collins. "We can't let them kill each other."

"Fuller won't let it happen," said Sam. "Hold tight a little longer, you'll see what I mean."

Sam turned to face Collins, seeing behind him Billy Odle in one cell and Bootlip Thomas in the other, each of them watching him intently. At the battered desk stood Carl Yates and Ronald Andrews, also wearing expressions of concern. "What kind of fresh riding stock have you got at the livery barn, in case I have to get the boy out of town?" he asked Yates.

"Don't worry," said Yates, "I'll slip out the back door and fix you up something. Your horse and another one will be ready when you are." He nodded toward Ronald Andrews as he continued talking to Sam. "The two of us ain't quitting on you, Ranger. Say the word, we'll help you bust this thing up and throw Fuller in jail for a spell."

"Much obliged," said Sam. "But Fuller being in jail won't solve this. The problem here is this town has neglected what's important for a long time. It hasn't cared for its people. It's been run by a sheriff who was owned by businessmen." His eyes cut across to Collins, whose eyes turned down in shame. "Now the sheriff is gone, and the businessmen are turned against one another," Sam added. "So the whole town is like a dog running in a circle snapping at its own tail."

"We're changing all that, Ranger," said Yates. "Just tell us what you want."

Outside a pistol shot resounded. Collins said, "For God sakes, Ranger, they're starting to kill one another! I've got to do something!"

"Stay where you're at, Collins. Don't play into Fuller's hands," said Sam.

Inside the saloon, Fuller, Booker and Asa Dahl turned toward the sound of the pistol crack out in the street. They hurried to the broken window and looked out. The men in the street who had pulled apart at the sound of the shot now stood facing one another, ready to resume their brawl. Fuller's eyes shifted to the jail. "I must've misjudged him . . . he ain't coming. What kind of lawman stands back and lets something like this go on?"

"I don't know," said Asa Dahl, "but we can't let this get any more out of hand."

"Don't worry, I'll handle it," said Fuller. He stepped over to the ledge of the broken window, then out onto the boardwalk, glass crunching beneath his boots. On the street a man wobbled back and forth on his knees, an arm across his stomach and a pistol smoking in his hand. Fuller reached down, twisted the pistol from his hand and lifted him to his feet. "All right, men, this has gone far enough. It's not each other you need to be mad at . . . it's that Ranger." His finger pointed toward the jail. "He's got that kid in there and won't even let us talk to him. No wonder everybody's getting testy. Authority is being taken away from you in your own town!" He looked back and forth at his possemen, who had been fighting with the townsmen. "You boys get back and settle down. The Ranger caused all this. Let's quit fighting among ourselves and get to the real source of the trouble."

"Now you're talking, Fuller." At first Fuller thought it was someone calling out in support, until he turned and saw Sam Burrack step down into the street and walk forward, the big pistol in his hand, cocked and ready, hanging down his thigh. "I *am* the source of your trouble. I think it's time we settled up between us." As Sam spoke, Yates and Andrews stepped out of the sheriff's office with their shotguns raised and ready. Behind them came Selectman Collins carrying a pistol in one hand and a rifle in the other. He moved away from Yates and Andrews until the three of them held the street covered from twenty yards away.

Fuller stood silent for a moment. He had planned on the Ranger breaking the fight up. Now that Sam hadn't fallen for doing things his way, Fuller was grasping at straws: "You wouldn't have lifted a finger if these men killed one another out here! You wouldn't have given a damn, would you, Ranger?"

"Not particularly," said Sam. He motioned the townsmen to one side, out of his line of fire. Fuller's posse stood their ground. Fuller spread a smug grin. "You're outnumbered, Ranger, with or without those three backing you, and with or without the rest of these townsmen backing me."

"I've been outnumbered before," said Sam. "It's not going to mean anything to you, though, once the lead flies. If these men want to die over me killing you . . . I reckon it'll be up to them."

A couple of the possemen wavered and moved an inch. But Fuller called out, stopping them. "Stand fast, men, he's bluffing."

Beside Fuller, Red Booker looked uncertain. The Ranger said to him, "What about it, Booker, am I bluffing?"

When Red Booker only bit his lip without replying, the Ranger said, "I called your colonel down fair and square . . . just him and me." Sam jerked his head toward Collins, Yates and Andrews twenty yards behind him. "They'll stay out so long as it's fair. Won't you, men?" he called out over his shoulder.

"So long as everything stays jake," said Carl Yates.

Sam saw the hesitancy in Colonel Fuller's eyes and played on it quickly, saying to Red Booker, "Is this the man you're going to follow, one that turns down a fight? Has to back himself with a whole posse, to settle with one man?"

"Don't try turning my own men against me, Ranger," said Fuller. "I gave you a chance to cooperate with me. Now we're all going to take you down. Then I'm going to question that kid, my way. He'll tell me what happened out there when they stole those horses . . . he'll tell me where that Injun is hiding, too."

"Then draw your pistol and fire," said the Ranger in a resolved voice.

"What?" Colonel Fuller looked surprised.

"There's nothing more to talk about, Fuller," said Sam. "So let's get to it."

Fuller batted his eyes in disbelief, starting to see Sam was not bluffing, and that these long odds didn't bother the Ranger at all. "Holster your pistol first, Ranger. I'm no fool. Let's keep this fair and square."

"You've got a posse backing you, and you're talking about fair and square?" said Sam. He shook his head, raising the big pistol slowly. "This is the best you get today, Fuller—"

"Wait! This isn't the way to conduct a gunfight!" Fuller took a step back, his hand curling around the butt of his pistol, yet making no attempt to draw it. He saw the Ranger had already gotten the drop on him. "I'm not ready yet!" Fuller blurted out, looking baffled.

Sam kept his big pistol cocked and leveled on Fuller's belly from twelve feet away as he spoke to Red Booker and the rest of the possemen. "Did you boys hear that? He's not *ready*. What about the rest of you?" His words were directed at Red Booker although his eyes never left Fuller's face. "Booker, what about you? Are you *ready*, since your boss seems to be running a little behind?"

Booker seemed disgusted at Colonel Fuller. "Jesus, Colonel, you let him just walk up and get the drop on you."

"I—I didn't know." Fuller was dumbfounded.

"You're supposed to know," said Booker in a harsh tone. He looked at the Ranger and slowly raised his hands chest-high in a show of peace. He glanced at Collins, then at the two blacksmiths, then back to Sam Burrack. "This is your show, Ranger. All me and the boys want to do is get out of here. We'd have been gone long before now if it hadn't been for him."

"That's what I figured," said Sam. He let his pistol barrel lower an inch.

"But, what about the Injun?" asked Fuller, still not ready to give up whatever might be left of his authority. "The boy knows where he's—"

"Aw, hell, Colonel," Booker snapped. "All that boy ever meant to you was a way to get at the Ranger! Well . . . we see how that turned out." He looked around at the men and asked, "Any of you see any reason to stick around here?"

The men stood back and let down their guard, their hands falling away from their pistols. Now that Fuller appeared to be crushed without the Ranger even firing a shot, the townsmen shook their heads and mumbled under their breath and began to disperse.

"Looks like you win, Ranger," said Red Booker, treating Fuller as if he were no longer there. "We'll be clearing out as soon as we get our horses and our prisoner."

"Bootlip's not going with you. I talked it over with Collins," Sam lied. "Hubbler Wells is going to hold him for trial when the circuit judge comes through."

"Whoa, wait a damn minute, Ranger," said Booker. "Now you're meddling with our bounty money. We won't stand for that."

"Hubbler Wells has a right to hold him," said Sam. "He admitted he came here to rob the bank. If the town wants him, they've got him." Again Sam called out over his shoulder, this time to Selectman Collins. "Ain't that right, Sheriff?"

"That's correct, Ranger Burrack," said Collins, having heard nothing of the sort until this moment.

"But we're the ones who caught him," Red Booker said, thumping himself on the chest. Behind him, the possemen began to spread out.

"Makes no difference, he's staying here, Booker," said Sam. "You can collect your reward after the town gets through with him. But not before."

"This ain't right, Ranger," Booker said, relenting under Sam's cold stare and dead-steady pistol barrel.

"Call it a penalty for overstaying your welcome."

The Ranger turned slowly back and forth, facing the rest of the men. "Collins and I will both sign an affidavit saying you caught him. If the Midwest Bankers' Association needs any more proof, they can contact me in Arizona."

"And I've got your word?" Booker asked.

"You've got it," said Sam.

Colonel Fuller tried cutting in, saying, "You can't trust this sneaking son of—"

"Shut up, Fuller!" Red Booker cut him off. "If we'd left here when we should have, Bootlip Thomas would be going with us. I'll take the Ranger's word. He'll see to it we get paid. If we don't, it's coming out of your part, for keeping us here."

"You'll take *his* word?" Fuller rebuked him. "Don't start getting the idea that you're running things now, Booker. Don't forget who the bankers hired to run this job! I brought this posse together!"

"Midwest Bankers' Association will pay whoever brings in the meat," said Red Booker. "Now keep running your mouth and see if we don't cut you out altogether." As Red Booker spoke, three of the possemen closed in quietly behind Fuller, anticipating his next move.

"Why you backstabbing bastard!" Fuller bellowed. His hand snatched at the pistol on his hip, but before he could raise it, the men behind him grabbed him and wrestled him to the ground.

Red Booker saw one of the men take Fuller's pistol away from him, then another man booted Fuller in his ribs, causing him to roll into a ball on the cold ground. "That's enough, let him up," said Booker, stepping in and shoving the men to one side. He lifted Fuller to his feet, then turned to Sam as Fuller staggered in place. "All right, Ranger, we're settled up. Go on about your business. We'll do the same."

Sam stepped inside the sheriff's office first; Yates, Andrews and Collins came in behind him, looking back at the street as the townsmen and possemen began to drift their separate ways. "Whew," said Collins, running a trembling hand across his forehead through a cold sheen of sweat. He collapsed back against the closed door. "I never want to go through something like that again!"

Carl Yates and Ronald Andrews looked a little less shaken, but not much. They stood close to the battered desk and laid their shotguns down atop it. Andrews then went to the window and began keeping watch on the street, making sure everybody did as they said they would. Carl Yates looked at Bootlip Thomas who stood staring through the bars on his cell and said, "Well, outlaw, looks like this is your lucky day."

"Huh?" Bootlip looked puzzled.

"We changed our minds, Bootlip," said Sam. "Hubbler Wells is going to keep you here for a trial. I didn't think you'd mind."

Bootlip Thomas let out a long sigh. "Lord, I sure do thank you, Ranger," he said.

"Don't thank me, thank the town sheriff," said Sam, a trace of a smile on his face. "He's the one who calls the shots around here, for the time being at least."

Collins shook his head with a short nervous chuckle. "You came up with that one out of the blue, Ranger. I wish you'd mentioned it before we got out there," he said.

"To be honest," said Sam, "I didn't think about it until we were out there." He looked at Bootlip Thomas. "But that's okay. Maybe the judge won't hang him—maybe a few years in prison will cool his heels."

Bootlip Thomas nodded, looking down at the floor. "I'll take it like it comes. But I appreciate you not letting them tote me out of here in a flour sack, Ranger."

In the cell next to him, Billy Odle had been standing silent, watching and listening. Finally he said to Sam, "You mean Colonel Fuller's posse is gone? Just like that?"

"They're not gone yet, but they're leaving, Billy," said Sam Burrack. "As soon as they're gone you're free to go, too."

Billy Odle looked lost. "Go where?"

"Go see about your ma for starters," said Sam. "The main thing is, you're free to do what suits you." Sam didn't want to hold the boy to any conditions or appear to offer him any lectures, even though he wanted to. Instead, he stepped over to the window beside Ronald Andrews. "Did you put my horse out back like you said?" Sam asked him.

"Yep, yours and the big gray the Indian was riding," said Andrews.

Sam nodded. "Looks like I won't be needing them now."

Chapter 18

Asa Dahl hurried out the back door of his saloon and came straight to the hotel. Having watched everything from the hotel window, he'd backed away to the counter and stood there with a bitter expression on his face. As Sam walked through the door, Dahl made sure he kept his hand away from the pistol shoved down inside his waist belt. "I want you to know I had nothing to do with that," Dahl said, as if expecting the Ranger to say something about it.

Sam looked at him and said as he walked across the floor to the stairs, "I never figured you did, Dahl." He stopped at the stairs with one hand on the banister. "I don't have you pegged as a man who does something face to face in broad daylight. I see you more as the kind of snake that might slip out of the shadows and stab a man in the back . . . more than likely while he's sleeping."

Asa Dahl's face swelled red, but he had the good sense to keep his mouth shut.

Sam stood long enough at the bottom of the stairs to let him know that he had an opportunity to respond. Then, when Dahl lowered his eyes in submission, Sam offered a trace of a wry smile and walked up the stairs. Tinnie met Sam at the door to Hattie Odle's room and stood in silence for a moment looking at him. Then she threw her arms around him and shook her head against his chest. "Sam, I watched it from the window. I . . . I was so worried."

He held her close to him, yet he felt awkward doing so. "Now, now . . . There was nothing to worry about, Tinnie. Collins and the blacksmiths had me covered." He waited for a second, then held her back from him at arm's length. "Besides, I'm not used to folks worrying about me . . . it throws me off."

He noticed a tear in her eye. She touched a finger to it and collected herself. She seemed surprised by his words. "Well, then, I'm sorry, Sam . . . but I *was* worried. I still am."

"Thanks," he said, his voice almost a whisper. This time it was he who put his arms around her. "It feels good, Tinnie, someone worrying about me, I won't try to deny it." A silence passed, then Sam added, gently, "But this isn't the time or place."

"When is?" she whispered,

"I don't know." The silence returned and they stood in an embrace until he finally said near her ear, "How's Hattie doing?"

"Better than I am, evidently," Tinnie sighed. Taking a step back, she turned her face up to him with a tired smile. "Don't worry, she's getting better and better. She's over the opium. Now it's just a matter of willpower." She shrugged. "Some people have it, some people don't. We'll have to wait and see. What about her boy, now that Fuller and his men are gone? Is he going to be safe around here?"

"As safe I can make it without staying here from now on, guarding him. He'll hear some unkind remarks I suppose, after being involved—we'll just never know how much, unless he tells us. And that ain't likely."

"Think Collins can keep the peace here?" Tinnie asked. "Don't forget he was on the other side, wanting to prosecute Billy only a couple of days ago."

"Collins seems to have taken on a keener sense of right and wrong." Sam smiled. "Sheriffing does that to a man, if the man has good in him to begin with. I think he'll keep things in order here until the circuit judge arrives. It'll be up to the judge whether or not Billy Odle is charged with anything. My guess is, he won't be."

"So Billy and his ma both get another chance," said Tinnie.

"Yep," said Sam.

"Maybe we ain't such a bad town after all," said Tinnie, "most of us, anyway. At least some of us started helping once we saw the problem."

"That's all you can ask of folks, I reckon," Sam said. "It's a shame nobody saw it sooner. Maybe if the woman got help sooner, the boy wouldn't have gone so far for attention. That's all this was, a scared, lonesome boy wanting somebody to tell him he's worth something."

"Do you think he sees it now, Sam?" Tinnie asked.

"Some, maybe," Sam replied. "As much as we can expect of him. It didn't take him overnight to get cut off from the rest of the world. It'll take him just as long for him to get connected back to it."

"Is he listening to you now, Sam?" Tinnie asked.

"Not enough," said Sam. "He's still impressed by that outlaw, Willie John. As long as he still thinks he's a part of the outlaw world, it'll take some doing to ever jerk his head down out of the clouds."

"And you, Sam?" she asked. "What will you be

doing now? The snow's not too deep to travel, but it is winter out there. Willie John's gone. He could be headed in any direction. Will he keep till spring?" She offered a suggestive smile.

"Until spring? I doubt it," said Sam. He stepped forward, turning, slipping his arm around her waist. "But what's a week, more or less?"

"That's what I say." Smiling, Tinnie gestured a hand toward a door at the end of the hall. "I took a room all for myself," she said, "away from the other girls. I hoped you might be staying for a while."

Down in an alley off the main street, Willie John watched from around the edge of a shipping crate as Ronald Andrews led the horses back to the livery barn. Willie had slipped in only moments before, long enough to see the last of Fuller's men file out of town and head southwest. They were still after him, he supposed. Willie allowed himself a slight grim smile. He was still one step ahead of them. He glanced back and forth once more, then hurried in a crouch along the back of the buildings and through the corridors of long drifts of snow, making his way toward the livery barn.

Ronald Andrews stopped long enough to step inside the mercantile store and purchase a fresh twist of chewing tobacco. He paid for it and bit off a chew as the store owner's daughter rattled on about all the excitement earlier in the street. Andrews tipped his hat to her, put the tobacco inside his shirt pocket and excused himself. He continued on to the livery barn, leading the horses and working on a jawful of chewing tobacco.

In the back of the darkened barn, Willie John eased the door closed behind himself and crept into an empty stall, his pistol in his hand, his wound throbbing from all the exertion. He crouched down and waited. In moments, light sliced in across the floor as Ronald Andrews entered and dropped the horses' reins long enough to turn and close the door. Willie John watched through a crack in the stall planks, seeing Andrews turn and lead the horses past him to the next stall.

Willie listened to Ronald Andrews unsaddle the Ranger's horse and hang its bridle outside the stall on a peg. Then as Andrews closed the stall gate and led the dapple-gray to the next empty stall, Willie slipped out of his hiding place and moved in behind the stallion. He hurried along the gray's side until he could raise the pistol and jam the tip of the barrel into Andrews's spine. "Stop right here, blacksmith," he said, his voice like the low hiss of a coiled snake.

Ronald Andrews froze in place, the gray's reins dangling from one of his raised hands. "You're the Indian, ain't you?"

Willie John snatched the reins from his hand and nudged him sharply with his pistol barrel. "Don't worry about who I am. Get in that stall. Hurry up!"

"You're not going to shoot me," Ronald Andrews said matter-of-factly. "You don't want to bring that Ranger running, do you?"

Willie John didn't answer. "Is that posse still here?"

"Nope, you just missed them," said Andrews. Willie was amazed at this man's calm, unshaken manner. "The Ranger threw them quite a going-away party, though. You might've gotten a kick out of it."

"I saw the last of them leaving," said Willie John. He lifted the pistol from Ronald Andrews's holster as they stepped inside the empty stall. Owing to the unusually placid manner of the man, Willie John asked, "What's your name, blacksmith?"

"Andrews," was all Ronald Andrews said, reluctantly.

"Andrews, huh?" Willie John reached around Andrews and ran his free hand across his belt, checking for any more pistols. "That's not always been your name though, has it? You haven't always lived here, have you?"

"What's it to you what my name's always been . . . or where I've lived, or how?" There was no fear in Ronald Andrews's voice.

"All right," Willie chuckled, "I see through you, *Andrews*. You've done some long-riding in your time."

Andrews fell silent for a second, then said, "I was a no-good sonuvabitch like you half my life. But I straightened up, been upright ever since. You need to kill me? Go on with it. I ain't built to beg."

"I ain't going to kill you, Andrews . . . not unless you make me do it." Willie John kept the pistol jammed into his back, but he did ease his finger off the trigger. "Tell me what's happened to that boy?"

"You mean Billy Odle? Nothing, yet. Fuller's men wanted to eat him for breakfast, but the Ranger stopped him. Why? What's your big interest in that kid?"

"Never mind my interest," Willie snapped, nudging the barrel when it appeared Ronald Andrews might turn his head facing him.

"You don't have to poke me with that damned pistol," Andrews said. "Keep doing it, and we'll go out of here locked at the horns like mountain rams. You want to know about Billy, I'll tell you, but no more back-poking. It shortens my temper."

"Good enough," said Willie, easing his grip a little more. "I feel sorry for that kid. He's young and stupid . . . and I worried about him getting in trouble."

"You mean for helping you escape?" said Andrews. "Hell yes he got in trouble for it. I rode out and saw what happened to Old Man Renfro. I tried to help him out some—told them no kid Billy's age could've done it. They believed me . . . the Ranger did, anyway. That's the only one who counted. I figured he'd get a couple of more people on his side, enough to keep Fuller from hanging the boy." Andrews shook his head. "What the hell did you mean by dragging that kid into all this? Poor little bastard . . . his ma's a whore, his pa's a convict. Damned if you didn't come near getting him stuck with horse theft and murder. What's wrong with you?"

Willie John started to offer some sort of excuse, but he realized there was no answer for what this former outlaw had just asked. There wasn't meant to be. "I did it because I still am what you used to be . . . a no-good son of a bitch," said Willie John. He let down the hammer with his thumb as quietly. But still Ronald Andrews heard it.

"So the Ranger kept them from lynching the kid? Maybe he ain't such a devil after all," said Willie John.

"Oh, the Ranger's a devil all right, depending which side of hell you live on. Make no mistake about that. He's out to kill you graveyard dead."

"I'm not worried about who kills me," said Willie John. "I know somebody's going to. I'm just putting it off long as I can. Do you know what I mean?"

"Yep, I sure do," said Ronald Andrews. He let out

a breath. "I felt the same way before I gave it up. Toward the last I believe I might have even been wanting somebody to do it, just to get it over with. It's a sad state when going to hell looks no worse than what you've got here."

"That's enough," said Willie John. "Get over there closer to the wall."

"How hard are you going to crack me with that thing? Did I make you mad, blaming you for what happened to the kid? Too damn bad if I did. You asked for it, getting him all excited thinking he's—"

"Naw, I'm not mad over any of that," said Willie John, cutting him off. "If I take it easy on you, will you do what you can for that boy?"

"It would be easy to lie to you right now, tell you I will, Willie John," said Andrews. "But the truth is the kid won't have nothing to do with me . . . or nobody else in this town for that matter."

"Because of his ma?" said Willie John.

"Yep, that's the whole of it." Ronald Andrews sounded ashamed. "Hell, I never stopped to think about it, you know? She was selling, I was buying. Never gave any thought the kid might be understanding what was going on. Now I feel awful about it, but it's done. I can't change it. All I can do is see my mistake and try to fix it. Can you damn me for that?"

"Nope, I reckon not." As Ronald Andrews spoke, Willie John drew back the pistol, ready to knock him cold. But right before he started to swing, he stopped himself and asked, "Tell me something, Andrews, when you gave it up, how'd you go about it?"

"I just quit one day," said Andrews. "I was supposed to meet some boys from up at Wind River, getting set to raise some hell down along the border.

I spent a week fighting with myself over it. Come the day, I just didn't show up. I came north, been up here ever since. I just let time and distance swallow me up, so to speak. Whoever I was back then is dead, the way I look at it. Anybody who knows me now, wouldn't guess I was ever that person."

"Has it been worth it?"

"Worth it? Hell, I don't know," said Andrews. "I'll always miss it . . . taking what I wanted any time I wanted it . . . doing what suited me any time it suited me. You think it's easy working for blacksmith wages after all that? Worth it? Ha! You try it a while, then you tell me. What you're really asking is do I think you can do it, give it up and never look back. Well, I can't answer that for you—nobody can. It's like asking can you outrun your shadow. I told you I'll do what I can for the kid if he'll let me. Now go on, crack me in the head, get it over with. You better make it good, too. I've worked too hard at being straight to have somebody here accuse me of helping you escape."

Willie John drew back again, this time sending a hard blow to the back of Ronald Andrews's head. Andrews fell forward and down, against the wall of the barn, then sank to his knees on the straw-covered floor. He swayed back and forth until Willie John reached out with a boot and shoved him forward. "There, *Mister Andrews*," Willie said. "You talk too damn much, anyway."

Morgan Aglo, Joe Shine, Texas Bob Mackay, and Tack Beechum sat atop their horses three miles outside of town, behind a snow-covered pile of brush along the flatland trail. They watched Willie John ride toward them from the south along the snowy trail, raising a fine white drift of powder in his wake. "What the hell is he doing coming back?" Morgan Aglo asked himself aloud, straightening in his saddle and squinting for a better look at Willie John.

"If you ask me," said Joe Shine, "that Injun ain't acted right since we took up with him."

"I didn't ask you, Joe," said Morgan. He settled down onto his saddle and waited while Willie John rode the last hundred yards.

"I don't like this," Tack Beechum said, sidling his horse up close to Aglo. "He's suppose to scout things out and wait for us there, give us some cover when we come out of that bank."

"Well, thank you for reminding me, Beechum," said Morgan Aglo in a sarcastic growl. "I had plumb forgotten he was supposed to do any off that." He gave Beechum a harsh stare and jerked his horse away from him.

"Maybe somebody spotted him," said Joe Shine.

"Yeah, maybe," Aglo grunted.

Texas Bob Mackay just sat quietly observing the men from a few feet away.

When Willie John cut off from the trail and guided his horse over toward them, Morgan Aglo and Joe Shine widened the space between them to allow Willie John in. But Willie John stopped his big dapple-gray short of the men by five feet and turned his horse sideways to them, his right hand resting atop his pistol butt. "What's wrong, Willie?" Morgan Aglo asked, looking him up and down. "You ain't supposed to be out here."

"Nothing's wrong," said Willie John, patting the dapple-gray's withers with his rein hand. Steam blew from the big animal's nostrils. "I told you I wanted my stallion back . . . and I got him."

"Damn it!" said Aglo, "I'm talking about the bank! You was supposed to stay there if everything was all right. What the hell are you doing coming back here unless it's to warn us something's wrong?"

Willie John offered a thin straight smile. "Take it easy, Aglo," he said. "Everything's fine in Hubbler Wells. The town's still there, the bank's still there. All you four have to do is ride in and rob it."

"What about the bounty posse?" Aglo asked.

"The bounty posse was pulling out as I got there. The town's a duck in a shooting gallery. I came for my stallion, and that's all. I scouted the town for you as a favor. When you ride in, get off this trail, swing wide around and come in from the south. Now I'll take my leave and wish you the—"

"Huh-uh, I don't think so," Tack Beechum cut in. "You rode here with us, you're staying with us. How do we know the posse really left town?"

A tense silence set in. Even Willie's horse seemed to freeze in place at Tack Beechum's words. Texas Bob caught the hard look on Willie John's face and whispered, "Jesus."

"Easy now, boys," Morgan Aglo finally said, barely above a whisper. "If Willie says the posse left, that's good enough for me." He gave a slow nod toward Tack Beechum, saying to Willie John, "Don't you mind Beechum here, Willie. He's just a little over cautious. He wasn't calling you no liar."

"That's funny," said Willie John, "I could've sworn he did." His voice was cool and level, but his eyes were ablaze and fixed on Tack Beechum's.

"Don't do me this way, Willie," Morgan Aglo coaxed, keeping his voice calm and unheated. "One shot out here and we can kiss Hubbler Wells good-bye." He slowly turned in his saddle and said to

Tack Beechum, "Beechum, if Willie says the posse left town, it left town. Do you understand me, man?"

Beechum was ready to do whatever it took to get things settled with Willie John. "Yes, I understand." He spoke to Willie John in a level tone, saying, "No offense intended. I spoke out of turn and I apologize for it."

Without acknowledging Beechum in any way, Willie John backed the dapple-gray a step at a time until he was ready to turn it away toward the trail. Then he said to all four of them, "Good luck, boys. Maybe I'll see you in Old Mex."

"Whoa, Willie," said Aglo, "what about the Ranger? Is he going to be there waiting for us?"

"Not if you do like I told you," said Willie John, the big stallion stepping high-hoofed and restless beneath him. "Like I said, swing around wide and come in from the south. By the time you get there, the Ranger will be gone." The stallion reared up and rolled its hooves in the air, then came down at Willie's command and bolted away.

Morgan Aglo grinned and watched for a moment. Then he said to the others without turning to them, "Well, boys, you heard him. He's got it all set it up for us."

Chapter 19

Only a few minutes had passed when Ronald Andrews dragged himself to his feet and stood on shaky legs, steadying himself against a grain bin until he caught his balance. A swirl of confusion clouded his mind. Then everything came back to him as he shook his head and rubbed his eyes. "Damn it," he murmured, his hand dropping to his empty holster. He forced himself forward and staggered to the sheriff's office with a hand pressed to the swollen cut on the back of his head.

At the sheriff's office, Carl Yates hurried over and caught Ronald Andrews just in time. Andrews had swung the door open and fell against the frame. "Give me . . . a hand," he said, his voice sounding like a drunkard's.

"God Almighty, Ronald!" Yates looped Andrews's arm across his shoulder and guided him to a wooden chair. "What the hell has happened to you?"

As Selectman Collins moved in with Yates and helped get Andrews seated, Bootlip Thomas called out from his cell, "Look, his hand's bleeding!"

"No, it's not." Ronald Andrews shook his head and slumped forward. Yates and Collins both saw the swollen welt left by the pistol barrel at the same time. "Aw hell," said Yates. He and Collins looked at one another. "Who did this, Ronald?" Yates asked, leaning down for a closer look.

"The Indian . . . caught me by surprise," Ronald Andrews managed to say. "He . . . came back for his horse."

"On no!" said Collins. "I better go get the Ranger." He turned a full circle then asked Yates, "Where did he go?"

"He went to the hotel," said Yates. "Him and Tinnie Malone has been getting pretty close, if you know what I mean."

Collins winced at the thought of disturbing the Ranger. Then he looked around the office as if noticing for the first time that Billy Odle was gone. "Where's that crazy Odle kid?" he asked hurriedly.

"He went to see about his ma," said Yates, whipping his bandanna from around his neck and shaking it out. "Go get the Ranger, Collins," he demanded. "And hurry it up! We can't have that murdering Indian running loose around here. I'll get some cold water on Ronald's head and come join you."

Andrews snatched the bandanna from Yates's hand and said, "Don't worry about my head. Go on with Collins."

Once Collins and Carl Yates were out the door, Ronald Andrews pushed himself up from his chair and reached for a pitcher of water sitting near the wood stove. He poured water on the bandanna, then squeezed it and held it to the back of his head. Bootlip Thomas called out from his cell, "Looks like Willie John got you a good one, huh?"

Ronald Andrews gave him a flat stare, the intensity of it causing Bootlip to take an uncomfortable step back from the bars. "I been waiting for the right time to ask this," Bootlip said in a hushed tone. "Don't I know you from somewhere?"

Andrews took a step forward and said in icy reply, "No . . . You've never seen me before in your life, mister."

There was mettle in Andrews's words, enough to send Bootlip Thomas another step back. "Oh . . . well, my mistake," he said, "I meant no harm by it."

When the urgent knocking resounded on the hotel room's wooden door, Sam Burrack grabbed his shirt and his Colt. "Who is it?" he asked, catching a glimpse of Tinnie Malone as she rose quickly from the bed, snatched a sheet around herself and moved to the other side of the room.

"Ranger Burrack," Yates called out, "Indian Willie John is back. He busted Ronald Andrews in the head and left him laying in the barn. Ronald said he came back for that dapple-gray of his."

The door swung open so fast, Yates and Collins jumped back from it a foot. Sam stood with his shirt unbuttoned and his thumb across the hammer of his Colt. "Where's the boy?"

"Billy?" said Carl Yates. "The last I knew, he was coming here to see his ma." Yates jerked his head toward Hattie Odle's room down the hall.

Collins saw the look on Sam's face and said, "We'll go get him."

"Good," Sam said with a nod, "I'll be right with you." He closed the door slightly, and turned to Tinnie as he stepped over to the chair and picked up his gun belt. "You heard them, I reckon."

"Yes, I heard," she said. She drew the sheet more securely around her and offered a half-hearted smile.

Nodding toward Sam's feet, she said, "You didn't even get your boots off."

"Next time?" he asked.

She watched him stuff his shirt into his waist with one hand, his other hand holding his gun belt and pistol. "Sure, next time," she said.

When Sam got to Hattie Odle's room, Collins and Yates were bringing Billy Odle out into the hall. "Ma's asleep," Billy said to Collins. "Can't I wait here and see her when she wakes up?"

"The Ranger said come and get you, Billy," said Carl Yates, his hand on the boy's shoulder as if to keep him from bolting away. Yates saw Sam walking toward them and said to Billy Odle, "Here he comes now."

"Did you tell him?" Sam asked.

"Nope," said Carl Yates, both he and Collins shaking their heads. "All we said is that you wanted to see him."

"Tell me what?" Billy asked looking up at them, his eyes shifting back and forth as they spoke.

"Willie John came back for his horse," Sam said to Billy Odle. He saw Billy's eyes light up, and he added quickly, "I wanted to make sure you were still here, Billy."

Billy couldn't keep the excitement out of his voice. "You think he came here for me? Came back here to take me with him? Maybe he's looking for me right now." As he spoke, his eyes darted back and forth along the hall as if Willie John might appear.

Sam looked at Yates and Collins, then down at Billy Odle. "No, Billy. Willie John got what he came for, so he's gone now. But, to be honest, I thought you might have seen him and tried to follow him.

That would have looked real bad on you, if you had."

"Oh . . ." Billy looked disappointed. His eyes lowered. "Well, you can see, I'm still here."

"Yes, and we're all glad of it, Billy," said Sam. He leaned down to talk to Billy at face level. "Now, I want you to come back to the sheriff's office with us for a while. You can come back and see your ma at supper time."

"But why? You said yourself, Willie John got what he came here for . . . He's gone now."

"Just in case, Billy," said Sam. "If he would happen to pull something before leaving town, we want to be able to say where you were. We wouldn't want anybody pointing a finger at you, saying you was a part of anything, would we?"

"No, we wouldn't," said Billy Odle, but Sam could see the excitement return to the boy's eyes at just the suggestion.

"Come on," said Sam. "Go along with Collins and Yates, help them keep an eye on things for a spell, all right?"

"All right," Billy nodded.

Sam straightened up and said to Collins, "Why don't you and Billy go on. Yates will be right along."

"Sure," said Collins, seeing the Ranger wanted to talk without the boy hearing him. "Come along, Billy."

As soon as the two were headed down the stairs, Sam turned to Carl Yates, asking, "Does anybody else know about this yet?"

"No, just Andrews, Collins and me—now you and Billy, of course."

"Good," said Sam. "We'll keep it that way for

now. We'll have time to warn everybody if my hunch is right. I don't want to cause anybody to go running out thinking they're going to track down Willie John and leave this town unguarded."

"I don't understand," said Carl Yates, cocking his head in curiosity. "You're expecting trouble? You figure there was more to it than him coming here to get his horse?"

"Yep, I think so," said Sam.

Yates looked puzzled.

"Think about it, Yates," said Sam. "If he caught Andrews off guard enough to knock him in the head, he could have gone on and killed him. He could have dragged him into a stall, covered him with straw . . . it could be tomorrow before anybody knew about it, even longer before they realized Willie John had anything to do with it." Sam shook his head. "Nope, Willie John knew what he was doing. He might have come to get his horse, but there was other things at work, you can bet on it."

"I see," said Yates, getting the picture. "Think it's the bank again? Think there's some of the Ganstons' men left, they're going to take another run at it? They sent Willie John to get you out of town first?"

"That might be part of it," said Sam. "I think Willie John needs to let me know he's still around. Needs to make sure he gets me back on his trail."

"He does?" Again Carl Yates looked puzzled. "That makes no sense to me at all. Why would he want to get you on his trail?"

"I didn't say he *wants* me back on his trail," said Sam. "I said he *needs* me back on his trail."

Yates considered it, then said, "Hell, that still makes no sense to me, unless he's trying to get himself killed."

Sam Burrack didn't answer. He walked over to the stairs and headed down. Carl Yates followed until they got to the front door of the hotel. Then Sam turned and said, "I'm going to ride out of here to the north, just far enough to be seen, then I'm coming back. You and Collins get the townsmen ready."

Carl Yates hesitated for a moment then said, "Would you do us a favor, Ranger?"

Sam looked at him. "What's that?"

"Will you let us handle this on our own? The town needs to do something right, to make up for all that's gone wrong."

Sam thought about it, then said, "All right, I'll ride out like I said. I'll listen for the shooting. If none of the outlaws come riding out, I'll figure you and your townsmen got all of them and I'll go on after Willie John. Fair enough?"

"Yes," said Yates. "I sure appreciate it, Ranger."

Sam nodded. "Just be sure you get every one of them. If one rides out of here, I'll have no choice but to take him down and haul back here."

"Don't worry, Ranger, we'll take care of them," said Yates.

"And no matter what happens, keep a close eye on the boy," Sam said.

"Want us to jail him for his own good till you get back?" asked Yates.

"No," Sam said adamantly, speaking over his shoulder as he walked out the door. "I could be gone a long time. Keep him at the sheriff's office, but don't jail him. Besides, I'm afraid we'll get him too used to looking at the world through iron bars. All we can do for Billy Odle is make sure he's getting a fair shake. We can be his friends. But from now on, the rest is up to him."

*   *   *

Once Morgan Aglo and his partners had swung wide
of Hubbler Wells, they stopped to rest their horses
before riding in. From the cover of a short rise in the
land, Joe Shine stepped his horse up carefully and
looked out across the snow. After a moment he called
back to Morgan Aglo and motioned him forward.
"You've got to see this, boss! That Injun was right.
There goes the Ranger headed out after him!"

"How the hell do you know it's the Ranger?" Aglo
asked in a gruff tone, punching his horse forward,
then jerking it to a stop beside Joe Shine. He looked
out across the snow, squinting against the dim glow
of sunlight through the gray sky.

Shine said, "I just figure it is, boss. Willie said the
Ranger would be riding out, tracking him. It sure
looks like that rider is dead on Willie's trail to me."

Morgan Aglo studied the rider's bearing from afar,
the way the man sat his saddle, the way he rode tall
and smoothly even in the foot-deep snow. A rifle
was across his lap. "I reckon you're right for once,
Joe. I'd make him for a lawman, sure enough,
whether Willie had tipped us off or not." Morgan
Aglo thought things over for a second, then said, "Of
course, if he hears shooting from town he'll come
back."

"Yep," said Joe Shine, "and we'll be long gone by
then, if we know what the hell we're doing."

"Uh-hmm," Morgan Aglo nodded, seeming to
only half hear Joe Shine. "I wonder why that Injun
didn't go ahead and ask us to ambush that lawdog?
It would've been easy enough."

"I don't try to figure out how that Injun's mind
works," said Joe Shine. "I have a hard enough time
figuring out what I'm thinking."

"That sounds like a terrible affliction," said Morgan Aglo, giving a sly grin, putting aside what Willie John might or might not have been thinking. "Suppose having a bunch of money in your pocket would cure it?" He backed his horse as he spoke.

Joe Shine returned the grin, jerking his horse back with him and saying, "Hell, I'm convinced it would."

The four riders gathered into a loose formation and rode forward at an easy gait, saving their horses' strength for the ride back out of town. Nearing Hubbler Wells from the south, Morgan Aglo took note of the many fresh hoofprints headed in the opposite direction. "Willie John was right again," he said to the others beside him. "Looks like that bounty posse decided to find themselves a warmer spot to lay up in." He looked back and forth at the faces of Joe Shine, Tack Beechum and Texas Bob Mackay, steam swirling in their breath. "Boys, it's our lucky day!"

A half mile away, Sam Burrack turned his horse around and headed back, careful to keep himself from being seen on the rolling flatland. He'd caught only a fleeting glimpse of fine powder drifting upward like dust across the top of a low rise, but that was all he needed. He circled southward on his way back until he came upon the fresh tracks left by Morgan Aglo and the others. Then he heeled the horse forward, the rifle coming up from his lap. He levered it with the snap of one hand and kept his thumb across the cocked hammer for safety.

In Hubbler Wells, after checking on Ronald Andrews, Selectman Collins and Carl Yates left Billy Odle with him and hurried to the saloon, waving down as many townsmen as they could on their way. As the townsmen gathered near the bar, Collins

stepped up onto a chair and called out to them, his
voice charged with fear and excitement, "Everybody
listen up . . . We've got more outlaws heading this
way!" His eyes went to Darton Vittitow who pressed
a palm to his forehead in disbelief. "That's right, Mr.
Vittitow, the Ranger says they'll be here to try and
rob your bank again."

"Poor Timothy," said Vittitow. "I don't think his
nerves will be able to stand this. Why in the name
of God do they keep doing this?"

"I don't know, sir," said Collins. "The Ranger says
they're doing it simply because they know they can.
I believe him. The word is out on us—we're a losing
town that's about to go under. We've still got a bank,
but we won't for long. They figure to rob it now
while the pickings are still good." His voice took a
fury. "It's like getting a lousy pack of hungry dogs
on your trail—they can't stop until either they've ate
you up, or you've put them out of their misery. The
important thing is that we need to be ready when
they get here. Show them we've got some fight in
us, with or without the posse, with or without the
Ranger. Maybe if we handle things right for ourselves this time, it will be the last we see of them."

"What, are you asking us for help, Collins?" Asa Dahl
called out in a sarcastic tone. "Now that you and that
Ranger are scratching each other's backs, maybe you
ought to rely on him and leave us alone. You refused
to cooperate with us when we needed your support.
Where's your Ranger now that you need him?"

"He'll be here if he can," said Collins. "He rode
out to throw these men off, make them think he was
leaving town."

"What the hell's that supposed to do for us?" Asa
Dahl growled.

Collins gave a him a cold hard stare, the first he'd ever given anyone that he could recall. "Look, Dahl, I'm not going to explain this to you. I'm sheriff until somebody's elected to take the job. You can either back my play on this or not. I'm not out to convince you whether or not you should." His eyes went across the others as he continued. "This town belongs to all of us. If we want to keep it we better be ready to join together and fight for it. If not, we might just as well turn tail and clear out of here, leave this place standing empty in the wind. Right now, we've got men coming to take what's ours. Are you going to help me stop them or not?"

The townsmen looked at one another and nodded their support. "Give us a couple of minutes to arm ourselves," said a voice from within their midst. "We'll be right behind you!"

"Good," said Collins. "Get any horse away from the hitch rails and leave no wagons on the street for them to use for cover. It's bad enough we've got so much snow piled up . . . they'll use it if they can."

"Ha!" said Asa Dahl, listening to Collins shout orders. "You men must be out of your mind. This man is no lawman." He looked at Darton Vittitow. "If you're smart, you'll take your money out of the vault and hide it someplace until these men have come and gone. Everybody lay up until they've left here." He swung a pointed finger at Collins. "But whatever you do, don't listen to this fool! He's a two-bit lackey I brought here when I came to Hubbler Wells—a tinhorn I figured would make a good politician, to help me run my business! Look at him close, boys. Is this the kind of man you want to follow?"

The men turned their questioning gazes to Collins who stepped down from the wooden chair and slid it away from himself. He took a deep breath and said in a level tone, "It's true what he's saying. I've been nothing but a sold-out fool ever since I first ran for office here. But by God, this is my home! I'm not asking you to stand up to these men *for* me . . . I'm asking you to stand up to them *with* me. That's the only difference you'll see in me today." His eyes went from man to man in turn, then stopped on Asa Dahl. "I hope that difference is enough. If not, I'll go out there alone. Live or die, from now on I'm not looking at what's best for me. I'm doing what's best for my home."

"And we're with you!" cried a voice above the roar of approving townsmen. They hurried away to get their weapons, spilling out through the doors onto the snowy street.

Asa Dahl chuckled under his breath, picked up a shotglass full of whiskey and raised it toward Selectman Collins in a mock salute. "I hope you know what you're doing," he said.

"No," said Collins. "To be honest I'm not sure I know exactly what I'm doing. I just know I'm doing what I think's right for a change . . . what these people hired me to do, not what best suits your needs."

"Then you've let that piece of tin on your chest go straight to your head," said Dahl. "Be careful it doesn't end up getting you killed."

Chapter 20

Morgan Aglo stopped his horse at the beginning of the main street into Hubbler Wells. He looked all around at the high mounds of snow where the townsmen had cleared a wide path the length of the town. With a broad grin, Aglo raised his pistol from his holster and said, "Now, boys, this is what I call a hospitable bunch. They've cleared the way out of town to keep our horses from breaking a leg."

"Thank you kindly, Hubbler Wells," said Joe Shine in a lowered voice, raising his hat toward the empty boardwalk. Tack Beechum and Morgan Aglo muffled a laugh. Texas Bob Mackay only looked back and forth without a trace of humor, wondering why no one looked out from the windows or doorways, why not even one horse stood at the hitch rail out front of the saloon.

"I've seen empty towns before," he murmured to himself, "but this one takes the all-time prize."

"What's that?" Morgan asked, turning in his saddle toward Texas Bob Mackay, barely hearing his words. "Did you say something, Texas Bob?"

"I said maybe I best stay back here and keep guard, make sure nobody's up to something."

Morgan Aglo looked him up and down, then flagged him forward with his pistol barrel. "Naw, we need you up here in front, Texas Bob, just in case your old bounty-hunting habits turn too powerful for you to resist."

"What?" Texas Bob's face turned red with rage.

"You heard me," said Morgan Aglo. "Don't go thinking about reaching for that pistol."

Texas Bob let his hand move away from his pistol butt. "That's a hell of a way for you to talk to me, Aglo," Bob responded, "after all I went through to come up here and join you boys."

"All the same, get on up in front here," said Morgan Aglo, angling his horse away from Texas Bob and keeping his eyes on him. "Boys, keep ole Texas Bob in front of yas at all times. He could get amnesia on us, forget who he's riding with."

Texas Bob Mackay had all the insults he could take. Again he started to reach for his pistol, but Tack Beechum and Joe Shine already had theirs out, cocked and pointed. "You heard him, Texas Bob," said Joe Shine. "Just do what you're supposed to do and everybody'll get along fine. You didn't think you could hook right up with us after riding with a bounty posse and expect to be treated like a long-lost brother, did you?"

"You son of a bitch," Texas Bob snarled.

Inside the saloon, Selectman Collins held an arm out to his side as if keeping the men behind him quiet. "Here they come, men," he whispered. "Everybody get ready . . . It's not going to be like the last time. We're not going to lose a man, and none of them are getting away."

Beside him, Darton Vittitow leaned forward and peeped out around the corner of the door, gripping a shotgun tightly in his thick hands. "What in the world are they doing out there? It looks more like they're getting ready to fight one another!"

"Everybody just hold on tight," said Selectman Collins. "Let them get closer to the bank. We'll catch them in a cross fire." He looked over at the alley beside the bank building and saw Carl Yates and a half-dozen townsmen crouched back out of sight from the street. In the dusty window of the sheriff's office, Ronald Andrews stood watching with apprehension as the four horsemen moved their horses along the cleared street. Speaking under his breath through the window pane and toward the saloon, he whispered, "Come on, Collins, make your move! Don't wait around!"

Billy Odle slipped in beside Ronald Andrews and looked out, cutting his gaze toward the four horsemen.

"Who is it out there? It's not Willie John, is it?" Billy asked, sounding hopeful.

"Stay back, Billy." Ronald Andrews drew him back from the window. "Willie John's not out there. I already checked. Willie's gone for good, if you want my opinion."

"No he's not," said Billy, stuffing his hands down tight into his trouser pockets, giving a sullen look toward Bootlip Thomas as if looking for an ally.

But Bootlip Thomas only shook his head. "He's telling you right, Billy. This town has seen the last of that Indian for a while. If he's smart he's headed for the border right now."

"I don't believe he came here just for the horse," said Billy. "He came here thinking I was in trouble. He was going to bust me out of jail if I was under arrest. Lucky for everybody I wasn't."

"Kid," said Ronald Andrews, "there's so much you don't know, it's hard to know where to start."

"There's nothing you can tell me," said Billy. "What do you know about people like Willie John and me? You're nothing but a blacksmith—not even a real blacksmith at that. You're just a blacksmith's helper."

Ronald Andrews shot Bootlip Thomas a guarded look, then picked up a rifle from atop the desk and levered a round into the chamber. "I guess you're right, kid. I'm only a blacksmith's helper—what do I know about outlaws?" He walked back to the window and looked out. "Yates asked me to stay put here with you, Billy. So I'm going to try. But from the looks of what's getting ready to happen out there, I'm going to have to leave you here on your own and go help them. Will you be all right if I have to do that?"

"I can take care of myself," said Billy.

Bootlip Thomas cut in, saying, "Billy, he ain't asking if you can take care of yourself. He's asking if he can trust you, you hardheaded little peckerwood. Don't you have enough sense to see everybody here is doing their best to help you? All you're doing is acting like an—"

"That's enough, Bootlip," said Ronald Andrews. "Billy has to make his choice just like the rest of us did."

"Yeah," said Bootlip Thomas. "I wish to hell I'd had the people on my side back when I was a stupid kid starting out." He gripped the bars and shook them. "Is this what you really want, boy? You want to end up like this? Or like Willie John and the rest . . . on the run, never knowing where the next day's going to take you?"

"That doesn't sound so bad to me," said Billy Odle. "Going where I want to, when I want to . . . doing whatever I want to once I get there." He looked Bootlip Thomas up and down. "As far as ending up like you . . . I'm not going to. You wouldn't have, either, if you'd been smart."

"Why you little . . ." Bootlip Thomas stopped himself from saying more than he wanted to by kicking the bars hard with his stockinged feet. Then he turned, grumbling to himself, stomped over to his bunk and flopped down on it.

Ronald Andrews shook his head and looked out through the window, seeing the four riders move their horses forward at a slow walk, riding abreast in the middle of the cleared street. Around them fresh snow began falling. Large flakes clung to their collars and hat brims. "Come on, Collins," Ronald Andrews whispered again to the cold window pane, "For God sakes, make your move . . . make it now. Don't let them get between your men and the men in the alley. They'll have you cutting each other to pieces, you damn fool."

But inside the saloon Collins waited, keeping the others behind him with an outstretched arm. Across the street in the alley Carl Yates did the same, waiting for Collins and his men to make the first move as Morgan Aglo and his outlaws moved slowly in between them. Seeing what was about to happen, Ronald Andrews said to Billy Odle, "Boy, I sure hope you're worth all this trouble."

"Me?" Billy looked astonished. "I never caused any of this!"

"Hell, of course you didn't," said Andrews, a sarcastic snap to his words. "Now stay right here." He raised his pistol from his holster with his right hand

and moved to the door, his rifle hanging in his left hand already cocked and ready. "Somebody's going to have to keep this town from shooting itself to pieces." He swung the door open and stepped out quickly, as if afraid that taking time to consider his action might cause him to change his mind.

At the sound of Andrews's pistol fire, the four outlaws' horses stopped at once, Morgan Aglo's big dun rearing and trying to turn in mid-air. Without warning, Ronald Andrews charged forward from the boardwalk, hoping the sight of him would cause both Collins and Yates to bring their men out of hiding and rush the outlaws. But as one of his shots hit Joe Shine high in the shoulder, Ronald Andrews heard not a sound from the townsmen. "My God, what's he doing?" said Collins, staring as if frozen in place.

Before flying backward from his saddle, Joe Shine had managed to draw his pistol and get a shot off. The bullet whistled past the side of Ronald Andrews's head, yet Andrews never flinched. The pistol in his hand kept firing until it clicked on an empty chamber. Then Andrews let the smoking pistol drop to the ground and swung his rifle up into play. Two of his pistol shots had hit Tack Beechum and unseated him. Another shot had barely missed Texas Bob Mackay and caused him to spin his horse in the street as he drew his pistol. Beside him, Morgan Aglo had righted his animal and brought his pistol into the fray.

When Texas Bob Mackay's horse had turned full circle, his shot hit Ronald Andrews low in the left side, the impact twisting Andrews sideways before catching himself and returning fire with the rifle. Morgan Aglo's pistol shots hit Ronald Andrews like maddened hornets.

"My God, men!" cried Carl Yates, seeing the shots from Morgan Aglo and Texas Bob overpowering Ronald Andrews. "What are we waiting for? They're killing poor Ronald!"

Carl Yates sprang forward, the men right behind him, firing on Morgan Aglo and Texas Bob Mackay as the outlaws' shots sliced and punched Ronald Andrews. Morgan Aglo let out a tortured scream and kept firing as bullets ripped through his body: "*Aii-ieeee!* You sonsabitches, we ain't even robbed nothing yet!" His voice sounded wild with rage at the unfairness of it.

Texas Bob managed to turn his horse even in the hail of fire. His last bullet had hit Ronald Andrews straight in the teeth, and ripped a gaping hole in his cheek. Andrews had staggered in place and caught himself, managing in his dazed state to remain on his feet, a cold gray numbness settling over his senses. Badly wounded, Morgan Aglo scrambled across the ground to ally himself with Joe Shine as Collins and his townsmen spilled out through the doors of the saloon. Through the heavy gunfire Morgan Aglo called out, "Don't worry, Joe, I'm coming!"

Badly wounded himself, Joe Shine looked forward across the body of Tack Beechum at the street full of angry guns facing him and cried out with tears in his eyes, "Damn it to hell, Morgan! This ain't fair!" Large snowflakes fell peacefully onto both the dead and the dying.

Thirty yards along the street, with bullets whizzing past him, Texas Bob Mackay threw his arm back and fired the remaining shot from his pistol, then let it fall from his hand. Fresh blood was pouring freely down into both of his boots, and most of his clothes were stuck to his body. He was not at all surprised when something like a hammer blow hit him in the small of his back and seemed to lift him up from his saddle just long enough for his horse to run out from under him.

Seeing the world slow down around him, Texas Bob felt himself float down to the ground among the gentle snowflakes. He began planning how he would explain to everybody that this was all a mistake—that he was riding with Fuller's bounty posse. That this was just his way of getting in with the outlaws, gaining their trust. See, he wasn't an outlaw. *Hell no!* He never had been . . .

When Texas Bob hit the ground, the firing behind him stopped, or at least he could no longer hear it. All he could hear was a low dull roar, like some distant wind across a dark bottomless chasm. Strangely though, he could hear the sound of boots walking toward him, their hard soles making a crunching sound on the cold earth. Texas Bob rolled over onto his side and made a pistol of his steaming bloody hand and raised it toward Ronald Andrews.

"I'll shoot," Texas Bob warned, seeing the terrible face loom above him. Even the veil of slow falling snow could not soften the harshness of the rent flesh, the shattered bone fragments, the steam billowing grotesquely from the fresh wounds.

"No you won't . . ." Ronald Andrews's voice sounded muffled and guttural, coming from the numbness of his mouth and the dazed state of his mind. He staggered back and forth in place, his pistol hanging aimlessly in his hand.

Texas Bob clicked his thumb back and forth as if this make-believe pistol might actually fire. Then he sighed deeply and let his hand fall to the ground. Somehow, even through Ronald Andrews's bloodied face and torn flesh, Texas Bob saw something familiar—the face of someone out of his past. He tried to smile, wanting to make sense of this new twist on things, thinking perhaps this was someone who might awaken him now and tell him this was all a bad dream. "I—I know you . . . from somewhere," Texas Bob managed to say.

"No," said Ronald Andrews, "you don't know me." He found that speaking took little effort even with his teeth broken and his cheek turned inside out.

"Hell yes . . . I do," said Texas Bob. "You're just . . . an outlaw yourself . . . you always was."

With much effort Ronald Andrews extended the cocked pistol, holding the tip of the barrel no more than six inches from Texas Bob's forehead. "You don't know me from nowhere." The pistol bucked once in Andrews's hand, slamming Texas Bob backward to the ground, a wreath of blood and bone matter splattering out beneath his head on the fresh white snow. "You never did."

"Lord have mercy, Ronald," Carl Yates said in hushed tone, having witnessed the shooting of the outlaw. Then he gasped in disbelief and horror as he slid to a halt, seeing Ronald Andrews's face as Andrews turned toward him, raising the pistol in his direction.

"Ronald it's me, Carl! Put the pistol down, please!" He saw the strange look in Ronald's eyes, the dazed look of a wild animal with a paw pinned in a steel trap. The look chilled Carl Yates to his bones. "I'm here to help you! For God sakes, drop the pistol!"

"I can't," Andrews said in his wounded muffled voice.

Yates noted that the pistol had been recocked.

Dropping it was a dangerous proposition. "I mean just lay it down easy! Get rid of it!"

"I can't," Ronald Andrews sobbed, streaming blood from the gaping hole in his cheek. "I've tried . . . I can't."

"Listen to me, Ronald," Yates said quickly, seeing that in his wounded state Ronald Andrews was far past any level of logic or reasoning. Ronald Andrews was functioning now on raw human instincts, nothing more. "Don't try to talk. You've got to lay the gun down and let me help you. Get a hold of yourself, man! You've been hurt, real *real* bad!"

"I know it," said Ronald in his guttural shapeless voice, all air and life seeming to have left him. He staggered closer to Carl Yates, raising the cocked pistol slowly with a shaking hand. "I ain't going back . . ."

In the street between the saloon and the sheriff's office, the shooting had ceased. The townsmen from both sides of the street had drawn in cautiously around Morgan Aglo who rocked back and forth on his knees, a long red string of saliva bobbing up and down from his bloody lips. The fresh snow surrounding him was a widening red slush. His failing eyes went to the bank building. "How much . . . money, was we . . . talking about?"

But the townsmen turned quickly away from the dying outlaw without offering an answer when the single pistol shot resounded up the street. "Oh my God!" said Collins, not believing his eyes. "Yates just shot Ronald Andrews! Shot him dead!"

"Never . . . mind that," Morgan Aglo said, his dying voice going lower. "How much . . . money?"

· "Shut the hell up and die, you lousy bandit!" said a voice. A boot swung around, kicked Aglo in the back of his head and sent him sprawling facedown on the cold, rutted street. He laid helpless, blood spouting from his gaping mouth, the dimming world above him growing smaller and farther away.

Chapter 21

Collins and the rest of the townsmen hurried to where Carl Yates was kneeling beside the body of Ronald Andrews on the cold ground. As the men drew close around Yates, they saw him reach out with his gloved hand and wipe the flakes of snow from Andrews's face and close his dead blank eyes. "What happened, Carl?" Selectman Collins asked in a gentle tone of voice.

"I didn't shoot him," Yates whispered, having heard what Collins had said moments ago.

"I'm sorry, Yates," Collins offered. "I heard the shot and looked down here—"

"He shot himself," Yates said, not seeming to hear Collins's apology.

"Lord have mercy," whispered one of the townsmen, wincing at the sight of Ronald Andrews's mangled cheek, the rugged bullet hole in the side of his head, the streak of blood on the white frosty ground. "The poor ole boy . . . He must've plumb lost his mind, running out there that way, then getting his face shot off like that. I reckon you can't hold it agin' him for taking his own life. No doctor could ever made him right after this." He gestured a hand toward

Ronald Andrews's face, then looked away as it pained him to see it.

"He jumped right out there and called it on," said Collins shaking his head in amazement. "What on earth do you suppose made him do that?"

"I reckon we'll never know," said Carl Yates, standing up and rubbing his gloved hands together. "Ronald was a good helper and a damn good fellow . . . but I have to say, there was a side to him that I never understood. Seemed like he would only let a person get so close, then he'd back off real quick. He had things he didn't want folks to know, I reckon." Yates shrugged and added with sad finality, "Well . . . they'll never know it now."

"Come on, Yates," said Collins. "Let's get you looked at." He nodded at a spot of fresh blood on Yates's coat sleeve.

"Oh, that's not my blood, Collins." As Carl Yates spoke he felt himself up and down, as if having to make sure he hadn't been wounded.

"Look who's coming," said one of the townsmen, "now that the shooting's over and we don't need any help!"

At the far end of the street, Sam rode his horse forward through the falling snow, his rifle butt propped on his thigh, his thumb still across the hammer. When the gunfire had stopped, Sam's first thought was to ride out in search of Willie John before fresh snow covered his tracks. Yet he couldn't leave without first checking on the town. When he stopped his horse a few feet back from the body of Ronald Andrews on the ground, Carl Yates looked up at him, grief-stricken.

"That's Ronald laying there, Ranger," Yates said, gesturing with a hand. "We don't know what happened . . .

He just jumped out front ahead of everybody and commenced fighting them by himself."

Sam shook his head slowly, showing his regret, then looked along the street at the bodies of the outlaws. "Are the rest of you all right, Sheriff?" he asked, his gaze going to Selectman Collins.

"I believe so," said Collins, cutting a glance at the men around him as if asking their opinion. Their heads nodded in agreement.

"Where's Billy Odle?" Sam asked, looking toward the sheriff's office where the door stood wide open.

Seeing the door at the same time, Collins said, "Oh, the door? I expect Ronald Andrews left it open in his haste. He wasn't himself I'm afraid . . . not after that Indian busting him in the head."

Sam heeled his horse forward quickly, leaving Collins, Yates and the townsmen standing in the street. Outside the sheriff's office he swung down from his saddle before his horse completely stopped. He ran inside, his rifle hanging in his gloved hand, and looked at Bootlip Thomas who stood with his face pressed between the bars, trying to see out through the open door. "Is—is it all over out there, Ranger?" Thomas asked.

"Yes," said Sam. "Where's the boy?"

"He's gone," said Bootlip. "I hollered, but they didn't hear me for all the shooting."

"Did he say anything first?" Sam asked hurriedly.

"Nope . . . but he didn't have to. He's been acting real squirrelly ever since he heard about Willie John coming back."

Behind Sam, Carl Yates hurried inside the office and looked all around, understanding right away what had happened. "Blast that boy! Ranger, I'm awfully sorry! There was just so much going on.

Poor Ronald was keeping an eye on him, but I reckon Billy lit out of here as soon as Ronald stepped out in the street! I take the blame for Billy running out."

"Save your breath, Yates," said Sam. "You've done the best you could. Nobody's to blame for Billy's actions anymore, except Billy himself."

"I wasn't going to tell you this, Ranger, but I reckon I better," said Bootlip Thomas. "The boy took a pistol out of the desk drawer before he left." Bootlip nodded toward a wooden peg on the back wall of the office. "He also grabbed a belt full of bullets down from over there."

Sam gave Bootlip a hard gaze. "And you weren't going to tell me about it?"

Bootlip looked ashamed. "I sort of promised him I wouldn't. Then I got to thinking about it. I don't want to see that crazy kid get himself killed." Bootlip shook his head. "I don't know what it is about him. I reckon he reminds me of myself back before things got out of hand."

Sam let out a breath and with it the hardness in his eyes seemed to diminish. "I know what you mean, Bootlip." He looked at Carl Yates, then at the men outside on the boardwalk who pressed close to the doorway, staring in at him. "Billy has that effect on all of us. Thanks for telling me about the pistol."

"You'll try not to shoot that worthless little peckerwood, won't you, Ranger?" Bootlip pleaded between the bars.

"I'll do the best I can," said Sam. "If he gets with Willie John, there's no telling how this will turn out."

"I'll go with you, Ranger," said Carl Yates.

"Much obliged," said Sam, "but you're needed here right now. Get this town settled down."

"If I hear much shooting out there, I'm riding out to you, Ranger," Carl Yates said.

"The snow's bad, Yates," said Sam. "If you come looking, make sure you let me know it's you coming up behind me . . . and make sure it's me you ride up on."

"I will." Carl Yates swallowed a dry knot in his throat, then stepped quietly to one side of the open door as Sam walked past him. Between the door and the hitch rail, townsmen cleared a way for him, watching closely as Sam swung up into his saddle and urged his horse forward to the livery barn. The men still did not move. They stood staring as Sam walked into the barn, then came out a moment later, remounted and rode away in the falling snow.

"Lord have mercy," said Kirby Bell under his breath, "I'd hate to be in that boy's shoes once the Ranger catches up to him."

"Sam Burrack won't hurt that boy, Kirby," said Carl Yates. "You heard him, didn't you?"

"Ha! Yeah, I heard him," said Bell. "But he's going to skin Billy Odle alive when he catches him. The way that kid's been acting, it won't bother me one bit."

"Hush up, Bell," said Carl Yates. "If that's all you've seen out of the ranger, you're blind as a bat. He'll bend backwards to keep that boy from harm."

"Yeah? Then you better hope that boy doesn't raise a pistol toward him. If he does, my money says the Ranger will shoot him dead." He looked around at the others for agreement. A few heads nodded; others looked away.

"Sometimes you get on my nerves something awful, Bell," said Carl Yates. He spit and wiped a hand across his mouth. "Come on fellows," he added, "let's get Ronald Andrews out of the cold. It tears me up to see him like this."

"Ronald was a good and decent man," said Kirby Bell, his voice softening. "That's one thing you and I can agree on."

Once outside of Hubbler Wells, Sam Burrack followed the prints as far as he could before the falling snow began filling the tracks left by Billy Odle's running horse. Yet, halfway across the flatlands between Hubbler Wells and the line of low hill surrounding the basin, Sam stopped his horse and gazed out across the smooth surface of snow before him, his vision eclipsed by a swirling white veil. In the ringing silence he heard the slightest sound of a horse nickering, far off in the distance.

"Billy Odle!" Sam shouted, knowing full well that this was a dangerous thing to do, letting whomever was up ahead know his position. But for the kid's sake he had to risk it. "It's me, Ranger Sam Burrack. Stop running, Billy. Let me talk to you."

For all Sam knew the sound could have come from Willie John's horse. Or, at best, it could tip Billy Odle off that he was being followed. With a gun, in this weather, there was nothing to say that a harebrained kid like Billy Odle couldn't shoot him from his saddle, the same as any grown man. "I must be as crazy as he is," Sam murmured to himself. Hearing no response, Sam heeled his horse forward in the direction the nickering had come from.

But before he had gone fifteen feet, the flat distant sound of a pistol shot rolled in, muffled by the snow. Sam didn't even flinch. Instead he shook his head and heeled forward in the same steady pace, knowing that the pistol was far out of range. That in itself let him know for certain it was Billy Odle. Neither Willie John nor any other outlaw would have done something so foolish. Sam allowed himself a trace of a smile. All right, now he had the boy responding to him, he had to keep it this way.

"Billy, listen to me . . . You're not getting away. You might as well give this up."

His answer was another pistol shot. He studied the sound closely, gauging the distance. Then he followed the sound another twenty yards before calling out again. "Billy, stop shooting at me. Let's talk."

Of course, the one thing Sam didn't want was for Billy to stop firing the pistol. But he didn't want Billy to know. Bootlip Thomas had said Billy took a belt full of ammunition from a peg in the corner. Sam wanted to keep him shooting just enough to bring him in closer. Once he got his tracking paced just right and got ahead of the time it took for the fresh snow to fill the hoofprints, he would quit calling out to him. He would slip in closer following the hoofprints and catch Billy Odle off guard—he sure hoped so, anyway. Otherwise . . .

Sam didn't want to think about that right now. If his hunch was right and Willie John was somewhere out there waiting for him, there was no way Sam could let Billy Odle come between him and what he had to do. He'd given the kid every break he could afford. Now it was down to living and dying. Sam knew that, and so did Willie John, he thought. He heeled the horse forward, knowing that as surely as he and Billy could hear one another out here, somewhere—up in those hills, no doubt—the Indian was waiting, watching, preparing himself to bring this thing to a close.

*   *   *

Willie John stood beside his big dapple-gray stallion on the edge of a thin cliff where he'd guided his horse at the sound of the first pistol shot from the flatlands below. From this distance he had not heard Billy's horse nickering. But by the time the third shot was fired he'd heard the slightest trace of the Ranger's voice calling out to Billy Odle. Willie John put two and two together and nodded to himself, almost smiling, picturing poor, dumb Billy Odle down there shooting at the wind.

This Ranger was smart, Willie John thought, getting the kid to fire the pistol, bringing him in closer that way. But then Willie John had long since decided that this was no ordinary man, this young Ranger. That's why he'd led the Ranger into this to begin with. It was time to settle all accounts. Willie John raised his rifle and fired a shot into the air. Then he climbed atop his dapple-gray mount and heeled it forward along the ridgeline. One hundred yards along the ridge he slowed long enough to fire another rifleshot, then heeled forward again. He knew full well where Billy Odle was going. He might as well let the Ranger know where he stood on things . . . add something interesting into the mix.

At the sound of the second rifle shot, the Ranger's eyes went toward the hills beyond the swirl of white snow. It was Willie John, there was no doubt about it. He had suspected it upon hearing the first shot. The second shot had only confirmed it for him. He rose forward, knowing that the rifle shot was Willie speaking to both Billy Odle and himself. The Indian was telling Billy where he was headed. At the same time he was inviting Sam to follow. All right. Sam raised his rifle from its boot, levered a round into the chamber and laid it across his lap. He needn't reply, he thought. Willie John knew his answer. Sam kept his horse moving along parallel to the spot where the last shot was fired.

Less than two miles ahead of Sam Burrack, Billy Odle had stopped his horse stone still at the sound of Willie John's first rifleshot. He'd sat astonished, his mouth agape for a moment until it dawned on him who it was up there. There was no question it was Willie John. He was there in the hills some-where, listening, figuring out what was going on . . . giving him a signal. Billy Odle's face lit up in a smile. Willie was headed for the ruins where Billy Odle had left him. Billy knew it. He gigged the tired horse forward in the falling snow.

In his excitement, and with the white swirl of snow obscuring his vision, Billy did not see the riders sur-round him from ten yards out and close in like a silent pack of wolves. Only when his horse rose up in fright and let out a long whinny did Billy Odle see what was about to befall him. But by then it was too late.

"Got him," said Red Booker, jumping his horse forward and catching Billy's rearing horse by its bri-dle as it touched down.

"Get off me!" Billy Odle shouted. The pistol was still in his hand. He jerked it up toward Red Booker's face, his thumb trying to cock the hammer.

A hand seemed to come out of nowhere. "I'll take that," said Colonel Fuller's voice. Fuller snatched the pistol from Billy's hand so fast, Billy was powerless to stop him. He darted a glance back and forth, wild-eyed at the closing circle of drawn guns pointed at him.

"Stay back! All of you! I'm warning you—" Billy's words were cut short when Colonel Fuller's gloved hand came around in a vicious slap that lifted him from his saddle and landed him flat on his back in the snow. Billy laid addled, shaking his head, trying to keep from going unconscious. Through a mental fog he watched Colonel Fuller step down from his horse and walk over to him. Fuller took his time, drawing a long skinning knife from its sheath behind his back. Billy only moaned and ran a cold hand across his face, trying to clear his mind. Then he managed to spit a long stream of blood from his split lip.

"That's it, wake up, boy," said Colonel Fuller. "You don't know how long I've been wanting to do this." He slapped the wide blade against his gloved palm and looked down at Billy with a crazed look on his face, a cruel smile forming on his tight lips. "You think you're a tough young man? A real outlaw *desperado*? All right, then, it's time somebody treated you like one." His knife hand made a quick slash across Billy Odle's stomach. Billy saw the blade coming and tried to jerk back away from the sharp steel. He managed to pull back far enough to keep the wicked knife from opening his stomach, but he felt cold air on his skin where the front of his coat and shirt were laid open.

"You ain't ducking this, boy!" said Fuller, drawing back for another swing. "I've got all day!"

"Stop it, Fuller!" shouted Red Booker.

"Like hell I will," Fuller gasped in reply. He took a step forward as Billy Odle scooted backward in the snow.

"I said stop it! Leave him be, Fuller!" Red Booker shouted, hurrying in, catching Fuller's wrist in time and twisting it back in an armlock. As his free hand cocked his pistol and jammed the tip of the barrel beneath Fuller's ear, Booker hissed, "Don't make me splatter your brains out! I'm running this show now. I'll say who dies, and when. Now drop it!"

"Red, please," Fuller pleaded, not giving the knife up right away. "You've got to let me field-dress this little son of a bitch! You've got to . . . for all the trouble he caused!"

Red Booker put more pressure on Fuller's wrist, the pistol barrel jamming harder beneath the colonel's ear. "I'm too close to catching that Injun to let you ruin the deal. I didn't pull out here and sit waiting in the cold for nothing. Now drop it or die with it in your hand."

Colonel Fuller relented, letting the big knife drop to the ground near Billy Odle's side. Before Billy could make a grab for the knife handle, Red Booker clamped a boot down on it, calling out over his shoulder, "Some of you get down here. Grab this kid and hold onto him."

When three men stepped in and yanked Billy Odle to his feet, Red Booker stepped away from the knife, picked it up and pulled Colonel Fuller away from the others, out of sight in the thickening cover of falling snow. He shook him, saying, "Damn it, Fuller, I told you not to start giving me trouble! I'm running this posse now. I'm not letting you kill this two-bit punk kid and keep me from getting Willie John!"

"Please, Booker!" said Fuller. "You've got to let me slice him apart! I don't care about nothing else. This is your posse now, that's fine! But give me the kid!"

"I'll use that kid when the time comes, Fuller. He's not worth a thing to me dead."

"You're crazy, Booker!" Fuller snapped at him. "Willie John won't let himself be taken over that kid.

He'd watch you turn that boy into blood gravy before he'd give himself up!"

"We'll see," said Red Booker. He shoved the colonel back a step, then said, "Are you going to settle down and not give me any more trouble over that ragged-assed kid?"

Colonel Fuller spit and put the back of his gloved hand to his lips. Steam gushed in his breath. "To be honest, Red, I don't think I can."

"Is that your last word on it, Colonel?" Red asked.

Colonel Fuller only nodded, his eyes blank, not seeming to even see Red Booker, but instead staring past him through the swirling snow to where he'd last seen Billy Odle on the ground at his feet.

Nells Kroft helped push Billy Odle back up into his saddle. As Red Booker came walking over to them, Kroft blew his steaming breath on the tips of his fingers sticking out of his ragged gloves and said, "Hey, Red, where's the colonel?"

"He ain't coming with us," said Red Booker. He looked from one set of knowing eyes to the other. In one hand he carried the big skinning knife, in his other hand the leather sheath. The blade of Fuller's knife was streaked with fresh blood. "Anybody got something to say about it?" Booker shoved the knife into the sheath and stuck it down behind his belt. When no one offered any more on the matter, Red Booker nodded and stepped up into his saddle. "Good. Then let's kill that Injun real quick-like and head on out of here."

Chapter 22

Tinnie Malone stood at the window in Hattie Odle's room and stared out into falling snow toward the unseen hill line. It had been a few minutes since she'd heard the last distant sound of a gunshot. Still she peered into the impenetrable white swirl and listened closely as she tied the string of her wool cloak about her neck. Behind her, Hattie Odle washed her face in a pan of water and dried it on a soft white towel. Hattie took a long coat down from a rack in a corner and walked to the bed where she had laid out the rest of her clothes.

"If you're going, I'm going with you," said Hattie. "Just give me a moment to get dressed."

"No," said Tinnie, turning around from the window. "It's better that you stay here."

"It's my son out there," Hattie responded. "I should be the one going to look for him."

Tinnie considered it for a second, then said, "All right. But you'll have to be the one to ask Carl Yates. He only agreed to let me ride along with him because I'm taking a horse sleigh from the livery barn, just in case the Ranger or Billy is out there hurt and needing help."

"I'll ask him," said Hattie, hurrying into her clothes, her face turning drawn and ashen at the thought of something happening to her son.

Both women were waiting with their winter cloaks and woolen mufflers on when Carl Yates knocked on the door. He saw right away what the women had in mind, and he said, "Whoa now, ladies." He cut his eyes to Tinnie. "I said you could ride along and bring the sleigh. But it's too dangerous for both of you to be out there."

Hattie Odle started to speak, but Tinnie's words jumped in ahead of her. "Carl, for God sakes, it's her son out there. She's got a right to go along with us. Besides, if he's hurt and gives you a hard time, maybe it would be better having her along."

Carl Yates relented slowly. "Well . . . all right, Hattie, come on with us. Let's get a move on."

As they walked out the door and toward the stairs, Hattie said sidelong to Tinnie, "Thanks, but I thought you said I'd have to ask him for myself."

Tinnie Malone smiled kindly. "The truth is, me and the rest of the girls feel like we've got some making up to do with you, Hattie. We saw the hard times you was having, and the way Asa Dahl was treating you. But we just turned our heads . . . and I'm sorry."

Hattie replied, "You needn't apologize. None of you owed me anything."

"Yes we did," said Tinnie Malone. "There's some things we all owe one another without it ever being asked for, or ever being expected."

As they descended the last three steps, walking ahead of Carl Yates, Tinnie and Hattie saw Asa Dahl standing at the hotel counter with a cup of coffee and a cigar. When the two women reached the bottom of the stairs, Dahl set his coffee cup down and stepped over in front of them, blocking them from the front door. "Tinnie, this has gone on long enough!" he growled. Although he'd been sipping coffee, Tinnie smelled whiskey on his breath. "You abandon this woman and her little outlaw son right now, or you can kiss your job with me good-bye forever!"

Before Tinnie could answer, Carl Yates stepped around from behind her and Hattie Odle and shoved Asa Dahl back a step. "Get yourself out of our way, Dahl. We don't have time to deal with you and your spite. If the truth was told, you're the one who caused this town to turn into such a sorry, don't-give-a-damn place to begin with."

Asa Dahl stiffened for a second, then retaliated, saying, "Oh yeah? Well then, since we're standing here speaking our minds, let me remind you that there is a four-dollar beer tab at my place right now with your name on it."

"Here, you puny bastard!" Carl Yates reached into his vest pocket, snatched out some wrinkled dollar bills and threw them against Asa Dahl's chest. "Now get out of our way before I knock you cockeyed!"

Asa Dahl stepped aside letting the money fall to the floor. He said to Tinnie as she walked past him, "Don't forget what I said—you're fired."

"Sure, Asa." Tinnie shrugged. "But me and the girls all talked it over, and if I leave, they all leave with me. Now chew on that while you figure how to explain to all the miners and cowboys passing through that your whole flock of soiled doves has flown the coop."

"You women can't leave my place," Dahl shouted. "Where else can you ply your profession, out in a tool shack, like this woman?" He pointed a finger of condemnation at Hattie Odle. "You do that, and you'll all end up just like her!"

Tinnie stopped and made it a point to look Hattie Odle up and down as she said to Asa Dahl, "Oh? She doesn't look any worse for the wear . . . once she got your dope out of her system." Dahl looked stunned. "That's right, Asa," Tinnie continued, "I know who was behind selling the opium in this town. You never fooled me, or any of the girls. We're all fed up with you anyway. Maybe I'll gather them all together as soon as I get back, tell them I'm fired and see what they want to do about it." She turned and started to walk out the door as Carl Yates held it open.

"Hey, wait, damn it!" said Asa Dahl, his voice suddenly sounding concerned. "Tinnie, you're not fired . . . hell, can't you see I've been drinking? Go ahead and befriend this woman far as I care. It means nothing to me."

"Too late, Asa," said Tinnie, guiding Hattie through the door then following her. "I've decided to take it on myself to see if we can turn this town into something better . . . and get rid of the likes of you." She grinned. "We've all seen what happens to a town when it's pulled apart in every direction by a snake like you. Now stand back and watch what happens when everybody starts pulling together." She started to slam the door in Dahl's face, but he caught it with the heel of his hand and called out as Carl and the two women walked away toward the livery barn, "You've just got a bad attitude right now, Tinnie . . . but watch, you'll come back to me, wanting me to keep you and the others on." Tinnie didn't look back.

* * *

Sam Burrack stood at the spot where the posse's hoofprints had left the snow upturned, the falling snow not yet having covered them. He saw the spot of blood Billy Odle had spat upon the ground. Taking note of how his horse kept poking its muzzle in the same direction as if sniffing something unseen, Sam held his thumb across his rifle hammer and walked forward cautiously. He saw the dark shape of a body lying facedown on the ground, snow already starting to cover its back. He hurried forward, keeping the horse's reins in his hand, careful not to lose the animal in this kind of weather.

Sam turned Colonel Fuller's body over in the snow and looked at the deep red-purple gash across his white throat. Sam's expression remained fixed, neither surprised nor repulsed by the shameless face of death. Yet, finding Fuller's body gave the Ranger cause to consider Red Booker's thinking. The man was running out of tolerance, losing his self-control. This was something a man couldn't afford to let happen to himself on a manhunt, Sam thought. Booker had turned on one of his own now, the colonel at that.

Looking back down at the shocked expression frozen onto Colonel Fuller's bloodless face, Sam knew that Red Booker himself hadn't been fully aware of what he was doing when he slashed a blade across the colonel's throat. Now Booker would be even more dangerous in his dealings with Billy Odle. Booker wouldn't realize it until it was too late, but the longer it took for him to end this hunt, the more desperate he would become.

Sam turned his eyes to the weather, wondering if the snow had begun to slacken. Then he turned his eyes in the direction of the disappearing hoofprints—

the same direction Willie John's rifleshots had come from earlier.

"Well, Willie John," Sam said under his breath, "looks like you and I are going to get a chance at one another. But it ain't going to be the way you planned it . . . me, neither, for that matter." He stepped back up into his saddle and looked down again at the blood in the snow as he pushed the horse forward. "Billy boy, I sure hope you're worth all this . . ."

Over a mile ahead and up in the deep hill paths, Willie John led his dapple-gray instead of tiring it in the deep snow or taking a chance on laming the animal on what unsteady elements of rock lay beneath the thick snow. But up here the storm had waned a little, offering some partial view of the gray sky; and farther ahead toward the old ruins, Willie John could tell the snow had just about stopped falling altogether. He looked back down toward where he knew the Ranger was following. Then he shifted his gaze forward to where he expected Billy Odle would be turning upward about now. He hoped that in his eagerness to join him, Billy Odle wouldn't risk his horse's safety.

Fifty yards farther up, Willie John stopped when he heard the faint sound of a voice drift upward from one of the lower paths. He halted and listened closely, until at length he heard the sound of horses. This was not the sound of Billy Odle's lone horse the way he'd expected, but rather the sound of many horses. The animals were struggling up toward him through the deep drifts. He looked back along his path at his horse's hoofprints. With the snow lessening, there was no way to hide his tracks. Somewhere out there Billy Odle was still trying to get up here, but Willie John couldn't worry about that right now. For all he knew, Billy Odle could be with whomever was down there—Billy could even be leading them here, he thought. Willie John hurried his pace. This wasn't at all what he'd had in mind.

On the lower path, Nells Kroft's horse slipped out from under him and lay thrashing in the snow, screaming long and pitifully, its foreleg broken and angled to one side, a silver of white bone showing through the skin. "Damn it to hell, Kroft!" Red Booker shouted. "Shut that animal up! You can hear it two miles off."

"But a gunshot would be worse," Kroft offered in a worried voice, jerking his hat up from the snow and slapping it against his leg.

The horse continued shrieking long and loud.

Red Booker yanked the big knife from its sheath and flung it down in the snow at Kroft's feet. "Shut it up now, Kroft!"

Nells Kroft looked at the big knife and felt his stomach turn at the prospect of using it. "Oh Lord, Red, I never . . . I mean, I couldn't just take that and—"

"Jesus Christ!" Red Booker cursed. His Colt flashed up from his holster and exploded. The horse's head fell to the snow, its screams silenced. "There, now we've tipped our hands to anybody up there!" He swung the barrel toward Nells Kroft, his thumb cocking it. Kroft's cold face turned stark white in terror. He caught a quick mental image of Colonel Fuller lying dead in the snow back on the flatlands. The thought of it sent a dark chill up his spine.

"Red, please!" Nells Kroft pleaded. "It weren't my fault the horse went down! Give me another chance!"

He backed up a step in the snow, seeing the hard killing look in Booker's wide red-rimmed eyes.

"I'm tired of giving men chances they don't deserve." Red Booker aimed the pistol at Nells Kroft, tightening his grip on it.

Beside Red Booker, Bernard Gift said with a blast of steaming breath, "Lord God, Red! Don't kill him! Look at him . . . it's Nells Kroft! He's been with us from the get-go!"

At the sound of Gift's voice, Red Booker swung the pistol at him, the barrel only a couple of feet from Gift's belly. "What is this, Bernard? Are you taking charge now?"

"No, Red . . . please," said Bernard Gift. "I'm just saying what we're all thinking!" He jerked a nervous nod toward the men behind them. "You're in charge . . . but damn, not if you're going to start turning against your own men! Look at yourself. You were all set to kill Nells, and now me!"

Red Booker calmed down, taking a deep breath and looking at the faces of the men, some of them sitting their saddles with one hand on their pistol butts.

Red Booker raised the tip of his pistol barrel and uncocked it. He spit and ran a gloved hand roughly across his face as if ridding it of cobwebs. Without facing Nells Kroft, he said, "Kroft, get mounted. Let's get going."

"Mounted on what?" Nells Kroft asked, his knees visibly shaking behind his trouser legs. He looked all around, gesturing with a trembling hand, his big eyes watering.

"Mullins," said Red Booker, "throw that kid off his horse and give it to Nells."

"Down you go, kid," said Herbert Mullins. He reached out with his rifle butt and unseated Billy Odle. Then he jerked Billy's horse forward by its bridle until it stood before Nells Kroft, saying with contempt, "There you are, fat man. Try to keep it between your legs."

"Obliged," said Kroft, embarrassed, taking the reins and stepping up into the saddle.

Herbert Mullins turned to Red Booker and added, "Red, if I can keep this bunch together for you, say the word. You've got enough on your mind trying to sniff that Injun out."

Red Booker just stared at him for a moment, then nodded. "Boys," he said, "Mullins is going to be doing for me like I used to do for the colonel. Don't give him any guff . . . just do what he tells you." Booker looked at each man in turn, then down at Billy Odle in the snow as if for a second he'd forgotten about the boy.

Mullins also looked down at Billy. Then he acted quickly, saying, "Kroft, you double up with the kid . . . you're the one got his horse. Go on, hurry up. Red wants to get going."

"Not so fast, Mullins," said Red Booker. His eyes riveted on Billy Odle as he stepped down slowly from his saddle. "It's time this boy started earning his keep." He stepped over and yanked Billy up by his coat collar. "I was going to keep you for the Injun when we got to him . . . but I reckon that dying horse and the gunshot changes things." He held Billy with one gloved hand as he jerked a nod upward into the hills. "You know where he's at up there, don't you?"

"No," said Billy. "Cross my heart, hope to die. I don't know where he is right now."

"But you know where he's headed," said Booker. "You hid him out before. He's got a safe hole up there and you're taking us to it, ain't you, boy?"

"No I—" Billy's voice stopped as Red Booker backhanded him across the face.

The men winced and looked at one another. Mullins saw their expressions and said, "So what? The little bastard deserves what he gets! Huh? Doesn't he?"

The men avoided Mullins's eyes, offering no agreement with him.

Billy Odle spat more blood on the ground, then looked up at Red Booker with tears streaming down his cold bruised cheeks. "You can kill me . . . I ain't telling. Willie John's my friend."

"Hardheaded little shit!" Red Booker slapped him again, this time sending Billy flying, landing six feet away, again spitting out a mouthful of blood.

Again the men grimaced and tightened their eyes and faces toward Red Booker. Booker stalked forward and loomed over Billy, snatching the big knife from its sheath again. "Boy, you will tell me what I want to hear, or I will take you apart one piece at a time, starting with your ears. You think the colonel was tough on you? You ain't seen nothing yet."

Now, even Herbert Mullins was getting nervous, seeing the expressions on the men's faces as they watched Red Booker run a gloved thumb along the cruel knife blade. "Uh, Red?" said Mullins. "I believe I can get us up to where that Injun is. Don't cut the boy . . . not yet, anyway. Like you said, we'll most likely need him for bargaining."

"What makes you think you can find the Indian?" Red asked, letting his temper ease down a notch as he turned away from Billy Odle.

"Well . . ." Mullins pointed upward into the gray sky, where it grew lighter along the high hill line. "It looks like the snow has let up there along the high trails. If we get up there pretty quick, we'll see any tracks that Injun left. After all the noise we've made, it'd be best if we swung wide and came up on another path, too . . . in case that Injun is waiting on us."

Red Booker thought about it, looking at the faces of the men staring at him. He needed a chance to wind down, seeing the boy wasn't about to tell him anything. He wasn't sure how the men would take it, him doing any serious damage to this kid. "Jesus," he murmured to himself. What had come over him, anyway? He was acting no different than Fuller. He'd have to be careful from now on not to let the boy get to him.

Billy Odle picked himself up from the ground, spat out more blood and staggered toward Nells Kroft atop the horse. Kroft lifted him into the saddle and sat him in front of him. "You best keep quiet and go unnoticed, boy, if you know what's good for you."

Red Booker stepped up into his saddle, then turned and looked at Billy Odle, his temper cooled some now, but still intent on making the boy tell where the Indian would be hiding out. "Think it over, kid," Booker said. "When we get to the top, if we've got no tracks to follow, you better be ready to lead us on. If not, you ain't worth us riding you double and wearing out a good horse." He looked at the other men's faces for any sign of support, but in the falling snow he wasn't sure what he read in their eyes.

As the horses turned off the path and headed farther around the side of the hill, Billy Odle leaned out one last time and spit blood down onto the turning hoofprints. Then he rubbed both hands in his eyes, drying them and saying over his shoulder to Nells Kroft, "Don't worry mister, I ain't causing no more trouble."

Chapter 23

At the top of the path, Willie John had ridden his dapple-gray along the high trail, then circled off and stepped down from the saddle. He led the horse back to where he'd started, carefully looking for footing on the steep hillside. Once back at the top of the hill path, he put the horse out of sight between two stands of tall rock. He waited there with his cocked rifle until he heard the sound of hoofs seeking purchase at the edge of the trail. He steadied his rifle along the side of the rock and took close aim.

Topping the edge of the path afoot, Sam clung to his horse's tail and let the big animal help him upward. As soon as he had stepped up behind the horse and onto the snow-covered trail, Sam immediately felt eyes on him from somewhere in the snow-capped rocks. There were hoofprints along the trail ahead of him, but something told him they weren't headed anywhere but off the trail a few yards up, before doubling back on him. He peered around the rocky hillside. *Yep, sure enough . . .* Willie John had jackpotted him. "Kid, I hope you're worth it," Sam murmured, losing track of how many times he'd said the same thing to himself throughout the day.

But Sam stayed at ease, taking his time moving around the side of the horse, letting his hand fall to the butt of his big Colt while he kept the horse between him and the watching eyes. A few feet ahead of him, Sam saw the only rock alongside the trail large enough to provide him any cover. He moved closer to it, hoping he could fling himself forward at the last second before a gunshot ripped across the trail. As for his horse, he could only hope he had time to slap its rump and send it back down the slope below the trail. Just as Sam got ready to make his move, as if having read his mind, Willie John called out, "Don't shoo the horse away, Ranger, you're going to need it."

Sam froze, staring straight ahead, not toward Willie John's voice, but listening hard for its direction. He'd managed to draw the Colt and cock the hammer. It hung down his thigh, his finger poised on the trigger. "You're Willie John?" he asked, both he and Willie knowing it was a pointless question. Sam knew exactly who was looking down the gun sights at him. "Looks like you've got me cold, Willie John," Sam added.

"Don't fool with me, Ranger," said Willie, a warning in his voice that surprised Sam. "If I wanted you dead, you already would be." Sam noted his voice had shifted to a different direction, a few feet to the left and higher up, behind one of the larger rocks, Sam thought.

"Then what is it we're doing, Willie John?" said Sam, still staring straight ahead, but with Willie John knowing full well that this Ranger was trying to locate him by the sound of his voice. "You know I've come to take you in, Willie John. What now?" Sam judged the distance to the rock in front of him; at the same time he tried to pinpoint the voice on the other side of the trail, getting ready to turn and throw lead at it.

But Willie had moved again since he'd last spoke, back down to where he'd been a moment ago, again taking aim with the rifle against the rock. "They've got the boy, Ranger," said Willie. "I thought you ought to know."

"Yep, I know it," Sam replied. "That kid's been leaving me a blood trail to follow ever since they overtook him. He even let me know when they took another path farther along. I hoped to get up here and get ahead of them. I believe that's what Billy was telling me to do."

"A blood trail, huh? Is he all right, you think?" Willie sounded concerned

"For now he is," said Sam, his mind at work on how to turn this thing around and get the drop on the Indian. "It looks like he's just sucking blood from a busted lip and spitting it out. He's a clever young man to even think of doing such a thing. He'll get by as long as he can . . . but let's face it, when they get to where it's up to him to tell them where you're at . . . ?" Sam took a breath then finished, "I figure he's got just enough gravel in him to die first."

"I think so, too." Willie John let his hands relax on the rifle. Again a thin tight smile came to his lips. It was a smile built not of humor but rather of some strange sense of pride. "Damn crazy kid."

Sam noted the change in Willie's tone of voice. He also noted that this time the Indian hadn't shifted positions. Sam readied himself to turn and make his play. Willie John continued, "I reckon maybe he does have the makings of an outlaw after all."

"Is that what you want to see him do, Willie John?"

Sam asked, taking a short slow step forward, just enough to swing the pistol clear of his horse when he took his shot. "You want to see him turn into an outlaw?"

"It's not up to me what he turns into," said Willie, putting up a front of toughness regarding the boy.

"No, I reckon not," said Sam. Then he added, "No offense, Willie, but it doesn't take much to be an outlaw . . . just a willingness to turn your back on everything and everybody who ever cared about you, and be willing to run until you run out of road."

"Look who's talking, lawman," said Willie John. "I've managed to stay alive all this time. I'm still calling my own shots."

"Really?" said Sam. "Then let's get down to why you led me up here. And don't deny it, you did put me on your trail."

"You're out of your mind, Ranger." Willie John dismissed the thought. "But the fact is, those possemen will kill that boy if something ain't done to stop them." As he spoke he noticed the slightest movement of Sam's hand, and he said hurriedly, his voice turning cold again, "Don't do it, Ranger. You won't be the first one who thought they caught me napping. I don't want to have to kill you yet . . . but don't push it." That was close, Willie thought, seeing the Ranger's pistol relax back down his thigh. This Ranger was good, Willie warned himself. He'd have to stay on his guard with this one.

"What are you proposing, Willie John?" Sam asked. "Some sort of alliance? The two of us against the posse? It won't work . . . I'm here to take you back. I'll have to get Billy away from that posse myself."

"Just you, by yourself? What if you miss your

chance, Ranger? There's nobody up here but you and me. Don't forget I'm the only one who knows the way to where Billy'll take 'em. That's if they don't kill him first. And let's face it, Ranger, if we don't make a truce here pretty quick, only one of us is going past this spot in the trail."

"That's how it looks then, Willie. The only way I'll work with you is if you toss out the gun and give yourself up. Then you can take me where they're headed . . . I'll handle it from there."

"I was thinking more like *you* drop *your* gun. When it's over I'll give myself up," said Willie John.

"Not a chance in the world, Willie John," said Sam. "See where that puts us?"

There was a silence, followed by Willie John saying in a resolved voice, "Then it's the kid who has to pay for us, Ranger. Is that it?" His hands turned steady on his rifle again, his eyes taking aim as he spoke.

"That's all I can give you, Willie John." Sam took a breath and let it out slowly, knowing the talking was through. Now came the killing.

"Then answer me one question—tell the truth on your word of honor," said Willie John. "Did you mean it?" He felt his finger tightening on the rifle's trigger, the center of the Ranger's back locked in his sights.

"Mean what?" Sam asked, readying his hand to make the swing and catch what sliver of a target the Indian's face would offer.

"That you would take me in if I threw out my rifle and helped you find the kid? Was that the truth? You've been on my trail all this time, just to *take me in*?"

Sam thought about it for a moment, then raised

his pistol slowly, only to lower it into his holster and turn to face the snow-capped rocks with his hands rising chest-high. "I was lying telling you that. We both know what I came here to do." He leveled his gaze toward Willie John. "Was it true you'd have given yourself up after the kid was safe?"

Willie didn't bother answering. He lowered his rifle and stepped out from behind the rock into full view. "I figure it's best if I got in front of them around these slopes. There's an old ruins in a cave at the top of that peak." He pointed toward a higher hill on the other side of a natural rock bridge. "I'll come at them from one side and you from the other."

Sam stepped forward and looked down the steep drop. "You're going to try to take a horse around these? The odds are long on you making it across this ice and snow . . . too long, in my opinion." Sam eyed the dried bloodstain on Willie's chest through his open coat.

"I know it's long odds. That's why I want you coming in from this side . . . in case I don't make it."

"In case you don't?" Sam looked skeptical and shook his head slowly.

"I know," said Willie, "but it's for the kid, right? Us giving him a chance to draw to a better hand than this world dealt him starting out?"

Sam stood silent, looking down the long slopes. Then he raised his face to Willie and said, "We've still got business, you and me."

"I know it," said Willie John.

Sam murmured under his breath, "I hope that boy is worth it."

"I've been saying the same thing to myself all day," said Willie John. "I figure if I get around in front of them, I'll fire two shots right together, get them following me in, keep them from killing Billy over him not telling where the hideout is."

"So, you're not even going to have the element of surprise," said Sam. "I don't like it."

"You don't have to like it, Ranger . . . you just have to go along with it."

Sam thought about Willie John's plan, knowing the Indian was right—that Billy Odle was probably going to die before he'd help the posse. Sam thought about the body of Colonel Fuller lying in the snow. Red Booker must be reaching the end of his tolerance for the kid as well. All things considered, Willie's idea was as sound as any. Sam nodded at the rifle in Willie's hands. "How are you fixed on ammunition?"

"I could use whatever you've got to spare," said Willie John, lowering the rifle all the way and letting it point down at the ground.

Sam stepped back to his saddlebags, raised the flaps and took a box of cartridges without letting Willie John see how much spare ammunition he had. When he'd shook out a handful of shining new cartridges and walked back and laid them in the Indian's hand, Willie John stepped back without taking his eyes off of Sam, saying as he pointed his rifle upward again toward the next rise of hills with one hand, "Where the trail breaks into a Y, go to the right. It looks like an old elk path, but it's really a footpath that's so old it's worn into the stone. Follow it out around the far side of the hills. By the time you get there I'll be waiting on the other side. The snow will be stopped by the time we're ready."

Sam Burrack only nodded. Then he stood watching for a second as the Indian slipped out of sight, into the fading swirl of white, like a wisp of smoke.

Chapter 24

Herbert Mullins led his horse down from the path along the side of the hills to where Red Booker and the rest of the men sat waiting atop their horses. "The path ends around there," Mullins said to Red Booker, his eyes shifting to Billy Odle's as he spoke. Red Booker also turned his gaze to Billy Odle as he responded.

"What do you mean it ends there? Ends how?" Booker asked.

Billy Odle fidgeted nervously in the saddle in front of Nells Kroft. Kroft's big arms encircled him, offering no chance at hurling himself from the saddle and making a getaway.

Mullins's eyes hardened on Billy Odle as he answered Booker. "I mean it just stops dead right there. It narrows, then stretches out around the hill. You can't see nothing at the end but thin air."

Booker shifted back and forth in his saddle, looking out toward the western sky where the setting sun peeked through the gray heavens just enough to cast a pale red glow on the far rim of the earth. "It'll be getting dark before long," said Booker. "I want to be in spitting distance of that blasted Injun before this day ends." A silence passed as a nerve twitched in his jaw. Then he looked at Billy Odle again. This time the blank expression in his eyes was enough to make the boy's skin crawl.

"Boy," said Booker, "I've given you every opportunity to cooperate with us. Now we've got to where the metal meets the bone." The big knife appeared in his hand in a streak of shining steel from the sheath behind his back. "Either you tell me right now which way to go . . . or I am bound to trim something off of you and stick it down in your shirt pocket."

Nells Kroft cut in. "But, Red! You said you was keeping him as a bargaining chip when we—"

"Shut up, Nells! I know what I said!" Red Booker heeled his horse up close to Kroft's, reached out and straight-armed Billy Odle from the saddle. Billy rolled in the snow at the gathered horses' hooves, the horses snorting their steaming breath down at him, stepping wide and making room for him in the snow. "But he's forcing me to do this! I can't allow myself to be backed down by no snot-nosed kid!" Booker swung down from the saddle with the big knife held tightly in his hand, and said over his shoulder, "Mullins! Get us a torch lit. When I'm done with him, stick the fire to his wound so's he don't bleed to death on us!"

"Boss," said Mullins, "this ain't right, us carving up a kid like this."

"You're my lead man, Mullins," Booker snapped at him. "Are you not going to do like I'm telling you?"

Herbert Mullins saw the look on the faces of the other men, and said, "Red, I'm just saying ease down, get a grip on yourself."

"Ease down? Get a grip—" Red Booker raged at

him. "Why you son of a bitch!" He threw the big knife down in the snow, and jerked his pistol from his holster, cocking it as he swung it up toward Mullins. But Herbert Mullins was not going to be shot without offering defense. His pistol also came up, cocked and pointed. Seeing the two men faced off and ready to kill one another, the others spread away from them in a wide circle. Billy Odle huddled farther down in the snow.

Red Booker started to yank the trigger. But before he or Mullins made their move, the sound of Willie John's rifle resounded twice around the elk trail from less than a hundred yards, causing all the men to flinch, and all of the horses to jerk back in fright. "What the hell?" said Booker, his pistol still aimed at Mullins.

Mullins lowered his pistol an inch. "There is something around there after all, Red," he offered. "Looks like I must've been wrong about the trail going off into thin air. I reckon I owe you an apology." Their eyes went once more to Billy Odle, seeing the stunned expression on his face.

"Dang it, Willie John, *why*?" Billy Odle shrieked toward the upreaching path circling out into the sky. "I wasn't going to tell! Why, Willie?" The echo of his voice rolled out across the canyon and came back as if mocking him.

Red Booker grinned at Herbert Mullins and said, "That's all right, Mullins, anybody could have made that mistake." He uncocked and holstered his pistol, picking up the big knife from the snow with one hand and grabbing Billy Odle with the other. He shoved Billy over to Nells Kroft who caught the boy and yanked him up into the saddle. "Save the crying, boy," Booker added. "There'll be enough time for that after we cleave that Injun's head off his shoulders." He chuckled, giving Herbert Mullins a wink. "If you behave, kid, maybe we'll let you carry the bag we take it back in."

Two miles farther down the trail, Sam Burrack had heard Willie John's rifle shots as well. He was surprised the Indian could have made it that far so quickly. Upon hearing the shots echo off the walls of snow-capped rock, Sam heeled his stallion upward, pushing the big animal hard, hurrying to catch up to the posse before Willie John ended up facing them alone.

When Red Booker and his men rounded the path toward the old ruins, he stopped long enough to look back and say to three men at the end of the line, "Hickson, Murry, Rudd . . . stay back here and keep a watch for that Ranger. I ain't getting this close to killing that Injun and having some lawdog step in and shoot him right under our noses." The three men drew their horses back and stepped down from their saddles, pulling rifles from their scabbards.

Hearing Red Booker's words, Billy Odle reacted violently, turning on Nells Kroft riding double behind him, shouting, "No, you're not killing Willie John!" As he shrieked, he pounded his fists into Nells Kroft's thick chest and struggled to free himself from Kroft's hold. "Willie John, they're coming! Run for it! Get away!" Billy screamed along the path ahead. The horse reared up, throwing Nells Kroft backward from his saddle. Billy Odle managed to hang on, and as the horse touched down he tried heeling it forward. But Red Booker was ahead of the move. He caught the horse by its bridle and checked it down.

Before Billy had time to make another move, Red

Booker snatched him up and pulled him over onto his own horse, across his lap. Billy kicked and thrashed wildly until Red raised him up and squeezed a tight forearm around his throat. "Keep it up, boy," Red Booker warned, "and you won't live long enough to see what's going to happen to your Injun friend." He looked down and saw Nells Kroft dragging himself up from the icy edge of the path, a terrified look on his face as he turned and looked back down the steep drop to the dark chasm that came close to swallowing him.

"Lord God!" said Kroft through steaming breath. He dusted snow loose from his chest.

"Yeah, you big idiot!" said Herbert Mullins catching the reins to the horse and holding it for Kroft. "You're lucky the boy didn't dump your fat ass for the buzzards!" He flung the reins down to Kroft. "Now pay attention!"

Less than thirty yards ahead, at the entrance of the cave, Willie John had heard Billy Odle's warning. "Sorry, kid," he'd said to himself. "There ain't no getting away this time." He stood at the entrance and listened as Billy Odle settled down and Red Booker's voice called out to him.

"All right, Injun, I know you're up there. Here's the deal. Give yourself up or I gut this little fool like a fish."

Willie John didn't answer. Instead he waited and listened, judging the distance of the horses drawing closer around the snaking trail. Only as the first horse came into sight did Willie back a step into the darkness and reply, "What makes you think I give a damn about the kid?"

Red Booker pushed his horse ahead of Herbert Mullins and called out to the black slash in the rock face, "Don't fool with me, Injun. I've been studying your moves from the get-go. I don't know what the connection is, but you don't want nothing happening to this boy, now, do you?" Booker stepped down as he spoke, dragging Billy Odle in front of him, using the helpless boy as a shield. Drawing his pistol, Booker stepped forward slowly, testing his hunch. He looked back and motioned for Mullins and the other two men to follow. Then he cocked the pistol and put the tip of the barrel to Billy Odle's head. "I'm coming in there, Injun. Do something stupid, and this kid's a dead duck."

"Why are you doing this?" Willie John called out from back in the darkness. "You've got me cornered now, why not let the boy go?"

"Because I want you to see his face when I blow his head off," Red Booker said, stepping boldly into the entrance, letting Willie John see him holding Billy against his chest, Billy's head jammed to one side by the pistol barrel.

Willie John winced at the sight, but then said, "He's not the first kid I've seen take a bullet. Turn him loose. Let's play this hand like men, face to face, guts up and bark on, the way they write about it in nickel novels."

"I don't get much chance to read, Willie." Red Booker spat on the ground, looking past the glow of a small fire. "I stay too busy hunting lousy bummers like you." He saw the big dapple-gray standing in the closer shadows, then he squinted, looking farther back into the deeper darkness. "Now show yourself or the boy dies."

"Don't listen to him, Willie, he won't shoot me," Billy Odle blurted out. "Even if he does, I don't care,

I'll—" His voice stopped abruptly, Red Booker's forearm clamping on his throat.

"He's one game little rooster, Injun," Red Booker said. "It's a shame what I'll have to do to him. But if you give yourself up, you've got my word I won't hurt him."

Willie John watched the other three men move into the cave and spread out, their eyes searching for any form of cover, finding none. "Do what you need to do," said Willie John, hoping his voice didn't betray his bluff, "so's we can run this string on out. The boy means nothing to me. If I have to I'll shoot through his belly to get to yours."

Red Booker let out a dark chuckle. "You better hope you mean it, Injun . . . 'cause I'm going to count to three. If you ain't stepped forward and pitched them guns down, I'm dropping this hammer on him. There'll be no second guess."

Willie John only stood rigid in the darkness, his rifle in one hand, his pistol in the other.

"All right, then, here goes," said Red Booker. "One!" His voice rang out in the cave. Willie John's dapple-gray jerked its head to one side and scraped a nervous hoof on the dirt.

"Let the boy go," said Willie John. "You don't have to die like cowards . . . just because you've all lived like ones."

"Nice try, Injun," said Booker, "but no takers." A breathless second passed, then his voice rang out again, "Two!"

Billy Odle squeezed his eyes shut against the coming explosion and said in a sobbing voice, "So long, Willie John, I just wish we could have—"

His voice was overcome by Red Booker's, calling out, "Three!"

"Wait!" said Willie John, all pretense gone, his voice urgent, desperate. "I'll do it . . . I'll drop the guns! Don't shoot him!"

Red Booker eased up on his trigger finger and let out a tight breath. "Say please," he said, spreading a smug grin, knowing he'd just won the standoff.

"All right, *please*," said Willie John in a defeated tone. He stepped forward into full view beside the fire. Behind him the dapple-gray shifted back and forth restlessly, as if knowing he stood in the line of fire.

"Now pitch them," said Booker, his pistol barrel still jammed to Billy Odle's head.

"It's done," said Willie John. He threw both guns to the ground, his arms falling slack and useless at his sides. "Now turn him loose, you're choking him."

But Red Booker only held a cruel fixed grin on his face and said to Mullins and the men behind him, "Come on up here, boys, we've bagged ourselves an Injun outlaw."

Willie John raised his hands above his head, staring at Billy Odle's pained face. "Turn him loose—he can't breathe."

"Huh-uh." Red Booker shook his head, still grinning as Mullins and two men ventured forward. "As much trouble as this boy caused us . . . I might just have to kill him anyway."

"You gave your word!" said Willie John, his hands clamping on the sides of his head in his rage.

"Yeah, but look who I gave it to Injun," said Booker, a dark chuckle in his voice, his arm still tight around Billy's throat. Billy seemed to go limp against him, ceasing to struggle. "I don't owe my word to no two-bit outlaw. I changed my mind, Injun!" As he spoke, Red Booker lowered the cocked gun away from Billy's head and leveled it toward Willie John.

"I thought you might," Willie said. His right hand went back behind his neck as quick as the strike of a snake, then shot forward fast now, the big knife streaking from his hand with the low whistle of sliced air. Even as Billy Odle felt his consciousness slip away, he heard the whir of the steel and the deep thump as it lodged to its hilt beside his ear—the blade fully buried in Red Booker's throat.

"My God, boys!" shouted Herbert Mullins. "He's kilt him! Get that damned Injun!"

Red Booker staggered backward, his pistol exploding aimlessly into the ground; and as Billy Odle slumped straight down onto his knees then fell over onto his side, Willie John made a dive for his guns, both the pistol and the rifle seeming to be laid out perfectly, in wait for his grasp.

Back on the path, fifty yards from the cave entrance, Sam Burrack sat atop his horse, looking down at the three riflemen who stood mid-trail facing him. When he'd rode up, he'd raised his hands chest high, offering no resistance that might start a shooting and tip off Red Booker before Willie John made his move. But at the sound of the rifle and pistol fire exploding from the cave, Sam brought his hands down as the men turned their attention away for just a second. "Man! They found that sucker sure enough!" said one of the gunmen. "Let's get around there!"

Sam saw their intentions in their eyes as they turned quickly back toward him, their rifles coming up cocked and ready. "Aw no!" one man shouted as Sam's Colt exploded three times like the beat of a terrible bass drum. One man managed to get off a round before Sam's third shot lifted him off the ground and slammed him backward alongside his companions. The rifle shot sliced along Sam's thigh just beneath the skin, then opened a wider wound where it came out at hip level.

Rifles fell to the snowy ground in a spray of blood as the men settled into their twisted poses of death. In the deadly silence that followed, Sam stepped his horse away, keeping his eyes and his smoking pistol on the three men until he saw there was no need to. Then he heeled his horse forward toward the sound of battle raging within the rocky hillside.

As Sam slid his stallion down at the cave entrance, Herbert Mullins came charging out, firing his pistol behind him into the darkness. Blood spewed from his chest with each beat of his heart. When he turned and saw Sam stepping down from his horse, Mullins let out a long scream and swung his pistol fire toward Sam. One shot from Sam's Colt silenced Herbert Mullins and left him flat on his back staring blankly up at the sky.

Inside the cave, the battle raged on. Sam limped inside, into the darkness, hurriedly but with caution, his boot filling with warm blood. Recognizing Sam, Willie John shouted from the ground on the other side of the low flames, "Look out, Ranger!"

Sweeping his pistol to his right just in time to see the rifle barrel swing toward him, Sam fired a shot at the same time as Willie John. Both shots found their target, spinning the gunman like a top as he melted to the ground. Sam moved back a step, his left hand clutching his bleeding hip, his pistol scanning the dark shadows.

"That's the last one, Ranger," said Willie John, rolling onto his side and standing slowly, having to use his pistol barrel as a short crutch to get him started upward. He remained in a crouch, staggering in place, his left hand cradling his stomach as if to keep his guts from spilling out. "Now . . . it's just me . . . and you."

"No, Willie John, not like this," said Sam, lowering his pistol, cutting a glance at Billy Odle lying on the dirt floor, rubbing his throat and gasping for breath.

"Don't worry . . . he's all right," said Willie. He tried to stand straighter but couldn't. "Let's . . . get it done."

"I said no, Willie John." Sam uncocked his pistol and holstered it. He wasn't going to tell Willie that from the looks of his wounds he'd be dead in a matter of minutes anyway. He watched the Indian weave a step closer to the fire, then stop and try again to stand erect.

"What about . . . that Ranger?" Willie John rasped. "I killed him, never gave him . . . a chance. And I liked it . . . liked the way he blew apart . . . when the bullet—"

"Shut up, Willie John," Sam snapped, cutting him off. "I see what you're doing. But I ain't going to kill you and that's final. Look at yourself. What would the kid think, me shooting you the shape you're in?"

"I've never . . . laid down easy, Ranger," said Willie John, his words becoming more labored. "I don't even know . . . how."

When Sam didn't respond, Willie John cocked the pistol and said as he raised it and tried to steady an aim, "Tell the kid to keep my horse."

Sam cut a glance to the body of the big dapple-gray lying dead on the ground in a wide pool of blood. "He's dead, Willie," Sam said as gently as he could, all the while raising his own pistol from his holster now, cocking the hammer. Without looking at the dead dapple-gray, Willie squeezed his eyes shut for a second, then reopened them and said, "Well . . . he was a . . . one-man steed. Anyway . . . it's the saddlebags I want the boy to have . . . buy him and his ma . . . a new life."

"Money . . ." Sam let his words trail. "I won't ask where it came from."

"Good," Willie said, his voice getting weaker. "I don't know why . . . but I trust you'll see he gets it."

"You're right—I will," said Sam. He waited for a second, then asked, "Are you sure we have to do it this way? I wish we wouldn't."

"So do I . . . but damn it . . . it's all I know." Willie John managed to swing the pistol up and pull the trigger. "So long, Range—"

The sound of two shots exploding at once caused Billy Odle to shake himself the rest of the way conscious. He stood up coughing just in time to see Willie John fall back against the rocky wall and sink to the floor, a smear of blood leaving a trail among ancient stick figures drawn on the walls by long-forgotten hands.

"Willie!" Billy Odle screamed, running to him. He threw himself down onto his knees in the dirt, pulling Willie's head into his lap. "No, Willie! No!" he sobbed, his arms cradling Willie's head. "Please don't die! Not now! I just now made it back here. We can ride away now! Please, no!"

"Come on, kid," said Sam, lowering a hand onto the boy's thin shoulder. "I know how much you thought of him, but he's gone. There's nothing you can do."

"Who killed him, Ranger? Who? It wasn't you, was it?" Billy Odle's whole body shuddered with grief as he looked up at the Ranger with tears streaming down his cheeks. The Ranger knew there would be no peace between him and the boy if he told him the truth.

"No, young man, I didn't kill him. It never got that far. I came inside the cave. A man rose up to fire without me seeing him."

He nodded at the body of the gunman on the ground, then nodded back at Willie John. "Willie shot him dead before I even got a chance. He saved my life, I expect."

"See?" Billy Odle said, his tears still running freely. "He did good. He could have kilt you, instead he saved your life. That's how he was, Ranger," he sobbed, his lips trembling. "See why he was my friend? My *only* friend? He's the only person who cared anything about me!"

"Yes, I see," Sam said, his voice soft and turning a bit too unsteady to suit him. There was no talking to the boy right now, no way to explain that no matter how highly he regarded Willie John, there were others who cared just as much for him as the Indian had. *Or were there . . . ?* He looked at the bloodstains, both old and new on Willie John's lifeless chest. Then he looked around the small darkened cave and at the bodies strewn about like rag dolls. He reached down and patted Billy's shoulder. Then he turned and limped outside, needing to get away for a minute to keep the boy from seeing his face until he collected himself.

Outside, Sam drew in breath after breath of cold, clean air. He walked to the edge of the high trail and looked down at the flatlands to the right toward Hubbler Wells. He saw the obscured sleigh wagon and the rider on horseback. Two women and a man.

He could guess them by name, he thought. Then he rubbed his tired eyes and walked back inside. "Your ma's on her way, Billy. Let's get things done here and meet her down at the bottom of the trail." His eyes went to the saddlebags, then back to Billy Odle. "You're going to be all right, Billy . . . you and your ma both."

But Billy didn't seem to hear him as he stared down at Willie John's face—the peaceful visage of an outlaw at rest. "I won't never forget you, Willie, I swear I won't," he whispered. "You'll always be my best friend. My only friend, I reckon." Billy got himself under control and wiped his nose on his coat sleeve. He seemed to consider everything for a second, then looked at the Ranger with wet glistening eyes and added, "Well, not my *only* friend . . . but my *best* friend, I reckon, don't you think?"

"Sure, Billy, if that's how you see it," Sam said. He stooped down beside him as he took the bandanna from around his neck and pressed it to the wound on the side of his hip. "It's a person's right to decide who's their best friend, I figure." He gave Billy Odle a tired trace of a smile. "But try to remember, some folks are your friends whether you realize it or not." He stood up with the bandanna shoved into the hole in his trouser leg.

"I don't know what that means, Ranger," Billy Odle said, his voice sounding more steady now.

Sam didn't answer aloud. Instead he limped over to the dead horse, crouched down and began loosening the saddlebags from behind the saddle. *But maybe someday you will, Billy*, he said to himself. Then he smiled and added, *Let's all hope so, anyway . . .*

"A writer in the tradition of Louis L'Amour
and Zane Grey!"
—*Huntsville Times*

National Bestselling Author

RALPH COMPTON

Charles G. West

**"RARELY HAS AN AUTHOR PAINTED THE
GREAT AMERICAN WEST IN STROKES SO
BOLD, VIVID AND TRUE."
—RALPH COMPTON**

The Blackfoot Trail

Mountain man Joe Fox reluctantly led a group of
settlers through the Rockies—and inadvertently into
the clutches of Max Starbeau. Max had traveled with
the party until he was able to commit theft and
murder—and kidnap Joe's girl.

Also Available

Thunder Over Lolo Pass
Ride the High Range
War Cry
Storm in Paradise Valley
Shoot-out at Broken Bow
Lawless Prairie

Available wherever books are sold or at
penguin.com

S805-111510

No other series packs this much heat!

THE TRAILSMAN

Follow the trail of Penguin's Action Westerns at
penguin.com/actionwesterns   S310-110310